Copyright © 2021 by Alyssa Lynn

All rights reserved.

No portion of this book may be reproduced in any form without written permission from the publisher or author, except as permitted by U.S. copyright law.

ISBN: 9798592436130

Contents

WARNING: This book contains adult content which includes graphic scenes and offensive language. The contents of this book may not be suitable for all readers.

Text design by Alyssa Lynn
Cover design and photos by Alyssa Lynn

This is a work of fiction. Names, characters, places, and incidents either are the product of the author's imagination or are used fictitiously, and any resemblance to actual persons, living or dead, business establishments, events, or locales is entirely coincidental.

Introduction

For anyone who has ever contemplated creating a commune with their best friends. This series is for you.

And hopefully the murder and mayhem that occurs in these stories remains to be nothing more than a story.

Other Titles

ALSO AVAILABLE FROM ALYSSA LYNN:

The Perception Trilogy
"SEEING DOUBLE"
"LOSING SIGHT"
"TUNNEL VISION"
The Communal Coven Series
"HALLOWED TRAIL"

"ENCHANTED CAVERN"
"SACRED BUNKER"
Novels
"CIRQUE DU SORCERY"
"DREAMING IN A WINTER WONDERLAND"
"MISCHIEF & MISTLETOE"
Novellas
"WHAT COULD HAVE BEEN"

"CINDY-RELLA'S BUNNY SLIPPER"
Short Stories
"CURBY"

PROLOGUE
(CALEB)

THE METALLIC TASTE OF blood was left pooling in the corners of Caleb's mouth after being hit in the face with a brick. The tension in the room was so thick, it could have been cut with a knife. Much like the knife Caleb was currently pressing to the throat of his business partner, Evan.

Caleb had been struggling for the upper hand for the last twenty minutes. Four fists, two knives, only one walking out of there alive, and if he wasn't able to get this back under control, it wouldn't be him. A big part of the problem was Evan leveling the playing field by holding the second knife to his throat. Fuck.

"Looks like we're at a stalemate," Evan hissed as the blood danced around his teeth.

"It does appear that way," Caleb groaned. His head was still clouded from the commotion and impact of multiple blows to the face, but he tried to remain cool and calm. "We could let this all drift into the past. You can do as I asked and just let me disappear without a word. Or we can stand here with knives at each other's throats, waiting to see which one will be walking out of here."

"I vote option B," Evan said. "But either way, you're not getting out of this."

"What makes you think that?"

"JT won't allow it," Evan said. Despite how relaxed Evan seemed during those moments, Caleb knew Evan was squirming. A laugh burst from his mouth, bloody spit flying toward Caleb. "Once you're in this business, you don't get to walk away. Not unless you're walking directly into your own grave."

Caleb knew he was right. He remembered the conversation he had when JT sat him down before he agreed to be a part of the crew. The Northwestern region didn't seem so intimidating, so it didn't take much convincing.

Caleb looked around the small room he and Evan were standing in. His chest hurt from the combination of blunt force and anxiety. He could drop his knife and give up. Just let Evan kill him and hope that someone crawled down the ladder someday and found his body. But something kept him fighting. Something had him wanting to see if Evan was wrong; that he could make it out of this alive.

It was bad enough that Caleb and Evan lost part of JT's precious shipment for the Northwest region. If it hadn't been for that, none of this would have ever happened.

Crisp, clean dope. Smack. Junk. Snow. It doesn't matter what it's called, the cops would still throw them behind bars if they were caught with that much heroin. To be honest, Caleb would've preferred the cops, or even the knife currently at his throat to the alternative - nothing would be worse than JT.

"We can make a clean break on this," Caleb said, once again trying to convince Evan they could walk away. "With the size of that explosion earlier, JT may already think we're dead. We can walk away and lay low. We've been doing that most of our lives anyway."

"You think you're so slick," Evan snorted. The sweat was causing his dark hair to cling to his forehead. "You don't know the first thing about lying low. You can't possibly think you're being all sneaky when you've told your brother about our job."

"Ash doesn't know," Caleb argued. "He has no idea what I do in my spare time."

"Like hell he doesn't! You may think you've done all this on your own. Or pretend like you have, but he's been on your heels since day one. The first time our product was stolen from you, you got out of that scuff with JT. It's no secret how."

The knot in Caleb's stomach twisted tighter and tighter with each word Evan spit at him. Nobody but JT was supposed to know that Ash was helping. They had a deal. A deal that was made years ago and hadn't been spoken of since Caleb got up from that couch in JT's office.

Caleb all but shuddered as he remembered that day. The first time he'd ever come in contact with JT since he was a kid. He walked through the front doors of the casino and headed straight toward the VIP Poker rooms. It was paid only and there was security everywhere. Ash told him where to go and who to ask for to get him to JT. Nobody there used real names and Caleb still wasn't sure which name was printed on JT's birth certificate.

The room was lit up with flashing LED lights and soft couches along all four walls. A small fountain trickled in the corner while low music played. The smell of cigars was the first thing that hit your senses as you walked through the doors. Much different from the place JT used to hide out in.

JT greeted him and gestured toward the seat on the couch beside him. Caleb didn't say anything, but obeyed and sat down, accepting the small whiskey glass that JT offered him.

"I hear you're looking to make some money," JT had said.

"I am," Caleb answered. He was told by his brother to use short precise sentences. Don't give any more information than necessary.

JT crossed one leg over the other and stretched an arm along the back of the couch toward Caleb. It almost made him squirm, but he remained still. "Any particular reason?"

"Everyone needs a little more spending money," Caleb replied, taking a sip of the smooth malt liquid in his glass.

JT huffed an amused laugh. "Ain't that the God honest truth." He waved his glass toward the man in the corner of the room who charted over a bottle and poured it into both cups.

"Thank you," Caleb said. JT smiled at the sincerity from the man sitting beside him.

"You seem like a nice guy," JT said, leaning forward and resting his elbows on his knees. He swirled his glass and the whiskey stones clinked around. "A little different from the scrawny terror you were as a kid. What makes you think you can pull off the jobs I need done?"

Caleb wished Ash was in the room with him. Ash always knew what to say to guys like JT. Caleb never had much experience with it and was always afraid he'd fuck it up.

"I blend in," Caleb said simply. "I don't crack under pressure. And I'm loyal to a fault."

"Is that so?"

Caleb stared at JT, not saying anything more. Then, JT nodded toward the man in the corner who whispered something into his head piece. Caleb was instantly nervous, but remained calm and kept his breathing under control. He just told JT that he didn't crack under pressure. Now was not the time to go back on his word.

JT stuck his hand out and Caleb instantly shook it.

"Eager to get started," JT said. "Shaking without a spoken word on the contract."

"I trust my brother," Caleb said. "If you're willing to get me onto your team. I'm willing to do what it takes to live up to my task."

JT smiled at him. "I like you, kid."

"I do ask that we keep my brother out of this," Caleb added before they dropped hands. "He has other things on his plate, and he doesn't need to be bothered with what I'm doing."

"We'll keep him on the back burner," JT said, still giving that eerie smile. "But once you're in with me, you're in. No matter how dirty your hands get in the process."

Caleb left JT's office after agreeing to all of the terms and conditions of working under him. And he did fine until the day he was mugged and had JT's product stolen from him. Ash got him out of it, but it was supposed to look like Caleb took the lashing for the loss. Ash was never there.

According to Evan, more people knew the truth and that didn't sit well with Caleb. But he had to continue to play it cool while he stood face-to-face with his partner. The person he thought he could trust up until about an hour ago.

"You're lying," is all Caleb said. "Nobody was involved with that mugging except JT and myself." His teeth were gritted as Evan pressed the blade harder into Caleb's skin. He swore it broke skin, but he didn't feel the warmth of blood so he kept the pressure steady on his own blade, not wanting to further the altercation.

"Believe what you want. Just know that you're better off dead. You're useless in this industry and if you do get out of here, you won't make it far before JT gets his hands on you and finishes the job."

Caleb knew JT was capable of ripping him to pieces with just the snap of his fingers. He didn't care to get his own hands dirty, so he used his mind-washed subordinates who were too afraid to say 'no' to any demand of JT's.

"He wouldn't find me if I ran," Caleb argued, though something in his gut said otherwise. His games of hide-n-seek were always him and his brother; never him and a drug lord.

"He has his ways," Evan said.

Caleb stared at Evan, actively hating him in that moment. Sure they'd had their moments before where they'd argue over stupid shit. But this was different.

When all hell broke loose at the docks the night before, Caleb assumed Evan would flee. He never thought he'd come face-to-face with him in the hideout. Hell, he thought for sure Evan forgot about that place altogether since they'd never had a reason to use it in the past.

Caleb's plan before running into Evan was cut and dry. Get to the hideout, formulate a plan while the chaos boiled over at the docks with JT, and go somewhere far, far away. Hopefully in the opposite direction of Evan.

When he opened the door to the hideout and slid down the ladder into the open area underground, the last thing he expected was to feel the explosion behind his eye as he took a blow to the face. His gaze met Evan's after his sight cleared and he knew in that moment that only one of them would be walking away.

As he stood with a knife to the throat of the only person who welcomed him into his career choice, he realized he was running out of time. Something needed to be done, and it needed to be done now.

"Here's what we're going to do," Caleb began. "We're both going to lower our knives. Then, we're both going to walk out of this shelter, heading in opposite directions for as far as our legs will carry us. Every man for themselves."

"You're a broken record, Cal," Evan hissed. "And besides. I know better. The minute I lower this knife, I'm done for. You act like this is my first day on the job."

"I mean it," Caleb said, trying to sound as convincing as possible even though he wasn't sure what his next move was. "We just need to make a break for it. Otherwise, the two of us will rot in here."

Caleb could see the muscles tighten in Evan's jaw and knew he had to go a different route to convince him.

"Look, Evan," he began again. "We grew in this business together. We have been best friends for years. We're professionals in positions that were never offered at our career fairs growing up. But we're holding each other hostage in an underground shelter that was dug out by a stranger we left for dead." He swallowed despite the dryness in his throat. "We can get out of this. We can *both* walk away."

Evan lifted a considering brow, but said nothing. Caleb was growing antsy.

"Remember that time we decided it would be a good idea to go spelunking?" Caleb asked. Evan's expression told him that he was in no mood to reminisce. "You fell and you fell hard, man. You kept yelling for me to leave you behind and go get help, but I knew that if we put our heads together, we could both walk away from that without anyone knowing we were in that cave." Evan's eyes shifted away, but he remained still with the blade to his neck. "This is that cave, Evan. We're in that exact same moment. We can both walk away without anyone else ever knowing we were here."

Evan looked back at Caleb and Caleb could feel the pressure ease against his throat. As Evan backed off, Caleb began to do the same.

"There we go," Caleb said gently as he kept his hands where Evan could see them. "Now, we will both just walk right out of here and never look back. Everything will be just fine."

Evan lowered his hand to his side, but kept his eyes on Caleb's every move. The look in his eyes told Caleb he was still unsure.

"I still don't know if I can trust you," Evan admitted with a shaky tone. "How do we both get to walk away? If you go first, how do I know that you won't lock the door behind you and burn this place to ash?"

"This is the cave," Caleb echoed. "If it makes you feel better to go first, then so be it."

"How do I know you won't stab me in the back?"

"You have to make a choice," Caleb said. "We took the first step and nothing bad happened. Now, it's time to put this behind us and run. Far and fast. Never look back."

Evan thought about it. Caleb could see the slightest bit of relief on Evan's face when he said they would never look back. He knew which buttons to press with Evan and that always impressed JT. Caleb knew how to read people. He could always say the right thing to make any situation turn out in his favor.

"Okay," Evan said. "But I'm going first. You don't move."

"I won't move," Caleb agreed.

"And give me your knife," Evan demanded as he extended his hand.

Caleb should have seen that coming. He should have known that he wouldn't have a weapon in his hands if he got Evan to agree to walk away.

Slowly, he nodded and extended his knife to Evan who reached out and grabbed it without hesitation. Evan slid Caleb's knife into his own sock and turned to ascend the ladder and exit their hideout. With every step, Evan looked over his shoulder to make sure Caleb hadn't moved as promised.

Caleb waited until Evan had ascended almost thirteen feet up the ladder before he reached down and picked up the brick that was beside his foot. With everything he had, he hurled the brick at Evan's legs and made contact with the back of the leg that Evan had all of his weight on.

Evan screamed out in pain as he fell to the ground. Caleb heard the *snap* when Evan landed and knew that both of his legs were now out of commission.

Knowing he had to act quickly, Caleb raced toward Evan and grabbed him by the shirt, pulling him away from the ladder while he howled in agony. His legs were wrecked and Caleb knew he wouldn't be walking anywhere. Nobody would hear him screaming and he would rot in their hideout, never to be seen or heard from again.

"Sorry," Caleb said, almost meaning it as he slid his knife from Evan's sock and squeezed it with relief. "But I know the truth about what you did."

Evan had tears of pain pooling in his eyes when Caleb knelt beside him.

"You wanted me gone," Caleb said through gritted teeth. "We both know you were the one to let the shipment location spill to the other side. You made it look like you weren't ready when the carrier pulled up to the dock. And you were the one who planted that bomb to try and get rid of me when I went to take over your station."

His fist began to throb after he slammed it into Evan's face.

"And we both know that if I wouldn't have brought you back to the ground just now, you would have trapped me in here and made a run for JT to tell him where I was."

Evan spat blood at Caleb despite the agonizing pain in his jaw. "You're worthless," he hissed.

"Am I?" Caleb asked. "Because out of the two of us, it looks like you're the one with two broken legs about to be left for dead." Caleb got to his feet. "You made me out to be the weaker link, and the worst part is; I started to believe it." Caleb spat back at Evan. "But now it's my turn to stand tall. I'm getting myself away from all this like I've wanted to since the beginning. I'm making a new start for myself and leaving you here to get what you deserve."

Caleb swung his bag over his shoulder and headed for the ladder. After his fingers touched the cool metal of the ladder, he kept his tone steady and said, "And this time, I'm not looking back."

Chapter One

GISELLE

I would say I'm warm and cozy in my bed as the sun comes up, but the claws digging into my side cancel that thought. Tarot, my asshole black cat, is snuggled up beside me using my body as his claw sharpener.

Not my idea of a good wake-up call.

Despite the pain in my side, I smile at the sound of the whispers coming from outside my door. The tiny whispers are made by two children who know that if they wake mommy before she's ready to get up; all hell will break loose.

Tarot stretches his furry limbs as he lets out a big kitty yawn and looks up at me, begging me not to move. It's as if he's saying "Just one more minute. Please, human? My claws aren't quite sharp enough yet."

I smirk at him and scratch between his ears. "Sorry, buddy," I whisper. "Sun's up. So are the kids. And my skin can only take so much of your kitty knives."

I swing my legs over the side of the bed and slip my toes into my fuzzy slippers. My best friends always make fun of me for having slippers on, regardless of how warm it is outside.

Call me weird, but I hate being barefoot inside. Outside is a whole other story though. Grass between the toes is life.

As I take two steps toward my bedroom door to grab my robe from the hook, I hear my oldest, Owen, yell, "Mom's awake!"

In all my seven years of being a mom, I've never come to find out how kids can hear the slightest step of a mother getting out of her bed or sitting down on the toilet. It's like they have a radar that sends out a message saying, "Code red! The keeper of our lives is on the move! This is not a drill!"

Owen comes running into my bedroom with his little sister, Abby, in tow. Their little arms wrap around me and I kneel down to their level to give them morning hugs.

"Thank you for letting mommy sleep," I tell them as they hug tight around my neck.

"We didn't want you to come unglued like you did last time we woke you up," Abby says in her sweet little voice. There's just something about the way a four-year-old talks that makes my heart melt.

"Mommy did come unglued." I laugh as I tuck her hair behind her ear and out of her face. "Because Mommy told you kids three times that I wasn't ready to get up yet." What they didn't know was that I was hungover because my two best friends can drink like fish.

"Sorry, Mommy," Abby says.

I kiss the top of her head and smile. "It's okay, baby girl." I ruffle Owen's hair and take in the sight of them, hating myself for once again feeling irritated that they look like their dad. "Who's ready for some chocolate milk?"

The two of them jump and clap with excitement, then race toward the kitchen. I walk out of my bedroom and head down the hallway with Tarot on my heels. He knows it's morning which means it's time for some wet kitty food.

What can I say? I spoil everyone around me.

Abby and Owen are running like rabid animals through the kitchen when Tarot and I walk in, so I turn on the TV and tell them to chill until I've had my coffee. They climb up together with their cups of chocolate milk that Owen poured for them and get cozy.

My whole world is on that couch.

Tarot rubs against my leg, but then I feel a claw poke through my slipper.

"Ouch! You little shit!" I squawk at him. He struts toward his dish and plops down like a king. I roll my eyes and walk over to him, scratching behind his ears. "You're a pain in my ass, but I still love you."

He rubs against my leg again like he understands what I said. Or maybe he can feel my witchy vibes and I can actually talk to my cat. Crazy thought.

I see yesterday's coffee mug sitting on the counter and put it into the sink, when I hear a crash from behind me.

My head falls forward and my eyes closed. I don't want to turn around. It's too early to deal with this shit.

Especially since I know exactly who the culprit is.

"Tarot!" I shout as I turn slowly to see what he broke this time.

Tarot is perched on the shelf in my living room. Usually, my author portrait in its perfect glass frame would be sitting on that shelf. But now, it's a furry little ass that I'm about to kick.

I go racing toward the shelf to catch him, but he leaps like a damn gazelle and goes racing down the hallway.

"Yeah! You better hide!" I snap.

The kids are looking at me weird, but go back to watching their TV show while I sweep up what's left of my favorite frame, making a mental note to sell my cat and use the profits to buy a new one.

Once I'm dressed and I pour my third cup of coffee for the morning, I see something out of the corner of my eye and walk toward the window.

Lexie and Wyatt, Kiara's kids, are out back playing on the jungle gym. Lexie looks toward the house and waves, so I sneak out onto the porch and get smacked with the summer Montana heat when I see Kiara walking toward my house with coffee in her hands. Her dirty blonde hair is in the usual bun on top of her head and her glasses cover her makeupless face. She's wearing denim shorts and a black tank top which show off her amateur tan, and she's barefoot as always.

"Giiiseeellllle," Kiara says, drawing out my name in a groan as a way of saying 'Good morning' to me. "It's too early for this shit," she adds as she steps up onto my porch. "But I knew if I didn't get them out of the house and into the fresh air to use some of that energy, I'd turn them into frogs."

"I see your craft is improving," I tease her, knowing it's not something we can actually do.

"Shut up," she says, darting her deep green eyes in my direction.

I laugh. "Momming is great, isn't it?"

"The best," she says with a sigh.

Before I can say anything else, Owen and Abby go flying past me and out toward the jungle gym with Lexie and Wyatt.

"I see your monsters are up too," Kiara says, sounding satisfied that she's not the only one up at the ass crack of dawn.

"They've been up for an hour. Tarot and I weren't quite ready to get out of bed yet."

"But it's Saturday," Kiara says, looking at her watch. "We only have about an hour until breakfast."

"I know," I say, downing the last of the coffee in my cup and wincing at how cold it got. "Is breakfast at your house or Jade's this time?"

"I was last week," she replies, closing one eye as though it helps her remember. "It's Jade's turn this week."

I nod. "Gotcha." We both look toward Jade's portion of the land we all bought together. "Her porch light is on which means she hasn't been up yet this morning to turn it off."

"It's not her weekend to have Piper, so I bet you're right. That lucky bitch is probably still in here, all cozied up in her bed."

"Lucky bitch," I echo. "It must be nice to sleep in sometimes."

"It's eight o'clock and you just got out of bed not that long ago." Kiara laughs. "Lexie had me up at five. Don't talk to me about wanting to sleep in."

I smirk. "Alright, you win. But I'm still going to whimper for a minute."

"Fine. Let it out," she says.

I let out a few exaggerated whimpering noises before I say, "Okay, I'm good now." Then, being the friend that I am, take her coffee cup and finish off all but a small sip.

"Bitch," she says with her eyes wide. "You realize I have the right to murder you now."

I shrug. "You won't. Otherwise, you'd lose your babysitter on grocery day."

She rolls her eyes. "And now I hate you even more." I give her a nudge and she grins at me. "I still can't believe we're finally here."

"I know," I breathe. "The three of us have been dreaming about this commune since the year after we met." I do a quick calculation before I add, "And it only took us four years to pull it off."

"Only," she laughs.

"It feels like just yesterday we were standing here with the contractor that you kept hitting on," I say.

I can feel her eyes narrowing on me as I continue to watch the kids play. "Don't give me that crap, Giselle. You act like you weren't over there practically nibbling on the foreman."

We cackle as the kids come running toward us and wrap around our legs.

"You're gonna spill my coffee," Kiara says, holding her cup in the air to avoid losing the last few drops I left of her morning brew.

"I have an idea," I say, giving Kiara a devilish grin. "Let's go see what Aunt Jade is doing!"

The kids all cheer and take off at a sprint toward Jade's house. Our houses are spaced out enough that the kids don't have far to go, but far enough that us three women can pee outside if we want and not be spotted through each other's kitchen windows.

"She's going to kill you," Kiara says, chuckling. "Have your magic ready to back you up."

"We three don't dabble in black magic. And even if we did, I'd still find a way to fuck it up."

"We three?" Kiara echoes. "Trying to talk fancy?

"Is it working?"

"Nah," she says. "You're still my peasant friend who doesn't use social media."

"Social media won't make me fancy," I say.

"It would be a start."

I laugh and shove her as we head for Jade's house.

The kids don't even knock as they head through the front door. Since the three of us live in the middle of nowhere, we never find a reason to lock our doors. The only strangers we encounter are the occasional hikers on the trail about ten yards away. Plus, the kids love the freedom of getting to visit all three of us whenever they want.

We're basically a giant mixed family.

Kiara and I are a few strides behind the kids as we enter Jade's house and the smell of breakfast food slams into our senses. Jade is at her standing desk in the foyer, frantically typing on her computer. She doesn't even look up at Kiara and me as we stand at the door staring at her.

Her house is probably the most chic out of the three of ours. Decorations are on point and pictures cover the walls in organized chaos. Each frame was hung using a level, of course. Book cases are scattered through every room, each one completely packed with novels that were written by her favorite authors, Kiara and myself included.

"Whatcha up to?" Kiara finally asks Jade as we continue to stare at her in complete shock that she's among the living.

Her counter is filled with food. Her air conditioner is already fighting the summer heat in her house. And it looks like she could pack for an entire weekend trip with the bags under her eyes.

"Working," Jade says. She picks up her cup of coffee and finally looks at us. "Oh! Hey, bitches! Good morning!" She lifts her glasses from the freckles on the bridge of her nose and rests them on top of her head, tucking the ear pieces into her deep red hair that she has pulled up into something that is beyond being classified as a messy bun. Her blue eyes are super bright today which means she's exhausted and hardly got any sleep. "When did you get here?"

I laugh, shaking my head. "We just walked in. So did the stampede of children that you obviously missed. What is going on here? It looks like you've already put in a day's work."

"Well, I kind of *did* put in a day's work," Jade says. "I didn't sleep last night. And you only sound shocked at my accomplishments because your ass crawled out of bed an hour ago."

"New book idea?" Kiara laughs, cutting me off when I open my mouth to defend myself.

Jade nods, looking back at her computer screen and frantically clicking her mouse. "It hit me like it always does." It's that redhead chaos coming out of her now.

"You were climbing into bed and just as you pulled the covers up to your neck to doze off, the characters started talking to you?" I conclude.

"Nailed it!" Kiara says.

"Why is it always like that?" Jade asks, resting a hand on her hip. "Why can't we, as writers, get a solid night's sleep?"

"Because characters don't like to be ignored," I say with a sigh.

"Remember when we first met and we were all pumped up to get our first books out?" Jade asks. "The feeling of 'I'm really going to do it this time' and 'I can't believe this is actually happening'."

The three of us laugh together, nodding and reminiscing on our memories of diving head-first into the world of writing.

"I remember you sitting down and writing your first book in twenty-four days," I say to Jade, shaking my head in awe of my friend. "I still can't believe you pulled that off."

Jade mimics my head shake making her ginger bun dance on top of her head. "Me either."

"And now look at us," Kiara says. "We've hit multiple best seller lists and finally have the commune we've been planning for years."

"Some days it still doesn't feel real," I say. "And speaking of what's real and what isn't," I add, pointing to Jade's hair. "What kind of mythical creatures do you have living in that mop on your head?"

Jade reaches up and taps her hair. Her eyes fall into pissed off narrow slits when she says, "You stay up all night working on the outline for a new series and tell me how *your* hair looks the next day."

"A new series?" Kiara says. "Do tell!"

Jade puts her hands up like she's just made a huge discovery. "Picture this. It's like the old day-time TV medical shows, but every character has a dark past! There's a ton of misunderstandings, murder, adultery-,"

"So you're basically writing an old day-time TV medical show," Kiara says, interrupting her whirlwind of an explanation.

Jade sighs. "Yeah." She runs her hand down her face. "I swear it sounded so much better in my head. Everything just came together and the next thing I know, I can see the inside of the hospital and I can hear the character's personalities." She lets her hands drop to her sides like a pouty teenager. "Come on, guys. It's gonna be good. I'm *really* excited about this one!"

"As long as you have a plan," I say, looking at Kiara in a way of telling her to shut up. "How much research is this one going to take? You haven't really written anything in the realm of fictional medicine."

"You have no idea," Jade says, squeezing her eyes closed as though she's in pain. "I filled my head with all the medical jargon last night. I literally have no more space in my brain. None."

"It's definitely a challenge, but you can do this, Jade," I tell her, walking across the room and peeking at her computer screen.

"I stayed up last night working on the lingo," Jade continues. "And tonight I'll do more research in the specialties themselves. Learn what it takes to make a great neurosurgeon or cardiothoracic surgeon."

"Big words," I giggle.

The kids come stampeding into Jade's foyer, complaining that they're all hungry.

"I guess we should feed these mongrels," Kiara says. Then, she looks at Jade. "You get Piper tomorrow at six, right?"

Jade nods. "As long as her moron father decides to drop her off on time."

"You're right," I say, nodding as I remember all the times Piper's dad showed up late and ruined our plans. "We'd better plan dinner for seven."

Jade smiles and rolls her eyes in agreement as Owen tugs at my shorts. "Alright, alright," I say to famished tiny humans. "The adults will move our conversation into the kitchen so you can all eat."

"I have to run to my house and grab the food I made," Kiara says.

I put my hand on my forehead. "Shit, so do I."

"I've got the twirps," Jade says, pouring herself the last of the coffee in her pot. "You girls go grab your things. I'll see you in a bit."

Kiara and I wave as we head out the door, but hear Jade yelling, "And don't forget the orange juice! I have champagne!"

Kiara and I low-five each other and sing in unison, "Authors love mimosas."

Chapter Two

GISELLE

I SWEAR MY CHEST is sticking to itself as I race around the playground, chasing Abby and Owen in the summer heat. Today's game is lava monster, and as always, I'm the monster.

It's times like these where I'm glad I don't smoke, but also wish my job as a writer was more demanding in physical activity. I'm huffing and puffing as I come around the corner and reach for Abby, making a mental note to invest in a standing desk or something.

Sounds of kid's laughter has me smiling big as I let out a loud *RAWR* and wrap my arms around Abby, both of us tumbling to the ground.

"Owen!" Abby screams in between giggles. "Help me! The monster got me!"

Owen comes around the corner and dives on top of us.

"That's not helping!" Abby shrieks as Owen sits beside her and laughs. "Owen! Get the monster!"

I begin tickling them both and their screams get louder. They climb off me and sprint toward the jungle gym, climbing to the top tier so I can't reach them when I finally catch up.

"You can't get us now, monster!" Owen shouts.

"You're lucky I don't have wings!" I shout back.

I reach for the ladder to climb up and get them, but Abby yells, "Monsters can't climb!"

"Stop making up rules!" I shout back, but laugh as I crawl back down from the first few steps.

"Just use your broom to fly toward them!" Jade shouts as she walks over toward us.

I stick my hand behind me and give her the finger so the kids don't see.

"She just gave me the middle finger!" Jade shouts to Abby and Owen as she points at me.

"Mommy!" Abby scolds, narrowing her eyes at me.

I wave it off and walk toward Jade, fighting for breath with my hands on my hips. "So glad you're here," I say sarcastically.

Jade sniggers. "Rough day?"

"Lava monster," I say, letting my head fall back while I catch my breath. "What's up?"

"I'm making the grocery run. I already got Kiara's list," she says, pointing toward Kiara's house. "I'm here to get yours."

"I thought it was my week to make the run," I say, trying to remember my calendar that's sitting on my desk.

"You did it last week," she says. "Kiara sent out the new calendar for this month. I can print one for you if you need it."

"That's why I thought this was my week. I'm probably looking at last month's schedule." I sigh as my breathing starts to regulate. "I'll print it. Thank God Kiara is as organized as she is. Otherwise, I'd go nuts trying to remember everything."

Jade laughs. "No doubt." She waves to Abby and Owen who are hanging out from the jungle gym, calling her name. "Where is your list?" she asks me. "I'll just run inside and grab it on my way to the truck."

"It's either on the refrigerator, next to the coffee pot, or beside my keyboard," I say, trying to remember where I left it.

"Got it," Jade replies.

"Or it could be on my end table in my room," I add, twisting my face in a way that says 'sorry I'm so unorganized'.

Jade holds up a hand to stop me from continuing my one-man guessing game. "I'll find it."

I hang my head. "I'm sorry!"

"We wouldn't be us if we weren't a complete train wreck all the time. I'll be back in a bit." She takes a few steps away and then turns back to me. "Don't forget! Tonight's a full moon!"

"Oh shit!" I say, realizing I'm far from prepared. "Can you add a few glass jars to your list of things to grab?"

"Mom! Don't swear!" Owen shouts from the top of the jungle gym.

"Sorry!" I yell back to him.

"It's okay, Mommy!" he yells, smiling at me.

"Yeah, Mom!" Jade teases. "And don't feel bad. Kiara forgot too."

"We're the worst witches in the world." I laugh.

"Ain't that the truth. See you when I get back."

She gives me a wave and passes Kiara on her way to get my list. Lexie and Wyatt come racing toward me and wrap their arms around me.

"Hey, kiddos," I say, hugging them back. "Lexie and Wyatt are here!" I shout to Abby and Owen. Then, I lean down and whisper, "Last one to the top is the lava monster."

The kids take off running and Kiara says, "What fire did you light underneath those two?"

"I made a race to the top so I don't have to play monster anymore."

Kiara laughs and folds her arms over her chest as we watch the kids run around. A loud beep sounds from the driveway and Jade is waving her arms out the window as she pulls away from the commune. We wave back and return our attention to the kids.

She must have found my list.

"You forgot about the full moon too?" she asks.

I nod. "I don't know how we're supposed to keep up with all of this."

"We're the worst witches ever," Kiara says.

"That's what I said!"

Kiara makes a gesture between the two of us that says we think alike.

After a few seconds, she sighs and says, "I need to go in and get some writing done on this new series I'm working on."

"The fairy tale?" I ask.

"Nope."

"The motorcycle club romance?"

"Nope."

I sigh. "Good lord, woman! Which one is it now?"

"It's new," she says as though it's no big deal. "I came up with it while I was in the shower."

"Did you get your notebook wet again?"

"Yep," she sighs. "I need to get a whiteboard or something in my bathroom. Between the water and the humidity, nothing allows me to take notes."

"Well, I saw online that they make these underwater pens and paper. Maybe try that."

"You're a genius!" she shouts. "Remind me to order one later."

"Sure," I say. "Now, I did you a favor so can you do me one?"

"Sure."

"Remind me to remind you that you need water-resistant paper and a pen."

"You're useless," she says with a punch to my arm.

"I never claimed to be helpful," I counter.

The kids squeal as they chase each other around the playground area of the commune. I love that they have a place to unwind while the adults can be free of entertaining them for a while. It also lets us practice our spells and rituals.

Not that we're black witches or anything. We basically play with oils, herbs, and crystals. Charge our moon water and keep crystals in our bras to help us feel better. We don't sacrifice cats to the gods or anything.

Tarot would have my head before I ever got close enough to hurt him.

"Are we meeting at our usual spot tonight?" Kiara asks.

"I would assume so. If nobody tells me where to go, I'll just assume we're meeting at the lake."

"Sounds good to me." We both try to muffle our laughter as Abby picks herself up from tripping over her own feet. "She's definitely your kid."

"That's for sure," I agree. I sigh and check my watch. "You go get your work done. I'll spend some time with the kiddos and we'll be over in about an hour to fire up the grill."

"Don't let the kids fire it up," she says, looking at me as though that was my plan.

"Just because *you* let them, doesn't mean I'm going to."

She shrugs. "Yolo."

"Oh shut up," I say, shoving her away from us. "Go make me proud and murder some people!"

"Thank God we're authors. Otherwise, we'd have the police called on us with the crazy shit that comes out of our mouths."

I nod and chuckle. "Not to mention our browser history."

Summer is nothing without the smell of a barbecue. Pops and sizzles are flying from the grill while Kiara and I sip at our wine spritzers. Watermelon is cut and displayed on a bright green tray that makes me chuckle.

"What's so funny?" Kiara asks, laughing even though she doesn't know the reason.

"Remember when Jade fought tooth and nail to get that stupid tray from that old woman at the yard sale last year?"

Kiara laughs harder now. "How could I forget? The damn thing wasn't even for sale."

Now I'm laughing just as hard as she is. "Right?! And the looks on their faces when they pulled all the baked goods off of it to hand it to Jade."

We're holding our stomachs as we cackle at the memory. That kind of laugh that makes you look like a seal while you clap your hands for no good reason.

I finally get myself under control and kick my feet up in the adirondack chair. I pull my sunglasses from the top of my head down to my nose and sigh. "This is the life."

"It sure is," Kiara agrees.

We sit and watch the kids play while the food cooks and enjoy the heat of the summer day when Jade's truck pulls in. She gives us a wave and grabs the few bags from the back before she heads into her house to unload.

"Doesn't look like she got a whole lot," I say.

"She didn't need meat this trip," Kiara tells me. "Her brother called while you were playing lava monster to let her know he got half a cow. It's already been cut and packaged, but he didn't realize just how much it was until it took an entire SUV to deliver it to him."

"Typical Vince," I say.

"Yeah, well, I'm not complaining about it because he offered some of it to us. We just have to go get it. I think Jade's planning to go meet up with him at some point to grab the things we'll eat. Unless he said he's stopping by. I don't really remember."

I smirk at her. "I hope he stops by."

Her eyes dart toward me. "Why?"

I shrug. "So that I can watch the two of you dance around the fact that you'd bang each other in a heartbeat."

Her jaw drops. "Take it back!"

"Will not," I tease, singing to her. "Kiara and Vince, sittin' in a tree."

A piece of watermelon comes flying at my head and I dodge it, thankful that she has terrible aim. "Anyway," I say, trying to compose myself. "We'll eat whatever she brings."

Kiara is still glaring at me, but says, "We sure will."

We're pulling chicken and hot dogs from the grill when Jade walks over with a beer in her hands.

"It smells like summer over here," she says as she lifts her bottle to her lips.

"You got that right," Kiara says. "We know how to summer it up."

Jade sets the pasta salad on the table next to the watermelon and admires her tray. I can see a smile tugging at her lips as though she's still proud of that day.

She takes a seat in her chair next to mine and looks at me. "How are you doing?"

I nod slowly. "I couldn't be better."

Kiara blows out a breath and shakes her head as she takes a seat beside us.

"What?" I ask, looking at both of them.

"Nothing," Kiara says. "It's just that you're a lying sack of shit."

"Am not," I argue.

"Are too," Jade adds.

"How am I a lying sack of shit?"

"Because we know that Mark has been calling you," Kiara says. "We know that you've had to block him on almost every form of communication imaginable. And we know that you're still waiting for those divorce papers to show up."

"How do you know all that?" I ask, feeling two inches tall.

"Uhh.. you told us," Jade says with a nervous laugh. "Not that it's funny, but sometimes I think you're in a whole other universe."

"She is," Kiara agrees. She walks toward the table and gets the food situated, adding more barbecue sauce to the chicken before returning to her chair. "Everything will work out the way it's supposed to."

"I know it will," I say.

Jade gives my knee a comforting squeeze. "You've got us. You have a beautiful place to live with two amazing children who have a fortress to grow up in."

"The dream of us being here isn't just for us," Kiara adds. "These kids have it so good out here."

I nod and smile. "You're right." My glass clinks on my teeth as I take a sip. "We did better than I thought we would. I just wish that my past wasn't still lingering like a dark friggin' cloud."

"We all have a past," Jade says. "You just need to learn how to cope. Whatever that may mean for you. It's different for everyone, but we all have things that we have to deal with."

"And we deal with it together," Kiara says, even though she won't look at Jade and me when she says it.

"That we do," I agree. "You two are the best wives a girl could ask for."

"Wives that don't put out," Jade teases.

We laugh and Kiara hollers for the kids to come eat. "No more negativity. It's a full moon tonight and we have all this amazing food waiting for us to eat it."

"Agreed," Jade says."

"Let's eat and maybe hit the trail for a while," I suggest. "Give the kids another chance to blow off some steam before we put them to bed and head down to the lake."

"We'll wait for it to cool off a bit," I hope," Jade says. "I've got sweat all over my lady parts and I'm dying to lose the bra and panties."

"You're always dying to lose the bra and panties," I laugh.

"You're not wrong," Jade smirks.

"We'll feed the kids, let the food settle while we hang in the air conditioning, and hit the trail later in the day," Kiara suggests. "It's the perfect evening for a family walk."

"Deal," Jade says, holding up a beer bottle toward Kiara and me.

We clink glasses and I smile at them. "Deal."

CHAPTER THREE

CALEB

I THINK I MIGHT die. Like, actually die. My tongue is sticking to the roof of my mouth because I ran out of water this morning. Not a good situation to be in when I'm cooking like bacon in this heat.

I don't know where the hell I am or how long I've been on this trail. All I know is that if I don't find water soon, it'll be the death of me.

Literally.

My body hurts from walking, but I've managed to focus more on the fact that with each step I take I'm getting farther and farther away from where I left Evan to die.

I still can't believe it came to that. Killing someone that I thought had my back. I guess when you're working in that industry, it's every man for themself.

Tough break.

Dry dirt is crunching under my shoes with every step I take. I have my thumbs looped through a backpack I found on the side of the trail that thankfully had a bottle of water, albeit warm water, and a granola bar tucked away inside.

Was the granola bar expired?

Yep.

Did I eat it anyway?

Sure as shit.

I'm wiping my brow when I hear voices in the distance. I squint and feel the sting of sweat coating my eyes.

Two people. A man and a woman. Laughing and having a good time as they wander down the trail on this scolding late afternoon.

What is wrong with people? They actually do this shit for fun? Who has time for that?

I guess most people have time to go out into nature when they're not smuggling drugs across state and country lines.

Crazy.

The woman smiles at me before the man does. He seems more skeptical and deems me a stranger rather than a potential friend. With the state I'm in, I don't really blame him. Shaggy hair, dirty face, tattered clothes from the briars I had to climb through to even find the safety of this trail.

I don't give him another second to judge me. I smile at both of them and nod my head. "Afternoon," I say, continuing to walk so I don't spook them if I stop and corner them.

The man seems to soften at my easy tone and echoes my greeting. The woman adds a soft, "Hi" as they skirt on by.

I wait until they're past me before I turn and clear my throat. "Sorry, folks, but I could bother you for just a second?"

The woman stops walking and turns toward me, but the man takes a few more steps before realizing he lost his companion to a raggedy stranger. Almost makes me smile at how naive this woman probably is.

She doesn't know I work in a world of murder and paraphernalia. But alas. Here I am. Left a guy for dead only a few days ago if I counted the sunsets properly. And the week before that I had baggies filled with God knows what to sell.

But to this lady in purple spandex and a blonde braid; I'm simply a hiker sharing their local nature walk.

"I'm sorry," I say. "I'm just not from around these parts. Is there a break anywhere on this trail to a small store or anything?"

The man turns his full attention toward me. I think something about a man asking for directions and showing what us tough males consider 'weakness', may have him softening up to me even more.

He points behind me toward the part of the trail they came from. "There's a small gift shop at the trail entrance," he says. "The CDT gets a lot of traffic. Tourists love to snag a magnet every chance they get."

"Or a beer koozie," the woman says, grinning at the man.

The man chuckles and pulls a dark green koozie out of his pocket to show me. "Couldn't help myself," he says. "We've been on this trail for two days."

The woman, still smiling, looks at me and asks, "How long have you been trekking?"

I smile at them both. "Far too long."

"It can definitely feel like that sometimes," the man says. "But just keep putting one foot in front of the other and it'll be over before you know it."

"We're heading to Canada," the woman tells me.

When she looks at the man, her blonde braid swings over the large bag on her back and lands on her chest beside a diamond necklace. What I would give to sell that necklace and use the money for a greasy burger and an ice cold beer.

The man clears his throat when he notices me staring at the woman's chest. "We're going to continue on our way now. Good luck to you, mister."

I give them both my best smile and turn to head for the gift shop, hoping they'll have more than a damn expired granola bar.

I've only passed four other people on the trail as I close in on the small gift shop. The sun should be setting in a few hours which will definitely cool it down a bit more, but I still need supplies to make it through the rest of the trip to wherever I'm going.

Who knows, maybe I'll end up working at this gift shop for the rest of my life. Shrivel up like an old man while I ask a twenty-something muscled up douchebag if he'd like a beer koozie souvenir.

Not that the couple I talked to earlier were full of themselves, but they sure were quick to judge a stranger.

Though totally accurate with their accusations in this case.

The small gift shop is tucked between a bookstore and a gas station. Pretty quaint actually.

Two young women walk out of the shop, but hold the door for me, smiling as I walk up to it.

"Thank you," I tell them, picking up my pace and cursing under my breath to people who do that whole 'I'll hold the door open for you even though you'll have to do that awkward jog to get to it so you don't make me wait' thing.

They continue their conversation about Jason and Irene as they walk away and I step inside, almost sighing audibly as the air conditioning hits my skin. My eyes slowly fall closed and I almost put a hand on my chest, much like those people do when they claim to find Jesus.

To each their own, I suppose.

"Excuse me," a lady says softly beside me.

I open my eyes and realize nobody can get out of the shop because I stopped the minute I stepped inside the door.

"Sorry," I say, feeling the desert in my mouth as I try to speak.

I offer a smile and hold the door open for them to walk out before I step farther into the small store. Trinkets of all kinds line the walls. Coolers are filled with every energy drink you can think of, along with sodas, juices, and three different types of bottled water.

Before I know it, my feet are in motion, carrying me toward the bottled water.

I open the first bottle without thinking and start to chug. My throat burns as I swallow each gulp of ice cold water. I can feel it running down the corners of my mouth, but I can't stop drinking.

The last time I had something cold to drink was the last time I went for lunch with Evan. Right before everything went south at the docks.

"Asshole," I say. Only it comes out like "abbsshoobbllbbee" because I have a mouth full of water, but apparently I was living in the moment more than I intended to because I said it out loud.

"Sir?" A male voice says, beside me before I feel a hand on my shoulder and jump to the side.

You don't touch a man without his knowing, especially a man that's been through some shit.

The man immediately throws his hands up in surrender and looks around the small shop. He's wearing a name tag that says Ian and I look at the water bottle in my hand, realizing I'm drinking merchandise before paying for it.

I slowly lower the bottle and swallow the water that I didn't dribble onto my shirt. "Uhh," I say, unsure of how to recover from my outburst while I was stealing water.

"Sir," he says again, lowering his hands. "We're going to need you to pay for that."

The man is looking at me like I'm a rabid dog. Can I blame him? Hell no. I rush into his store and have an 'I've met Jesus' moment when I was hugged by air conditioning. Then, I start chugging store products like a crazy person.

"I'm sorry," I say, trying to catch my breath from all the inappropriate water chugging I just performed. I look at the bottle and then back at the store clerk. "I um..." I reach into my pocket and pull out nothing. Then, I decide to do a sweep of the backpack to make sure I didn't miss any cash that may have been sitting in a pocket.

Nothing.

I hate that my wallet was lost at the docks during that whole fucking fiasco. It's made it impossible to eat over these last few days.

I feel my breathing starting to quicken as I look around without a solution. "I'm so sorry," I say, trying not to stammer. "But I don't have any money."

The man considers me for a second before putting his hands on his hips. He waves me up to the counter and starts counting coins out of the 'Leave a Penny' dish.

"You look like you're a bit out of your element here," the store clerk, Ian, says to me quietly. "Let's just get this paid for with what we have in this dish and you can be on your way. I don't want any trouble."

I nod at the man and offer him an apologetic smile. "I appreciate it, Ian."

The man seems surprised at my use of his name, then looks down at his name tag and nods before dropping the coins into his register. "Don't mention it. Be safe out there."

He gestures toward the shop entrance as a way of telling me it's time to go and I don't say anything else before walking back out into the scorching hot weather.

"Gross," I say to the Montana sun before I take a seat on a bench a few feet from the entrance. I'm grateful it's not metal because I can guarantee my skin would fall off my legs like a well-cooked rack of ribs.

I grunt as my ass hits the bench and I lean into it, letting my head fall back for a minute. The dirt on the trail wasn't too comforting when I took short breaks before continuing on my path to nowhere. This is like a vacation compared to what I've been doing.

And I even made a friend.

I salute the store as a way of remembering Ian before I get up and walk toward the gas station. As I open the doors and step inside, the clerk looks at me and smiles, though the smile fades as she takes in my appearance.

"I'm sorry," I say. "But do you have a restroom that's available to the public?"

Her smile grows wider, though more fake, as she points toward the giant sign that's hanging from the ceiling outside the bathrooms.

I wave and smile as I walk into the men's bathroom and drop my backpack on the floor inside the stall. I pee, wash my hands, splash some water on my face, and clean myself up as much as I can with a wet paper towel.

When I'm done, I walk down the back aisle, blindly pocketing something from the snack shelf while smiling at the clerk who can't see my hands, and then skirt out of the gas station doors.

Once I'm back on the trail, I feel my mouth watering as I pull the mystery snack out of my pocket. I read the wrapper and sigh. "A fucking granola bar."

Chapter Four

GISELLE

Squeals and squawks from tiny humans fill the air as we venture down the dirt path near the commune. We only pass two other families on our walk, neither of them stopping to talk to us which I'm always grateful for.

Accepting that there are other humans living on my planet? Sure, I can handle that. But having to talk to them?

Absolutely not.

"Be careful with that," I tell Abby as she picks up yet another stick along the side of the trail and starts swinging it around.

The kids each chose a stick to use as a sword and we only had one casualty as a result. All in all, not a bad walk.

Having the trail near the commune has been both a blessing and a curse for us. We use it for walks and to have some time to ourselves, but we also have times where stragglers from the trail walk into the commune not knowing it's our home.

Normally, it takes a police discussion and a gesture toward the NO TRESPASSING signs for them to leave, but we did have one time where the police were called to have a couple escorted off the property. I mean, I can't really blame the two strangers. They walked into a full moon ritual, and Kiara, Jade and myself were wearing nothing but our amulets while we chanted to the gods and goddesses. They told the police they were being pranked.

Before they left, Kiara whispered something to them that had them all but jumping into the back of the police cruiser to get away from us.

Who walks the trail that late at night anyway? There's bears and stuff.

"It's finally starting to cool off a little," Kiara says.

"Finally," I agree, fanning myself. "Today was a bit warm. Maybe next time we have a day that hits the high nineties, we don't barbecue outside."

Jade laughs. "I second that. My boobs are sticking to themselves."

"I can't wait to shower," Kiara groans.

"Alright, kids," I say, ignoring my whiny friends. "There's the fence." I point to the fence along the trail that shows we've almost hit the mile marker. "That means it's time to turn around and head back."

Wyatt begins to whine and Kiara gives him one look that makes him practically stand at ease.

We three moms have gotten pretty good at the death stare.

We swing the group around, making super loud engine noises to mimic a plane, and head back toward the commune. The kids all grab new sticks, despite being told not to, but we figure if the last casualty didn't scare them, maybe the next one will.

I'm all about lessons learned.

"It was a nice day," I say, admiring the beauty of the walking trail. "And I seriously love that we have this at our fingertips."

"You say that every time we walk it," Jade points out.

"I mean it every time I say it," I sneer.

"You know what else I love having at our fingertips?" Kiara asks. Jade and I don't need to have her clarify. We know what she's going to say, but we give her the wide-eyed look as though we're asking her to tell us.

"Nerds Rope," she says.

I wiggle my eyebrows at her like we always do when we talk about these special candies. They're not just any Willy Wonka sweets. They're made for those over a certain age who partake in extracurricular activities.

Jade grins. "What about the Sour Patch Kids?"

"Giselled finished those off during the last full moon," Kiara tattles.

I whistle and look around as though I'm innocent.

"You bitch!" Jade says as she punches me in the arm.

I shrug. "The Sour Patch Kids aren't as potent as the Nerds Rope." Kiara and Jade are now doubled over in hysteria. "Okay girls," I say, annoyed. "It wasn't *that* funny."

"Oh, but it was," Jade says, laughing to the point she almost has tears running down her face.

"You're right though," Kiara says, trying to catch her breath. "You probably should just stick to the Sour Patch Kids." She wipes an imaginary tear from her eye and flicks it to the side.

I hate that they still talk about that night. It was the worst night of my life. No exaggeration.

"I still can't believe you had that bad of a trip," Jade says, rubbing her side as though she has a cramp from laughing.

Good for her.

"How much THC is in the Nerds Rope?" Kiara asks.

"Four hundred and fifty milligrams," I say. "That's a friggin' lot!"

"Well yeah," Jade replies. "But you weren't supposed to eat a third of the damn thing. There are four hundred and fifty milligrams if you ate an EIGHTH of the rope."

"I didn't feel anything from my first bite," I say like a cranky toddler. "So, I took another bite."

"It has a sixty-minute reaction time, Giselle!" Kiara says, laughing again. "You just need more patience."

"I don't see that happening," I say with a snigger. "So, anyway. I think tonight, I'll just stick to wine. You two can dabble in the Willy Wonka drug candies."

"At least have a cookie or something," Jade says, looking at me like I'm being a party pooper.

"Alright," I say, holding my hands up as we continue our way down the trail. "I'll have a cookie from my bedroom drawer. It won't get me onto your level, but I'll still be high in the clouds."

"Just give it a bit to kick in," Kiara teases.

We come to the opening in the trees that leads back to the commune and the kids take off running toward the playground. There's a truck parked next to Jade's house and we pause for a minute to see who's here.

All of us rush toward the kids, but slow our pace when we see Jade's brother stepping out of the driver's side.

"He must have got a new truck," Jade says.

"It's about damn time," I mumble. "He can definitely afford a new one on that animal surgeon salary he brings in."

"He's a vet," Jade says with an eye roll. "Don't over play it."

"My bad," I reply. Then, I look around the property, but see no signs of a furry companion. "Where's Toast?"

Jade looks around the truck, but doesn't see any signs of the dog either. "Looks like he doesn't have him today. Odd. He takes that dog everywhere."

"He's a cute dog," Kiara adds. "I'd probably take him everywhere too."

"Maybe we should get a dog," I say.

"Yeah," Jade laughs. "Tarot would *love* the idea of sharing his castle with an annoying, energetic drool bag."

Kiara and I both laugh because we know she's right.

"I'll catch you girls in a few hours," Jade says. "Are we meeting at our usual spot by the lake?"

I nod. "Don't forget your glass jars."

"I won't!" Jade shouts over her shoulder.

Kiara sighs and crosses her arms. "She's going to forget them."

I laugh. "I know she will."

"Did you get the kids all tucked in?" Jade asks us as we meet by the walkway to the lake.

"Yeah," I say. "That walk really took a toll on Owen. He was passed out before the opening credits of his movie choice finished. Abby on the hand wanted another round of her pick before she fell asleep."

"Lion King?" Jade asks.

I nod.

"Did you cave?" Kiara asks.

I shake my head. "I didn't have to. The minute I went to put the movie in the player, I turned and she was sound asleep on the couch. I carried her to her bedroom and turned off the lights. You'd swear the kid was dead with how hard she was sleeping."

"I love the summer heat," Kiara says. "Knocks the kids right out."

"Same," Jade says. She sighs. "I'm ready for tomorrow night. I miss my baby girl."

I rub her shoulder. "I know you do. We all miss Piper. Abby made her a card this morning."

"But her birthday isn't for another six months," Jade laughs.

I shrug. "It's a get well soon card. She just wanted to make her something and Owen found the video on YouTube."

Jade laughs and I think my attempt to make her feel better actually worked.

"Any problems getting Lexie and Wyatt into bed?" I ask Kiara.

"Nope. Just as you said- the summer heat does wonders for getting them into bed at a decent hour."

I look at my watch; the only thing I'm wearing besides my robe. "It's after ten. I'm not sure I'd call that a decent hour."

Jade blows air out her mouth and waves a hand. "It's summertime. Let them be little."

We walk down to our spot at the lake where we can still see the houses and trails leading to the commune. It's far enough away that the kids won't wake up from our chanting, but close enough that we can be at the houses in no time if something happens.

Not to mention the fact that it's gorgeous down here.

We had the contractors add the pavilion at the last minute and we're super thankful we did. There's nothing like sitting by the lake on a rainy day without getting wet. Add a glass of wine or seven, and a good book. It's pure bliss.

I pull my glass jars from my bag while Jade pulls candles from hers. Kiara grabs the crystals from our outdoor altar and lights an incense stick.

"Any thoughts on spells for tonight?" I ask.

"Yes," Kiara and Jade both say in unison while looking at me.

I study their faces before I realize what they're up to. "No," I argue. "We don't need to do this again."

"Obviously we do," Jade says, folding her arms over her chest. "The last one didn't work."

"You need to let go of everything in the past and move forward," Kiara says.

"You do too," I counter, looking at both of them.

Kiara and Jade swap a look, but turn back to me.

"Tonight isn't about us," Kiara says, waving off my interjection. "We're fine. Tonight is about you."

"So, just let us do it, or we'll tape you to a chair and do it anyway," Jade says with a look that tells me she's willing to hogtie me with duct tape.

I put my hands up in surrender. "Fine, but I'm prepping my moon-water first."

"Deal," Jade says with a nod of satisfaction.

They're right and I know it. I need to be able to let things go from my past and move forward. It's just difficult. I go from being married with a family and a nice big house, to living with my two best friends and no husband.

Don't get me wrong; I'd rather be here with my best friends than back in that awful relationship. But still. Sometimes change isn't easy.

I grab my glass jars and hand two over to Jade because, like I predicted earlier, she forgot hers.

We dip our jars into the lake and fill them before we secure the lids on tight.

"I brought the tray," Jade says as she sets it on the wooden banister of the lake pavilion. "Do you girls have your crystals and herbs?"

"No herbs for me this time," Kiara says. "But I brought my amethyst crystal to put on top of my jar."

"Same," I say, pulling my crystal from the pocket of my robe.

"And this is why we're friends," Jade says, as she pulls a matching crystal from her robe pocket.

We put our jars on the tray under the full moon and surround the jars with the crystals we brought. We say a quick 'thank you' to the moon as we leave the jars to charge.

"And now," Jade says, "to call the quarters."

We joins hands and begin to chant in unison. "We call on the element of earth. Bring your stability and resilience to our magic tonight. We call on the element of water. Bring your fluidity and compassion to our magic tonight. We call on the element of fire. Bring the light and heat of your transformative energy to our magic tonight. We call on the element of air. Bring us mental clarity as we perform our magic tonight."

We release hands and whisper, "Blessed be," before we begin with our spells.

After an hour of chanting and singing and laughing, we thank our deities and return to the commune. Jade offers the wine for this evening and votes Kiara's balcony for the coven gathering.

"That was probably your best work yet," Kiara says with a toast to me.

I grin. "Maybe our spells worked this time."

"Let's only hope." Jade sighs. "I can't stand seeing you like this anymore. I miss happy Giselle."

"I'm happy," I argue.

"You're not happy," Kiara says. "You're more content if anything at all."

"Well, what's wrong with being content?" I ask.

"Because it's not you," Jade says, dropping her hands to her sides. "You were so gung-ho on getting rid of your lousy relationship. Then, when it finally happened, it was like you sank into nothingness. You're just coasting through life, waiting for something else to happen so you can focus on that instead of your failed marriage."

"Ouch," I say, not sure if I meant to say that out loud. Hearing it actually did hurt a bit.

"Sorry," Jade says. "I guess I don't really know how to soften things like that."

"It's not just that your marriage failed or that you're single now," Kiara says. "We all say that we don't need men in our lives because we're strong, independent women. Which we are," she adds, holding up a hand before Jade or myself lay into her. "But what if one day, the right one comes along? Are we going to be able to throw our independence aside and let someone into our family?"

I shrug. "I guess it would take a lot of discussion."

"Between who?" Kiara asks.

"All of us," I say.

"Ya know," Jade says, leaning her elbows on her knees. "As much as we joke that we're married, you don't have to get our consent to sleep with a guy."

All three of us laugh, understanding how we sound right now.

"I know that," I say, taking a sip of my wine, but laughing into my glass. "And it's not even a conversation that needs to happen any time soon. I'm still married."

"And what exactly are those documents you keep moving out of your way on your desk? Maybe a little something that came in the mail today?" Jade asks, with a sideways glance.

I grunt. "Okay, so I'm married for the time being." We all go silent for a minute when the snap in my tone kills the mood. I decide now is a good time to chug the rest of my wine. "I just don't think I'm ready to move on yet," I continue with a softer tone. "I need some time to be myself. Figure out what I want in life and kind of test the waters in the lake of solitude."

"That's annoyingly deep," Jade says. "Even for you."

"Anyway," Kiara says, cutting her off and chugging the rest of her wine. "I think it's time we call it a night. It's already closing in on midnight and our fifth kid arrives tomorrow."

"You act like you were there for the making of my child," Jade laughs.

Kiara winks at her. "Listen, witch. We were all there for the making of your child." She pats herself on the chest and pretends to sob. "In spirit."

We burst into laughter and gather the wine glasses before Jade and I head toward our houses. I grab the girls by the arm and whisper as though someone else can hear the conversation.

"Am I really in that bad of a place in my life?"

They chuckle and Jade rolls her eyes as she says, "Man, I hope the spell worked this time."

Chapter Five

GISELLE

It's been two days since our full moon ritual and I can't wait to see the girls this afternoon. I thought I was crazy when I woke up yesterday morning and felt like a whole new person, aside from the usual cat claws in my side. But today I know it's a fact.

I roll over and check the clock by my bed to see it's already early afternoon. I pet Tarot as I fling the covers off me and head toward the kitchen to make a pot of coffee.

"Good morning, Mommy!" Owen yells as he runs toward me and wraps around my legs.

"Good morning," I say with a kiss on his head. "But it's afternoon. Mommy only took a nap. Where's your sister?"

"Lexie came over and got her," Owen says. "They're playing at Aunt K's house."

I give him another kiss on the head. "Why didn't you go over too? I'm sure Wyatt would want to play."

"I told Lexie that I wanted to wait until you got up," he says.

He makes my heart melt. Abby is my wild child, and Owen is more on the mature and mellow side. When Abby was born, Owen wanted to learn how to take care of her on his own. He wanted to be the one to change her diaper and clean up her nursery. It was nice having the help, but I didn't want him to think he needed to be the one to do that stuff. Sometimes I think he grew up a little too fast. Though I smile a lot when we play lava monster and I get to see the little boy that Owen used to be.

"Well, buddy. I'm up now, so you can go over and play with Wyatt. Tell Aunt K I'll be over shortly. I just need to grab my afternoon cup of coffee."

I reach to give him a hug, but laugh when he bolts for the door and closes it behind him.

My coffee brews slower than ever today, but once my cup is filled, I walk over to Kiara's to meet with her and the others.

"Well, if it isn't Sleeping Beauty," Jade teases.

"I just needed a nap," I snarl.

"Drink your coffee so you can come join us in the land of the living," Kiara laughs.

"Hey, Piper!" I shout when I see her waving at me. I take a sip from my mug. "Glad to see she's still standing."

"Why wouldn't she be?" Jade asks.

"I don't know," I say. "Abby said something about Piper not sleeping because of the monsters under her bed. She mentioned it last night when she got home from playing at your house."

"News to me," Jade says.

"She may have just wanted to get a rise out of Abby," Kiara says. "Lexie made a comment about Piper thinking there were ghosts in our house too."

"It's fun having the oldest," Jade says with an eye roll.

We laugh and I look toward the trail with a sigh. "It's been pretty quiet these last two days. I'm surprised we haven't had anyone wander onto the property."

Jade throws her hands in the air and then brings them down, slapping her own thighs. "Now you've gone and jinxed us."

Now it's my turn to roll my eyes. "I didn't jinx anything. I'm just saying we haven't seen too many people over on the trail."

"It's not like there's someone at that exact spot on the trail every day," Kiara laughs.

"Well no, but it's the CDT," I echo. "It's the longest trail on the planet."

"It is not," Kiara says. "That's the Pacific Crest."

"Only until they finish the CDT," Jade adds.

"Listen to us, acting like we exercise," Kiara says, mocking all of us.

I chuckle. "So, I didn't get to chat much after the text that dinner plans were still good. Yesterday's kid-switch wasn't as bad as you were expecting?"

Jade shakes her head. "Not really. Though I need to stop sending her to her dad's house with her nice summer clothes. I swear, it's like there's a black hole at this house that sucks up everything I send."

"I don't envy you," Kiara says. "I'm glad I did the sperm donor thing."

"No, you didn't," I laugh.

"It sure feels like it sometimes," Kiara says. She looks at Jade. "At least your ex is the better out of all of ours."

Jade shrugs. "He's still a moron."

"Yeah," Kiara replies. "But he was always away on business. You could have at least had your personal space and lived off his wallet."

"Listen," Jade says. "You can't look at me and tell me that you think I'm the kind of girl who is happy just because my spouse has money."

"Well no," Kiara says. "But at least his issues weren't that he was cheating or that he was abusive."

She says this in a tone that says we know she's right.

Kiara's ex-husband was a violent drunk and always took it out on her. The first time he hit her, she figured it was a fluke and he would never do it again. The second time he hit her, she hit him back. But the third time he hit her, she wound up in the ICU.

I'm glad she stood up for herself when it came to that relationship. It was a giant leap for womankind.

"I know this," Jade says. "But we still didn't belong together. Regardless of how much money was in his wallet. I've had the opportunity to live a carefree life when it came to finances. Twice. And neither time, male or female, was I head over heels in love with them. Men are lazy and women are crazy."

"Now *that* is a quote that belongs on a t-shirt," Kiara says out of the corner of her mouth.

I nudge Kiara and nod toward Jade. "I'm glad that none of us are in unhappy relationships any longer," I say. "We've got each other and that's what matters."

"Girl's gettin' sappy," Kiara teases in a fake southern accent.

"Oh shut up," I snap.

"But seriously," Kiara starts again. "They were all deadbeats and I'm glad they're gone."

Jade claps her hands together and I jump at the sound. "While we're on the topic of deadbeats. Giselle, we have a homework assignment for you."

"But it's summer," I reply. "I don't do homework in the summer."

"You're going to," Kiara says.

I have a feeling the two of them were conspiring without me at some point.

"You're going to walk into your house," Jade begins. "Go into your office, or wherever they are laying now, and sign those damned divorce papers!"

"Yeah!" Kiara cheers. "Do it! Do it!"

My stomach tightens at the thought. I know they're right. They usually are, but I can't wrap my head around the idea of not being married anymore. I was married for nine years. That's not something you can just throw away.

And the worst part was that he was the one to send me the papers. Even after he was the one that cheated.

"Okay," I hear myself say. "I'll do it."

"The spell worked!" Jade shouts, getting to her feet and dancing.

Kiara joins her and they're now looping arms and dancing in a giant circle.

I get up from my chair and head toward my house, leaving them to party without me. Abby and Owen are waving at me, so I give them a smile and blow them a kiss. The separation never even phased the kids. They were so used to their dad not being home that they just adapted to a life without him.

Little do they know, if Mark would have had his way; the kids would be living with him and I'd be paying child support out the ass.

Thankfully the courts sided with me when it came to the custody side and I got them. Mark didn't even seem upset that he lost that fight.

I head in through the mud room toward the hallway and walk into the office. The minute I enter the room, I can already see the papers staring me in the face. Almost as if they know I'm intimidated by them. I practically see them shoving me in a locker and taking my lunch money, calling me a coward and taunting me.

The problem is, they wouldn't be wrong. I am a total coward.

I pick the papers up from the desk and grab a pen, but stop right before I turn to the first tab. I know if I sign these in here without them witnessing it, they won't believe I actually went through with it.

Lifting them off my desk, I tuck them under my arm and head back outside.

As the summer air tickles my sense, I wave the documents in the air causing Kiara and Jade to jump up and cheer for me as though I'd just won the superbowl.

"Encore, encore!" Kiara yells.

"Go for the touchdown!" Jade howls.

"Sign them! Sign them!" they both call in unison.

I lay the papers down on the table in front of them and use exaggerated motions to turn each page. I can't help but laugh at the way they're handling this moment in my life. It's like they're more excited than I am to get rid of the cheating asshole I call a husband.

Ex-husband.

Kiara starts yelling at the kids not to use sticks for sword fighting and something about them not learning their lesson on our last walk.

"I'm going to go chat with the kids and work in the garden," Kiara says, putting her hands on her hips. "It's my turn to do the picking." She points a stern finger at Jade,"You make sure she signs every single one of those damn papers so she can finally put this all behind her!"

Jade gives Kiara a thumbs up and Kiara walks away. I laugh and continue reading over the legal language on the document in front of me.

Just as I decide it's all legit, I touch the pen to the paper and I hear Jade say, "Can we help you with something?"

I reply," Not unless you want to sign them for me," before I realize she's not talking to me.

When I look up, there's a strange man standing in front of us. Looking at his face, I'd think he's no older than we are. But the way he's standing and hunching himself over, he's acting like he's in his late seventies. He's wearing a backpack and looks as though he hasn't showered in a week.

"I'm not sure," the man says in a low raspy tone. "I was just looking for a place to take a rest from the trail."

Jade looks at me like I was expecting him to show up. Then, she turns back to him and points to the NO TRESPASSING sign.

The man turns and looks at it, then looks back at us. I swear he looks almost heartbroken when he realizes this is private property. He looks past the sign like he'll die if his feet touch that trail again.

It makes my heart hurt and I don't know why.

"What's your name, mister?" Jade asks.

The man looks between the two of us and I want to threaten him when his gaze moves toward the kids. I have a weird feeling in the pit of my stomach, but I'm trying to give this guy the benefit of the doubt.

He didn't mean to find us. He just happened to stumble upon our commune while he was on the trail. Can't blame a man for being curious. He's one of many.

The man continues to look at us, and Jade repeats the question. "Dude, what's your name?"

He clears his throat and tries to smile, though it looks painful for him when he finally does. I notice that his eyes smile when his mouth does and it makes his whole face light up. At least the parts of his face we can see under all the hair and dirt.

"My name is Cal," he finally says, trying to stand up a little taller.

"Cal?" I say. "Is that short for anything?"

He loops his thumbs through the straps on his backpack and says, "It's short for Caleb."

Chapter Six

CALEB

I'M STANDING IN FRONT of two beautiful women and I feel almost intimidated. The redhead is looking at me like she could jam a dagger through my chest. The brunette is looking back and forth from me to the kids that are running around the jungle gym near one of the houses.

Then, it hits me. There's two women in front of me and three houses in my view. I'm guessing there's someone else wandering around somewhere.

I nod toward the two in front of me while keeping my eyes out for the third. Trying to stand up as straight as I can, I put on a front that says 'I'm not on the run from a psycho drug dealer. And I'm totally well nourished and hydrated. Not desperate in the least.'

"You know my name," I tell them, trying to keep my tongue from sticking to the roof of my very dry mouth. "Isn't it only fair that I get to know yours?"

The redhead shakes her head. "No need. You won't be here long enough to need our names."

That makes me laugh. The ginger attitude is strong with this one. "Well, alright then."

I want to tip my hat to them and be on my way, but I don't have a hat on, and the brunette decides to chime into the conversation.

"Come on, Jade. It wouldn't hurt to let him sit at the pavilion for a while and rest."

Ms. Feisty has a name. We're making progress.

"Shut up, Giselle," Jade snaps under her breath.

I put my hands up. "Ladies, please. I didn't mean to ruffle any feathers. For that, I'm sorry. I can't imagine it's easy to welcome a stranger into your conversation, much less your..." Do I assume it's their place of residence? It sure seems like they're cozy here. Jade doesn't even have any shoes on. Eh, what the hell. "Much less into your home," I continue. "So, I don't blame Jade for having her guard up."

"Don't say my name like you know me," Jade snaps.

"I'm sorry, Miss," I say, raising a friendly hand. "I'm just saying I'd do the same thing. Be guarded, I mean. And I commend you for having the blaze in your lady bits to stand up to such a ruggedly handsome man."

Giselle chuckles and Jade gives her a death stare. I can tell that I'm rubbing off on at least one of them.

Jade crosses her arms in front of her chest and pops her hip out while she leans all of her weight onto one leg. Kind of like the mean girls do in those movies when they're about to call the outcast something mean and degrade them a bit.

"No offense, *Cal*, but we don't know you from Adam. You could be a serial killer or a drug smuggler or a child rapist."

Okay, so the mean girl side definitely came out. I even got chills at the latter. Not a fan of anything to do with children and those who do deserve to have their fingernails ripped off one by one and jammed up their ass.

"Jade!" Giselle hisses. "Lighten up a bit."

I hate that they're kind of going at each other right now. Jade was right to judge me and hit the nail on the head with her hammer of possibilities when she mentioned drugs. I try to focus on maintaining a good image.

"Thank you, Giselle," I say. "But your friend is right. Quite honestly, I'd rather just make my way up the trail and see if I can stumble upon another group of super badass women who are as strong as y'all seem to be. Maybe someone who doesn't have a group of kids they need to protect in a mama bear fashion. Give you ladies a little peace of mind."

Just then, five children come racing around the playground area and head straight for us with another woman in tow. When the third woman sees me, she yells for the kids to freeze. The kids do as they're told and giggle from thinking it's a game. Like that toilet flush game that I used to play as a kid. Where you run around, but have to stand still when you get tagged, holding your thumb up for those still unfrozen to 'flush' you back into the game.

Super strange, but totally fun.

The smiles all fade from the childrens' faces when they're told to get inside Giselle's house. I'm impressed by the house the kids all run toward. Metal art pieces are strategically placed along the front of the house, and they're absolutely stunning.

Not that I ever worked with metal art, but I can appreciate a good piece when I see one.

"It's okay, Kiara," Jade says. "We've got it under control."

At least I know their names now. Each one is just as beautiful as the first. Though, if I must say, Giselle's smile is enough to make a sane man howl at the moon.

"I was just leaving," I inform Kiara as she holds her ground beside Jade and Giselle. "And I'm sorry to have made such a ruckus of your day." What a weird time to use that word for the first time. I could have said 'mess'. I could have said 'wreck'. But no... I said 'ruckus'. If I wasn't trying so hard to keep my composure, I'd smack myself for it.

"What's your story?" I hear Kiara ask as I turn to walk away.

"Pardon?" I reply, trying to make sure I heard her right. Between her and Jade, I didn't exactly get the warm and fuzzies. So for her to ask me personal questions instead of agreeing to send me on my way, I'm wondering if I still have a shot here.

"Your story," she repeats. "What brings you here?"

"He told us-,"

"I didn't ask what he told you," Kiara says, cutting off Jade with a wave of her hand. "I want to hear it from him. I want to know what he's doing here."

This one seems like a force to be reckoned with. I'm not quite sure where she's going with this, but I do feel that if I don't answer her, I'll be facing a world of pain.

"I have been on this trail for quite some time and just needed a place to prop up my feet. I saw the lake down there and thought it seemed like the perfect spot. Rest my feet and let my mind wander for a while."

"You didn't mention the lake when we asked you," Jade comments, narrowing her eyes at me.

"That's because I just now noticed it," I admit. "I was too busy answering your questions when I first got here to look around. Now, I'm kind of wishing I knew what it was like to use one of those nice plastic chairs over there and take a load off."

Giselle smiles, though this time directly at me. I swear my knees go weak for a few seconds. "I say he can prop his feet up for a while. He won't be hurting anyone down by the lake."

I smile back at her now.

"Don't get all smug just yet with your toothy grins," Jade says to me. "We take votes around here. You only have one."

"He has two," Kiara says flatly.

This takes me by surprise and I'm actually speechless. Kiara actually sided with me. I'm grateful.

I've been in those woods for so long and I just need to get off my feet for a while. The trail was only a blessing to me for the last day or so. The thought of getting off my feet for even thirty minutes brings a smile to my face, but not as big as the one that blooms when I think about getting to watch Giselle for a little while longer.

Kiara and Giselle granting me permission to stay seems to piss off Jade because she storms away and mumbles something about checking on the kids. I bid her farewell and thank her, despite her refusal to let me stay, and hope that I'll be here long enough to gain her trust.

A challenge that I'm not mentally prepared for yet.

I just know that I need a place to stay and I know for sure, JT will never find me here.

"Thank you," I say with a sincere smile. "I'm sorry I pissed off your friend."

"Eh, she's just like that sometimes," Kiara says. "That ginger attitude gets the best of her at times. But everyone needs a chance to prove themselves and I don't see why you can't be given one now."

Just as I'm getting ready to thank them for the thousandth time, I notice Giselle looking at my pack and her eyes growing wide in fear.

"Gun," I hear her say as she steps in front of Kiara, stretching her arms to either side of her, guarding her friend. "Alright, you have about thirty seconds to explain before I drop you to the ground, asshole."

I put my hands up without even thinking. "I don't even need thirty seconds. This here's for protection. I've been by myself the entire hike and I never know what I'm going to come up against." I swallow again, feeling the dry burn in my throat. "There's not even a bullet in the chamber."

Giselle looks over her shoulder and Kiara nods at her.

"But I do commend you for protecting your friend," I say, my hands still up in peace.

"I wasn't protecting her," Giselle says. "I was buying her time and creating a distraction."

In one quick move, Giselle steps to the side and Kiara is now standing in front of me with a gun pointed in my direction. I keep my hands raised and don't move.

Even though I'm super impressed by these Charlie's Angels type women. Damn.

"Listen, Kiara. Giselle…" I swallow hard, unable to believe what is happening right now. I'm less concerned about the gun being pointed at me and more concerned about how turned on I am right now. "I'll keep my hands raised. You can come take my gun and double check that there's not one in the chamber. That proves that I'm not lying and that I'm only using it for protection. Keep the gun. I'll even tell you where my ammo is and you can have that too. I don't mean any harm." I sound kind of pathetic, but I also know how to defuse a situation like this. Especially with women who have most likely never been in a situation like this before. "Like I said before, I just need to take some time off my feet before I continue on my path."

Kiara holds her position. "What's your end location?"

I shrug, hands still in the air. "Don't really have one."

Giselle's eyes narrow at me for the first time since I looked in the direction of the kids. "You running from something?"

"No, ma'am." Technically that isn't a lie. Because I'm *hiking* away from *someone.*

"Don't call me ma'am," Giselle says.

"Sorry," I say. "I was raised to say that to a woman I don't know." Can't really remember if that's a lie or the truth. I just know that when I talk to a lady, it always feels right to use that term. "Women are 'ma'am', and men are 'sir'. I apologize, I was just using it to show respect. I'll stick to first names."

Giselle's eyes soften at my reply and I can't tell if she's impressed or amused. Or both.

"Alright," Kiara says, lowering her gun. "Place your bag on the ground and take a few steps back."

I do as she asks and when I take a few steps back, I put my hands back up so my palms are facing them.

Kiara steps toward the bag, but keeps her eyes on me. She starts patting it down like she's airport security and pulls the pockets open so she can see inside before she reaches inside. She takes the gun and checks the chamber, showing it to Giselle who nods.

"As you can see, the gun isn't loaded," I say, gently. "The ammo is in the right front pocket of the bag if you want to take it. You can hold my things until you're ready to send me on my way."

Giselle steps up beside Kiara once the gun and ammo are secured. But Giselle looks confused when she pokes around inside. "If you've been on the trail for that long, why don't you have any supplies?"

"What kind of supplies?" I ask.

"A tent?" Giselle replies instantly.

I shrug. "I didn't expect to be on the trail this long. When I started, my mind sort of got the best of me and when I broke away from my thoughts, I figured I may as well just keep going. I sleep under the stars each night with my gun by my side in case anything with teeth and claws looks at me with hunger in its eyes. Building beds and shelter with sticks and branches gives me a sense of accomplishment before bed each night. I don't expect you to understand that, but I really enjoy getting to listen to the sounds of nature without being muffled by the walls of a tent."

I see a satisfied smile tugging at the corners of Giselle's perfectly glossed lips. "I can understand that. But it still doesn't make much sense to me."

"I'm sure you have things that don't make much sense to me," I counter.

She looks at Kiara and tilts her head in a way of saying I have a point. I'm not going to ask questions though. I need to get on their good side and I'm down to two out of the three. If I lose another one, my ass will be back on that trail without getting to test out that plastic chair by the lake.

"There's no food in this bag either," Kiara adds.

"I know," I say. "I ran out this morning. I figured I'd eventually find a place to buy something on this trail."

"You're an odd character," Giselle muses. I swear I see a gleam of amusement in her eyes. Almost like she's intrigued by me.

Hopefully that means she wants to get to know about me. Answer some questions about the mysterious guy who showed up on her property.

"I'm an open book," I say to them both. "I'll tell you anything you need or want to know." I look between them. "But can I ask a favor?" I clear my throat. "Maybe two favors?"

"What?" Kiara says. I can tell she's avoiding the urge to make a mean comment to me.

"Can I please lower my hands? Possibly get off my feet for a bit and have a glass of water?" I ask.

"That's three favors," Kiara says.

Giselle rolls her eyes at her friend and says, "Yes, you can lower your hands. We didn't tell you to raise them."

"No, but you pointed a gun at me. I always see the guys in movies raise their hands in the air. I figured it was my best bet to not get shot."

Giselle considers this. "Alright, I'll give you that one." She looks down at Kiara who is still rummaging through my bag and says, "You can hang out at the pavilion. But we're keeping your things inside one of our houses."

"And we're not telling you which house," Kiara adds. "If you try to sneak into one of our homes, you'll have to face Jade."

"And I promise you don't want to do that," Giselle says. "Jade can be a bit of a bear."

"To be fair, so can you two," I say, giving them a flirty brow raise. They both grin and I gesture toward the house that Jade disappeared into. "Again, I'm sorry for causing such a chaotic end to your day."

Giselle checks her watch and tilts her head at me. "It's only six."

"Good point," I say, unaware of what time it was.

I guess my common sense swam away with the realization that I could possibly make camp here if I play my cards right. I don't want to use these ladies, but I also can't take a chance of getting caught by anyone. The possibility that these women are tied to JT in any way is slim to none.

"Go on down to the pavilion. Prop your feet up," Giselle orders.

"No funny business," Kiara adds.

"Only serious business," I say, realizing by the look on Kiara's face that it's not time for jokes. Giselle muffles a laugh, and that alone makes me feel like I'm already sitting with my feet up and an ice cold beer in my hand. "I'll be down at the lake," I tell them both, and send a smile toward Giselle.

I don't give them a chance to change their minds. I head toward the lake to prop my feet up at the pavilion without giving them a glance over my shoulder.

Chapter Seven

Giselle

My heart is still racing from the commotion with the gun maneuver that Kiara and I pulled. We'd practiced it one night while we were drunk and swore we'd always have weapons scattered throughout the property in case there was a stranger that gave us the creeps. That drunken night with my best friends equalled a three-thousand dollar bill at one of the online gun stores.

Makes us feel better though. And proved today to actually be useful.

Thank you, tequila.

I walk into the kitchen after watching Cal head down to the pavilion. Even though his back was facing us, I smiled in his direction when he propped his feet up on the banister by the picnic table. It's my favorite seat in that whole pavilion because it overlooks the entire lake. And if you're there at the right time, you can even enjoy a quiet sunset.

As long as the kids are occupied, of course.

As I look around my kitchen, all eyes are pointed at me like gun barrels to an intruder. I get the feeling they're going to pummel me with questions and there's really no way to avoid it. I just helped a stranger.

I'm about to get some spiel about my naive side again.

I drop Cal's bag at my feet and cross my arms, ready to take the heat.

"What?" I breathe.

"Are you insane?" Jade squeals. "You know nothing about him! There are children here! He has a fucking gun!"

"He is simply propping his feet up at the pavilion. I watched him sit down. I'm aware there are children here, I made two of them." I lift the weapon in front of me and let it dangle from my pointer finger like I see the badasses do in the movies. "And the gun is no longer in his possession."

Kiara smirks and looks at her hands when Jade whirls toward her. "How did you let this happen?"

Hands go up as though Kiara's now the one being held at gunpoint. "I did nothing," she lies.

"You helped," I tattle.

Kiara gawks like I just told the teacher she cheated on her exam. "Well just run my ass right over why don't you."

"All I'm saying is that we should give him a chance," I say, cutting off Jade before she can go off the deep end again. "He's not going to be here very long. You heard him say it. He just needs a place to rest his feet and then he'll be on his way." My hands are now on my hips and I feel like I'm about to start yelling.

"Why are you so defensive over him?" Jade asks, her face squishing together like she's accusing me of something.

Kiara is still playing innocent and looking at her hands. "She likes him."

I give her a dumbfounded look. "I do not like him. He's a complete stranger. I don't even know him."

Jade points a finger at me as her jaw falls open. "You do! When he was making comments and being all snarky, you couldn't keep your smitten smile under control. You like him!"

I feel myself avoiding eye contact and wonder if they're right. I can tell I'm being defensive and I can't even stand to look at them right now. But I've hardly known the guy for twenty minutes. There's no way I could feel anything toward him.

Or his burly, muscular body.

"I just think he's funny," I admit. "That's all."

Jade howls with laughter and slams her hands together. "Mystery man has wrapped himself around your little finger." She clicks her tongue at me. "Oh, Giselle. What are we gonna do with you?"

Kiara laughs. "Maybe you should go on down and give him a little somethin' somethin'," she winks.

"I second that," Jade says.

"Now hold it!" I shout. "Just ten seconds ago you were telling me how terrible he was and how I shouldn't have even let him sit at one of our outdoor family areas. Who the hell flipped your lightswitch?" I huff out a breath. "Telling me to go down there and get my groove on."

"Get your groove on?" Jade echoes.

"I wasn't saying anything about a groove," Kiara says. "Though I do think you should take his soul with that mouth of yours."

I feel my hand cover my lips as though my mouth is some magic stone I just found in a cove of treasures. I'm not sure why she's saying that. It's not like blowjobs are taboo, or anything out of the ordinary. Yet my face is burning with embarrassment.

"Now, don't go blushing on us," Kiara says. "I've heard the things that come out of your mouth and they're *way* beyond anything that I just said."

I laugh and feel some of the heat fall from my face. "I'm done discussing this with you two. You're impossible. I'm going to go down there and have a rational conversation with him. Maybe he has some interesting stories to tell. Maybe I'll learn something. Maybe I'll come up with a new plot to my book."

"Your porn book," Kiara says, making Jade cackle.

"He doesn't even know where he's going," Jade chimes in once she gets herself under control. "What are you trying to get out of him? His number?"

I shrug. "It just nice to have a conversation with someone who isn't trying to get me to hop on the next dick that comes my way." I give them both a pointed stare.

"Pun intended on the dick coming?" Jade asks with an exaggerated wink.

I wave away her comment. "Fine, I find him interesting. And he doesn't seem like the kind of guy that is going to do anything to us. I think we should give him a chance."

"What are you going to do?" Jade asks, still chuckling a little. "Offer him the guest house? Let him sleep in the bunker?" Her and Kiara both share a look like they just told the best joke on the planet.

I wouldn't make him sleep in the bunker. That's used mainly for emergencies or for slumber parties in the winter when we're stuck inside anyway.

One of the best additions to the property, in my opinion.

When I cross my arms without replying, Kiara's jaw drops. "Giselle, that's a bit excessive. Don't you think?"

I stare at them.

"Okay, put yourself in our shoes," Jade says, her tone more serious now. "What would you say to one of us if we decided to take in the next stranger that wanders onto our property? What would you say if we let him around our kids and into our lives?"

"I would ask what your thoughts were behind wanting to invite him in," I say, unsure if I'm defending myself or being honest. "I would give the guy a chance before I lash out with harsh accusations about him being dangerous. And I would trust your judgment because I love you both." I breathe. "We practice the craft, ladies. We have ways of making things right and we're supposed to be handling things as they come our way. Open hearts and open minds. Everything happens for a reason and I feel that he was brought here for us to help him. Or maybe he's supposed to help us."

Kiara and Jade look at each other.

I brush off some imaginary dirt from my pants because I feel like my hands need to be moving. "Now, I don't know what he's done or where he's come from. But like you say," I point to Jade. "Everyone has a past and everyone deserves to right their wrongs. So, no matter what he's done or why he's here. How about we practice what we preach?"

Kiara hangs her head and I know Jade wants to, but has more fight in her. When she goes to hold her hand up, I cut her off. "It's a simple gesture from one kind human to another. He's a kind human until proven otherwise and I'm not turning away someone in need." I turn to Kiara. "Would you turn away an injured animal?" Kiara shakes her head. Now, it's Jade's turn to hang hers. "And you never know if those injured animals are kind or killers. We need to create a world where we don't treat everyone as though they've just slaughtered an entire family."

I see Kiara shutter at that, so I move on, trying to be less harsh. But I'm thrilled to have had the floor for this long. They usually would have cut me off by now.

"Be the change you wish to see in the world," I continue, now feeling like I've overdone it. "We say that more than we tell each other we love each other. So, I'm going down there to be a kind soul for him to talk to."

"Be the change? Kind soul?" Jade is now mocking me. "Did you just go all Gandhi on us?"

Jade always knows how to irk me. Bringing Gandhi into this conversation only because she researched him not that long ago for a book.

The things authors learn in research is astounding.

"I'm going to remain on my happy cloud," I reply. "Go do something productive. Like, maybe finish a book or something?"

I turn to walk out of the house and I hear Kiara yell, "I still say you should use your mouth on that injured animal! Bring him back to life!"

I slam the door behind me and head for the lake.

I'm on the small dirt walkway that leads from the houses down to the lake and I can't help but take in the view of a man sitting at our pavilion. The only other man we ever have here is Jade's brother, and he doesn't give me the same tinglies when I look at him that I get when I look at Cal.

"Hey there," I say as I walk up to the pavilion. He jumps and whirls around to stare at me. "I'm sorry," I say, freezing in place to let him realize it's just me. "I didn't mean to scare you. I just thought maybe you'd want some company."

He takes a few deep breaths and continues to watch me. "I'm sorry," he says, trying to catch his breath. "I must have been deeper in my thoughts than I realized."

I gesture toward the bench beside him when he gives me the nod of approval, I take a seat.

"Nice evening out there," I say, looking out over the lake.

"It really is," he says.

My eyes are on the gleam in the water, but I can see out of the corner of my eye that his attention is fully on me. "Did you figure out where you're heading?" I ask him.

Cal shakes his head. "Not yet. I'm a bit of a wanderer I guess. No idea where I'll end up or when I'll get there. I guess it takes a while to tame a wildflower."

When I see his face contort, I realize he didn't mean to say that. Laughter spills out of me before I have a chance to contain it. When I see the look on his face, I try to calm myself down. "I apologize," I say. "I just didn't expect that. And by the look on your face, neither did you."

"Maybe I'm more in touch with my feminine side than people realize," he says, giving me a flamboyant flick of his wrist. I laugh again and he lets his wrist fall to his lap. "Maybe I should have gone with 'wild animal' or something," he admits.

"You're something else." My smile is so big that it almost hurts. He's so easy to laugh with and I kind of hate that. This stranger has completely opened me up.

He gives me a big smile and, once again, it reaches his eyes. "So, what's your story?" he asks.

"My story?"

"Yeah. What brought you to this place in Montana?"

"My life did," I say.

Cal turns toward me and rests an elbow on the picnic table top. "Any specifics you'd like to share with the class?"

I feel the corners of my mouth twitch. He seems like such a free spirit and I'm so curious about him as a person. The only thing that bothers me is the fact that I'm most curious about how his lips would feel pressed to my own.

"Not particularly," I say. "I'm a bit of a wildflower myself."

Now it's his turn to laugh. "I don't know about that."

I sneer at him. "And what makes you say that?"

"Look around you, Giselle," he says, the sound of my name on his lips making me tingle. "You have this wonderful community that, I'm assuming you've built with your sisters-,"

"Best friends," I correct.

"Sorry. Best friends," he continues. "I'm assuming at least one of those little squirts was yours."

"Why assume I have children?"

"With the way you tensed up when I looked in their direction. Either you have tiny humans running around this area, or you're an extremely protective, and cool," he adds quickly like he doesn't want to offend me, "Aunt Giselle."

"You're very observant," I say.

"That I am. It's a necessity when you're out on your own like I am. Nobody is with me to cover my back, so I have to be ready for anything."

"I can understand that." It hits me hard realizing that with Mark, I was on my own for so long. He never had my back with anything.

Mostly because he was on his, being ridden by some tramp.

If that wasn't a Kiara thing to say, I don't know what is.

"It's like coming face-to-face with a spider," Cal continues.

My face twists with confusion. "What does that have to do with anything?"

"A spider," he repeats. "When I came into your commune, you three looked at me like you wanted to squish me."

"We don't kill spiders," I say, cutting him off even though I don't think that helps his point.

"What people don't understand," he continues. "Is that the spider is just as afraid of you as you are of it."

I tilt my head back and forth, considering his analogy.

"Not to mention the fact that there are three of you and only one of me."

"So you were a scared spider," I say, looking at him.

"I was a scared spider," he says slowly, confirming.

I smile. "I guess I didn't think of it that way." This guy is definitely not what I pegged him for. When he walked onto our property, he seemed timid, but only because he wasn't sure of the area and we were obviously two out of three badass women who scared him.

Obviously.

He was burly, rugged, and muscular with dirt and disheveled hair coating his face. I assumed a tough guy who had something to prove.

Listening to him talk, he seems much more than that. Almost poetic. But still rugged and sexy as hell.

"I kind of assumed that you have people coming onto your property on a regular basis," he says.

"We've had a few stragglers. But we rarely have any that take a seat and prop their feet up."

"I feel special."

I smirk. "You should."

He grins. "Well, there's no signage on the trail itself that tells people it's not a cut-off into another part of the woods."

"We have a giant sign as you walk into our yard that says it's a no trespassing zone."

"I mean, it's not giant," he counters. "And can you blame us for coming here? Once we realize it's not a gift shop or tourist area, we realize that people actually live here. And let me just tell ya, it's a golden location."

I smile, growing more and more proud of the place I've built with Kiara and Jade.

He stares at me for a minute and I feel restless. I cross my legs and clear my throat as I look out over the lake.

It's stunning.

"I make you uncomfortable," he says matter-of-factly.

"Do not," I argue, still not looking at him.

"Do so," he says. "And if that's not a toddler's quarrel, I don't know what is."

"I'm rubber, you're glue," I tease.

He laughs. Pauses a moment, then he asks, "Why did you come down here?"

I tuck a strand of hair behind my ear. "I just wanted to see how long you planned on staying. It's not like you can up and leave whenever you want. We still have your things inside."

"You know," he says, resting his back against the table. "When I woke up this morning, I never expected to become part of a hostage situation."

"That's not what I meant," I chuckle.

"I didn't say I was mad about it."

His eyes are gleaming when I look at him. I'm not sure if it's the glow of the setting sun hitting the water, or if he's enjoying my company. I'm really hoping it's the latter.

"Then, maybe I'll just keep your things for a while longer," I tease, feeling my cheeks flush a little.

"I'd like that."

"How about you stay for dinner?" I offer, unsure if I just jumped the gun.

He straightens himself and looks up toward the houses. "Really? What about Lucy and Ethel up there? They won't have me gagged and tossed into the basement somewhere, will they?"

"You act like you wouldn't enjoy that."

He shrugs. "You're right." He looks out over the pavilion banister and takes a deep breath. "I guess it couldn't hurt to stay for a meal before I head out."

I want to say something, but I don't know what. I want to fight him not to leave, but I don't know why. I want him to stay here, but I don't know where.

And I rarely get what I want... except in this moment when he says, "Unless you want me to stay longer than dinner."

I feel my heart fluttering like I gave a cage of butterflies a line of cocaine.

I smile at him. You have no idea.

CHAPTER EIGHT

CALEB

I sat dumbfounded on the picnic table after Giselle handed me a key and told me it was to the guest house. The conversation between us keeps replaying over and over in my mind just to make sure I didn't imagine it.

Asking me to stay for dinner. Offering me a place to sleep. Giving me a key to a part of her world.

And the look in her eyes... oh man. That sparkle when I accepted the key almost knocked the wind right out of me.

As I open the door to the guest house, I'm almost blown away. It's like walking into a five-star bed and breakfast.

Modern decor is scattered perfectly throughout the open-concept space. There's a large living area, dining area, and a kitchen that are done in black and white with pops of red throughout. Stainless steel appliances in the kitchen. Reclining sofa with a large wall-mounted flat screen TV. A computer in the corner of the room that sits on a black modern desk. And I'm sure this kitchen is fully stocked.

A guy could get used to this.

My stomach is growling and I check my watch to see that I only have about forty minutes until I'm supposed to be up at Giselle's patio for the dinner she invited me to.

Just as I'm racing toward the kitchen to get rid of the embarrassing grumble in my gut, I hear a knock on the door.

It's Kiara. I can't see through the door, but I know it's her from the instructions I was given after she came down to the pavilion.

Go to the guest house and walk inside. Latch the door behind you. I'll bring your bag down and leave it outside after I knock once. Give me thirty seconds to walk back up to the house before you open the door and take your things. If you open the door any sooner, I'll mace your ass. Oh, and I'm keeping your gun hidden as long as you're on our property.

These ladies are one of a kind, but I'm okay with it. I feel like they'll definitely keep me on my toes.

I still want to know how Giselle was able to sway the other two into letting me stay with them. Part of me doesn't want to question it, but another part of me feels like it's a bit sketchy.

Maybe they are tied to JT. Maybe someone called them ahead of time because someone saw me on the trail.

"No," I whisper to myself. "They aren't involved with any of it."

I shake my head and realize I have no idea how long it's been since I heard the knock. Fifteen seconds? Twenty? Thirty?

I'll ransack the kitchen before I dare open that door. I'm a mess as it is and I don't need to add pepper spray to my ensemble.

I don't even look at the container that's labeled 'Granola' because fuck that. I've had enough of that shit to last a lifetime.

I grab a small bag of chips and jam them down my throat, chugging one of the mini bottles of water in the fridge.

I hate mini water bottles. What's the point? Buy the regular size and drink the damn water.

I drink a second one and walk to the door to grab my bag, dragging it inside and latching the door again. I pull the clothes out of the larger compartment and thank myself for grabbing extra clothes when I left.

I also thank myself that I didn't wear everything I dragged through the woods with me. I wasn't sure if I'd be coming in contact with anyone important and would need a clean pair of clothes. Apparently I was prepared for this.

I take my razor and clothes into the bathroom and gawk at the design of the tile. It's almost as if this house was designed by Satan himself. Baphomet statue on the shelf above the toilet. Red and black roses, fake of course, in a vase above the sink. Pentagram rug at the base of the shower.

Yet it looks so elegant and I have to admit, I don't hate it.

Not to mention the fact that I'm far from picky at the moment. It could be a mud hole and I'd be grateful to stand under a hot stream of water.

The last time I showered was when I snuck into a gas station after hours and hosed myself down in the bathroom. Not much of a shower, but it was more than I'd had in a while.

This is going to be heaven and I'm going to savor every second of it.

There's a small radio on top of the toilet by the shower and I click it on while I scrub the dirt and grime off myself. I make a mental note to scrub the shower when I'm done. I can't believe how dirty I am.

That's a lie. I can. I've been walking a dirt trail for what feels like a lifetime.

I can't even remember how long I've walked. My calves ache and my skin is so dry that I could claw it open. There's a bottle of lotion on the vanity outside the shower and I don't care how strong the lavender scent is, I'm lathering my entire body in that shit. I'll smell like a woman so long as I'm not clawing at my legs.

When I step out of the heavenly water box that I wish I could have stayed in for another hour, I sigh with relief and I sigh loud. It felt better than I imagined.

I even scrubbed behind my ears like a good boy.

The thought has me reminiscing on my childhood when my mom would always check behind my ears to make sure I scrubbed. Somehow she always knew whether or not I did.

Moms are magic.

Then, I wonder where Ash is and what he's doing. I haven't risked reaching out to him for fear that I'd be traced and found by JT. I want Ash to know where I am, but I can't chance that his phone is tapped or someone is listening in on his calls through a wall or window.

I know he was taking care of mom before everything went down, but I don't think he'd be stupid enough to stay with her after I went missing. That's the first place they'd look, and I know they'd hold him as collateral.

Part of me wishes I was the one to stay with her. Even when he and I were kids, he was a daddy's boy and I always held tight to mom's leg.

Call me a 'momma's boy' all you want; I learned a shit ton from that woman.

I send up a quick prayer for my mom while I'm thinking of her. Ever since she got cancer, I haven't been over to visit. I was more concerned that JT would get wind of it and use her as a weapon against me. Everyone that knows me would know that my family is my only weak spot.

Once everything calms down, and I'm sure that JT won't find me or go after my mom; I'll make it my first priority to go see her.

The mirror is all clouded with steam as I step to the sink to shave and tame my mane. It doesn't take me too long since I'm in a hurry to see Giselle and get a real meal in my stomach, but I also try to do a decent job so they get to see the real me.

Or at least as much of the real me as I can share for the safety of them and their kids.

"You're a good lookin' guy, Cal," I tell my reflection as I tilt my head from side to side, making sure I didn't miss a spot. "Now, go get ready to 'wow' those ladies with your radiant personality."

Once I'm dressed and pleased with my final look, I give myself one last pep talk in the mirror before I walk out the door.

I feel like I haven't had a real conversation with human beings in months. The last time I talked to anyone, aside from Giselle earlier today, it was a discussion with a squirrel on where they keep their nuts and what they do if another squirrel takes them. They don't have guns or weapons they can use, so does it look like a chick fight with fur pulling and claw scratching?

Hard to say. The squirrel didn't talk back much.

I make sure to pack my things in my bag before I walk out of the guest house, just in case Kiara and Jade changed Giselle's mind on my staying here.

The key is tucked safely in my pocket and I begin my walk up the hill toward the three houses.

I'm only sure of which house is Giselle's because of the iron work that sits outside. They told me dinner would be on her patio, so I head in that direction and walk around back.

The kids are playing on the playground equipment and two of them look up toward me and wave. I wave back before I walk toward the stone patio across from the kids.

Jade is sitting on a cushioned chair with a beer in her hand and as I take my first step onto the stone, she gets to her feet. Her red hair doesn't look as messy as it did earlier. She must have straightened it because it's now in a ponytail, but it looks immaculate. She even did her makeup and changed into a white flowy shirt that she paired with black shorts.

She looks nice, and I'd give her a compliment, but she hates me.

I stop walking when she stares at me.

"Hi," I say, unsure of what else to do.

"Hi yourself," Jade replies in a much lighter tone than she was using earlier. She's giving me the up and down and I swear her mouth turns up in a smile like she's impressed.

Kiara comes out through the sliding glass doors that I assume lead to Giselle's kitchen, and places a large bowl on the cloth covered table.

She is in another pair of shorts with a different black tanktop. I'm wondering if that's all her wardrobe consists of. Her blonde hair is now down around her shoulders and I'm wondering if she's sweating balls just to have her hair down.

But then I notice the hair tie on her wrist and realize she's prepared.

"I hope you're hungry," Kiara says with a smile, also looking me up and down.

It makes me feel a little bit better that Kiara is somewhat nice to me. "I'm starving," I admit. I look around, but don't see Giselle anywhere.

"She'll be out in a minute," Jade says, taking a swig of her beer. I smile at her as a thanks for reading my mind. "You look less murder-y when you shave your face and wash your hair."

My hand touches my cheek and I grin. "Thank you?"

"That's Jade's way of saying you look nice," Kiara says. "You really do clean up well. Giselle will be excited to see the new and improved Cal."

I fight the urge to blush. It's not manly for men to blush. I already smell like lavender, I don't need to go any further down that trail.

I smile and Jade walks over to me, extending a bottle in my direction. "Beer?" she asks.

I nod and accept the drink. "Thank you." I twist the top off, grateful it's still sealed so I know they didn't poison me, and take a long drink. It's icy cold and feels amazing on my throat. The amount of water I drank in their kitchen and from the shower head doesn't even do justice to how I feel at this very moment.

Kiara waves for the kids to come over from the playground and I watch them flood the patio. The two that waved to me walk right up and grab my free hand.

"I'm Owen," the little boy says. His dark wavy hair falling into his face and covering his gorgeous hazel eyes. He has to be Giselle's son.

"I'm Abby," the girl next to him says. When she smiles, I see nothing but joy in her face. Her eyes match Owen's and I'm guessing she's his little sister.

"We're the ones that waved to you," Owen says with a grin. "Who are you?"

"I'm Cal," I say, smiling back at them. "It's very nice to meet you."

"It's nice to meet you too," Abby says. She has the sweetest little voice.

Talking to these kids is like having a dagger driven into my stomach when I think that I won't ever have children of my own. Not with the past I'm carrying around with me.

"I'm Piper," a girl says as she walks up to me. She's taller than the others, but not by much. I can tell she belongs to Jade, not just because of her red hair that matches her mom's, but because Jade gets to her feet and watches our interaction.

"Nice to meet you, Piper," I say, giving Jade a reassuring nod that I'm not going to hurt these kids.

Jade sits back down.

The other two were at the top of the jungle gym, but come running toward the huddle. I don't get their names, but Kiara smiles, so I have a feeling they belong to her.

"Those are my two," Kiara says, confirming my assumption. "Lexie and Wyatt. Always late to the party."

I laugh. "Well, hello, Lexie and Wyatt."

Wyatt sticks his hand out toward me to shake, but the kid doesn't look to be any older than four. I accept the gesture and he gives a nod before he walks toward Kiara.

"Dapper young fella," I say with a smile. Kiara smiles big and nods.

I hear Wyatt tell Kiara he's hungry, and when she tells him that it's time to eat, the rest of the kids rush over to the table and take a seat.

"Do you need a drink, Cal?" Kiara asks. I wave my beer at her. "Gotcha."

I look around again, but still no Giselle. I'm starting to wonder if she's melting down my gun and turning it into something else.

Jewelry maybe. They seem like they'd like jewelry.

Or possibly another masterpiece to join the collection she has outside her house.

Lexie shouts, "Cal! Come sit by me!"

Then Abby argues. "No! I saved him a seat!"

Wyatt and Owen shake their heads at the girls, and Piper doesn't seem interested in me at all. She gets that from her mother. Though, I think I made some headway with her because she handed me a beer.

"How about we let Cal sit with the grown-ups," Kiara suggests.

"Yeah," Jade adds. "He doesn't want to sit with you yucky little kiiiiids." She's singing as she teases them.

This gets them all riled up and Kiara glares at her. "I just got them seated and now you're getting them all wild again. Thanks, Jade."

"Sure thing," Jade says as she tips her beer bottle up.

"Take a seat, Cal," Kiara says, gesturing toward the grown-up table.

The adult seats are bright cushions against a dark wicker with tiny throw pillows that I always find useless. On these chairs, they look stunning. These ladies sure know how to decorate.

"This space is amazing," I say. "The guest house, the patio, your homes. Everything. Did you ladies plan all of this yourselves?"

Kiara nods. "We have been planning this commune for years. It's been an ongoing dream for the three of us ever since we met."

"Did you grow up together?" I ask.

"Nah," Jade says. "I made a post on a social media group about wanting to form a tight-knit writing family, and somehow got stuck with these two yahoos."

"You're authors?" I ask, impressed. "All three of you?"

"Best selling," Jade says, sharing a high-five with Kiara.

Now I'm beyond impressed, and a little intimidated. "How long after you met did it take you to make all this a reality?"

Kiara and Jade's eyes rise toward the sky where they seem to keep their invisible calculator.

"About six years," Kiara finally says. "We spent the first two years writing like crazy. We even took on a writing challenge to write one million words in a single year."

"I'm guessing that's a lot?" I ask.

"Well, it's the equivalent of about eighteen books in a single year," Jade says. "So, I guess you could say that's a lot."

"Jeez," I say, puffing my cheeks out. "That's more than one book a month."

"We've got a mathematician on our hands," Jade sniggers.

I laugh too. "Sorry, I guess I just needed to calculate that out loud. That's a lot of work." I take a drink from my beer. "Did you accomplish it? The million words in a year?" I look over my shoulder toward Giselle's house, but still nothing.

"We did," Kiara says, puffing out her chest like Superman. "And we take every opportunity to tell random people that we did it."

"Cashiers, produce stands, random hikers on the trail," Jade laughs. "We hardly let anyone get away."

"I wouldn't either," I admit. "That's quite an accomplishment. How many books do you have published?"

I go to take another drink from my beer and the sliding glass doors open behind me, cutting off the conversation. Giselle steps out onto the patio and I lower my bottle to look at her.

She slides the glass doors closed behind her and when she turns around to look at all of us, our eyes meet. I get a hint of satisfaction when her jaw drops as she looks me over and whispers, "Oh hot damn."

Chapter Nine

Giselle

Y OU KNOW THOSE TIMES you're standing on stage, ten minutes late for the presentation you didn't know you were supposed to give? And you're naked?

Oh, did I mention that's a nightmare?

Yeah, that's how I feel right now.

I hate that I just blurted that to Cal. And even worse, I did it in front of Jade and Kiara. My cheeks are on fire and I can feel my mouth gaping open in shock, letting everyone around me know that I didn't mean to compliment him out loud.

"Mommy said a swear," Owen says.

I laugh in spite of myself and rub the back of my neck which I notice is now sweating. I'm not sure how much of the summer heat is to blame for that.

"I did," I say to Owen. "And I'm sorry." I let out a deep breath and try to redirect everyone's attention. "Dinner ready yet?"

"You're *damn* right it is," Jade says with a smirk. She shoots Owen a look that says she's allowed to swear and he better keep his trap shut. They've had this discussion in the past. "Grab a seat," Jade chuckles. "I'll get you a beer. You seem to need one," she adds out of the corner of her mouth.

"Thanks," I say, anxious to get the bottle in my hands so I can fidget with something. I turn and look toward Cal. "You look... different."

"I look good," Cal says.

The corners of my mouth quirk up. I have to clamp my mouth shut from making another comment that will embarrass the hell out of me. "Mmhmm" is all I manage to reply.

"I hope you're hungry," Kiara says. "The kids all have their plates loaded and are digging in. Now it's our turn."

I try to ignore how I'm feeling when I see Cal's naked and very handsome face, while I pile a bunch of food onto my plate. I'm grateful for not being one of those people who can't have their food touching because my mind is elsewhere and it seems my macaroni salad wants to be one with my beans and weenies.

The four of us head back to the cushioned seats and plop down, our plates heaping with summer time nourishment.

"So, Cal," Kiara begins with her mouth full. "Where are you from?"

Cal takes a drink of his beer and I'm thankful he's not one of those guys who will give the world a show of his chewed up food while he talks.

"I'm from Wyoming, originally. But I moved to Southern Montana about six years ago. I lived there with my friend, Evan, for four of those years."

"Awe," Kiara whines in her usual mocking tone. "He actually has friends."

"Yes," Cal laughs. "I have friends. We didn't grow up together or anything. I just met him when I left my hometown and headed this way. Figured there'd be more to this state than a hardware store and one traffic light."

"So, you prefer the hustle and bustle?" Jade asks.

Cal nods. "I just like to keep my mind busy. Focusing on things other than my own problems became a hobby of mine, I suppose." He chuckles.

"You have a lot of problems?" I ask, my forkful of pasta salad paused halfway to my mouth.

He shrugs one shoulder like it's no big deal. "Everyone has their own internal battles. Some they talk about, and some they don't."

Kiara nods in agreement, but it sends a shiver up my spine. I want him to elaborate on it, but I also don't know if I'll like what I hear. Plus, he made it clear that there are things he doesn't talk about.

"You have any siblings?" Kiara asks.

"An older brother," he says. "His name is Ash, though growing up I called him 'Ashhole'. I haven't seen him for about a year or so because he tends to dance around to the beat of his own drum."

"He's a hippie?" Jade asks.

Cal almost spits his beer out. "Oh God no," he says, wiping the drip from the corner of his mouth.

I almost bite my lip at the thought of using my tongue to clean it up.

"He's far from a hippie. He just tends to go do his own thing and checks in to let us know he's not dead."

"My brother is kind of like that," Jade says. "He'll show up when it's convenient for him or if he needs something. Otherwise, I don't see him much."

Cal tilts his bottle toward Jade and they cheers to having something in common. It makes me smile seeing Jade coming around to him.

"What about your parents?" Kiara asks.

I feel bad that they're interrogating him, but he seems to be rolling with the punches. Maybe it's the fact that Jade's now handing him a third beer, or maybe he just feels comfortable around us. He could also be giving us anything we want because we're giving him a place to stay.

"My dad passed away when I was just a pup," he says. "Car accident. Mom is still home though. Her favorite things are naps and Lifetime Television."

"I'm sorry for your loss," I say.

I look at Jade, knowing she lost her father at a young age too. She was in her teens when it happened, but it's not easy to lose a parent no matter how young or old you are.

And Kiara's history with her father isn't something she really talks about. She said that she hasn't seen him since she was a kid. That's all we really know about it.

"I'm sorry too," Jade says, looking at me like she's about to open up to him. "I can empathize."

Cal gives her a look and a slow nod. "I'm sorry that you had to go through that."

The two of them chug their beer together and Jade hands him another.

"Well, why did you shave?" Kiara asks, changing the subject to a lighter tone. "Hoping that the other trail hikers won't be able to control themselves?

He laughs and touches his chin thoughtfully. "Well, can you blame me? I'm surrounded by three gorgeous women and I'm sure you don't want a caveman among your children."

"Some women like cavemen," I tease. Cal looks at me and I swear I notice a twinkle in his eyes.

Owen shouts from the table. "I'm done, Mom!"

Followed by Abby's, "Me too! I'm done too!"

And Lexie on cue with, "Can we go play now?"

I stand up and walk over to their table to analyze their plates. I give them a nod of approval and say, "Clean up and you can go play."

"Can Cal come play with us?" Abby asks, looking over to where he's sitting.

I glance at him and he smiles at the girls who are craning their necks to see him.

"I will definitely come play for a little while," Cal says.

The girls start cheering and the four of them take off running when Cal tells them he'll be the seeker and they can go hide.

"Sorry, ladies," Cal says to us. "But it looks like my presence has been requested." He finishes the beer in his hands and clinks his bottle with Jade's. She raises hers to him and gives him a nod.

Before he takes off running after the kids, he looks over his shoulder, gives me a wink, and I swear my heart jumps into my throat.

Jade and Kiara help me get my patio put back together while Cal is chasing the kids around the jungle gym. We manage to get through most of the cleaning, including the dishes before Jade dives into the topic of our caveman.

"You're smitten," Jade says to me.

I can't even keep myself from grinning. I laugh and take a sip of my beer. "Am not," I lie.

"Are too," Kiara chimes in.

"You know what?" I finally say. I tuck my tongue in my cheek while I contemplate. "Maybe I am."

Jade points an accusatory finger at me and her eyes go wide. "I knew it! You like him!"

"Sssshhh!" I growl at her, looking over my shoulder to make sure he can't hear us. When he doesn't seem to be phased, I look back at them.

"She likes him," Kiara echoes.

"What's not to like?" I ask somewhat quietly. "He seems intelligent. He's funny. Witty. Super good looking. And he's obviously self-sufficient if he can make it out on that trail for as long as he has."

"How long did he say he was out there?" Kiara asks.

I try to think back, but parts of the conversation escape me. "I can't remember. But that's not the point."

"I bet you want to see *his* point," Jade says with a wink.

A laugh bubbles up my throat. "I can't even argue that," I admit, feeling my smile continue to grow as I talk. "Is it so bad to find him charming? A complete stranger that I've barely known for a day?"

Jade looks at her watch. "Four hours to be exact."

"You're lucky the spoons are all clean, otherwise I'd be throwing one at you," I threaten.

Jade sticks her tongue out and give her the middle finger.

"No," Kiara says, interrupting our childish banter.

When I look at her I notice she's shaking her head. Not in a way that says she's arguing with us. She's shaking her head like she does when she's about to go off on a tangent about something.

"You know what?"

Yep... here she goes.

"Go for it, Giselle," Kiara continues. "You've worked hard for everything you have in your life and it's time that you have some fun. Having some fun with him would be no different than picking a guy up at the bar. He's a stranger that you've only known for a little while. And who knows how long he'll be here." Jade goes to comment on the length of his stay, but Kiara doesn't give her the chance. It's oddly satisfying. "Go get some!" she shouts.

"Get some what?" Wyatt asks as he walks into the kitchen, completely out of breath.

The three of us clamp our mouths shut. Kiara looks at her youngest and says, "Juice. Get some juice."

"I want juice," Wyatt says. "Or maybe some water."

I race to the fridge for the juice boxes and hand them over to Wyatt. "How about you offer these to everyone. Take a juice break. Is Cal still playing with you kids?"

Wyatt pops the straw into the top and takes a few big gulps. He's nodding as he drinks and I can see that his cheeks are a little red.

"He's great," Wyatt says in his little voice.

I give his shoulder a squeeze. "I'm glad you think so."

Wyatt takes off through the back doors and heads for the play area. I cross my arms and look out the window to watch the kids chasing

Cal around with their juice boxes in hand. It warms my heart for there to be a man on the grounds. The kids haven't had much interaction with any grown men, aside from the occasional visit from Vince.

"Seriously," Jade says. "Go talk to him. Kiara and I will keep Abby and Owen for the night."

"I second that," Kiara says.

"But what am I supposed to say?" I ask.

"Uhhh, maybe start with 'Hi, I think you're sexy'," Kiara suggests, almost a little too seriously.

I rub my hands over my face. "I think you two are forgetting the fact that I'm a little bit married?"

"In the midst of a divorce," Jade corrects.

Kiara points her thumb at Jade as a way of seconding her comment.

I roll my eyes at them. "What if he rejects me because of it? I'm used goods. Cheated on and tossed to the curb."

"But you're at least sexy used goods," Kiara says with a wiggle of her hips.

I love my friends for always knowing how to take a little bit of the edge off.

I fold my arms over my chest. "What happened to you two being against this? Accusing him of being an ax murderer?" I ask, resting my chin on my fist and staring at the girls.

Jade shrugs. "Maybe he's not so bad after all."

Kiara and I smirk at her. "Be careful," Kiara begins. "You may be mistaken for a person with a heart."

"Shut your trap," Jade snaps.

I laugh. "There's our girl."

Chapter Ten

Caleb

I'M OUT OF BREATH when Wyatt hands me a juice box. It's like getting a spritz of water from a squirt gun, but it's better than nothing. All I've really had to drink in the last hour or so is a few beers.

Maybe next time, I'll ask Jade for a water instead.

The doors to Giselle's house open and Giselle starts walking my way. Her face is glowing in the light of the setting sun and it makes it impossible not to stare. She must have noticed me looking at her because she gives me a small wave before hollering for the kids.

"Everyone up to my house," she says to the kids. "They're putting on a movie and the popcorn is already microwaved."

The kids start shouting and it makes me laugh. They're so much fun. Loaded with energy, yes, but still a lot of fun.

"Popcorn?" I ask. I lean against the jungle gym with the juice box straw in my mouth. Lavender lotion and a child's beverage; I've never felt so manly in my life.

"Kiara made some for the kids," she says.

I feel a little bummed when she makes it sound like I'm not getting to share a snack with them. I really didn't want to be stuck in the guest house by myself tonight, but I guess they want some family time. I can respect that.

"Sounds like a fun time," I say, trying not to sound disappointed.

As I'm getting ready to push myself off the jungle gym and head down to my solitude, Giselle walks over and leans beside me. The smell of her perfume rolls off her shirt and dances under my nose. She smells like heaven.

"I was wondering if you'd like to go for a walk," she says.

I'm completely surprised at the offer. These women offering me shelter and food was shocking in and of itself. But now Giselle actually wants to spend time with me?

As my mother used to say, you could probably knock me over with a feather right now.

"Cal?" she says, looking at me as though she's unsure if I heard her.

"Sorry," I finally manage to say. I look down at my juice box and then back at Giselle. "Yes. I'd love to go for a walk with you."

"You can bring your juice box," she teases.

I grin. "That's mighty kind of you."

We head out of the playground, past her house, and down toward the bridge to the lake. The summer breeze is blowing across the water and moving over the ground, making the blades of grass dance underneath it. It's a beautiful sight to see the reds and oranges reflecting off the top of the water while it ripples under the wind.

"It's a nice night," she says as we walk.

"It certainly is," I agree.

I can't believe how many details these three thought of when they built this place. Including the garbage can that was placed in the perfect spot for me to discard my empty drink box as we stroll by the pavilion.

"I can't stress enough how amazing this place is," I say, jamming my hands into my shorts pockets to keep from running my fingers through her hair.

"Thank you," she says. "It took us long enough to get ourselves to this point."

"It's a huge accomplishment." We take a few more steps and I walk a little bit closer to her. "So, how many books have you published?"

She looks at me, shocked at the fact I know she's a writer. "Kiara and Jade," I say, answering her internal question of how I found out.

She nods her head and looks down at her feet while we walk. "I have twenty-two books published. Seventeen hit the bestseller list," she says.

I have to stop walking. "That's... that's incredible. You're like, famous or something!"

She puts a hand on her chest and cackles with laughter. I watch her in amusement and find myself joining in. When she gathers herself, she says, "I'm not famous." She adjusts her hair and wipes the small tear from the corner of her eye. "But thank you."

"You're welcome," I say. "Even though that sounds so silly to say to someone who has published twenty-two books. I feel like I need a better reply."

"It's not stupid," she says. Her expression is filled with amusement and satisfaction. She's so humble, it's not even funny.

"What kind of books do you write?"

"Paranormal romance, mostly. Sometimes I dabble in other genres."

"Like what?" I've never really been interested in books. But in this moment, I'm the biggest bookworm on the planet.

"I wrote two fantasy novels. A few romantic suspense novels and short stories, and one science-fiction. After that, I realized my work needed to remain in the paranormal romance world. It's my favorite genre and the one I feel most happy writing. It's what I'm comfortable with."

"I see."

"Do you read much?" Her eyes focus on me and I feel like my answer is going to determine whether or not she pushes me in the lake.

"I used to," I say. "The time for reading kind of got away from me."

She nods slowly. "What is it you do for a living?"

"I work in sales," I say, thinking that's the closest to the truth that I can get.

"Sounds kind of-"

"Boring," I say, finishing the thought for her.

Her laugh flows out over the lake. It's the best sound next to the laughter of all those little kids up there cozying in front of the tv with their popcorn.

I'm not as disappointed that I didn't get to share that snack.

"I'm sorry to hear that you don't like your job," she says, sounding sincere when she says it.

What she doesn't understand is how much I truly hated my job. How much I truly hated what that life choice did to my mind. I became a completely different person once I sat in front of JT and agreed to be a part of his group. Agreed to his terms and conditions of how my life would be once I shook his hand and walked out of that office.

"Eh, most people hate their jobs," I say.

"I love mine," she counters.

"Well, yeah. You get to be famous."

She nudges me. "So, I'm assuming you quit your job?"

"What makes you think that?"

She looks around us. "You're walking around a lake at sunset with a woman you don't even know. You've been on the CDT and in these woods for God knows how long. I'm assuming a sales job isn't one that can be done remotely."

I let out a breath. "No, it's not a job that can be done remotely." Though that would make it easier to hide. "Customers tend to want to be face to face when they're purchasing something. Mainly to test the quality of the product and make sure it's a good fit for them."

This lying thing is actually easier than I thought it would be. I hate that I'm lying to her so much, but she's setting me up with questions that can be twisted toward the truth without giving away who I really am.

I wish I could be honest with her.

"That makes sense," she says.

We take a few more quiet steps and look around the path near the lake. There's a slight breeze blowing her hair off her shoulders and I'm jealous that the warm night air gets to kiss her naked skin and I don't.

"Can I ask you something?" she asks.

My heart skips a beat, but I know my options are limited with answers. "Sure."

"You said earlier that everyone has internal battles. That some are better left unspoken." She clears her throat and looks down, like she doesn't want to look me in the eye when she asks her question. "What is the internal battle that you won't tell us about?"

She looks back up at me when she asks and I can tell she's afraid of what I'll tell her.

"I'm not asking to be nosy," she continues. "I'm only asking because I have this awful feeling in my stomach that I need to clear. My mind is clouded for reasons I can't quite decipher, and I just need to make sure that the limb I'm going out on doesn't snap under my feet."

"You sure do have a way with words," I say.

"I'm an author," she counters.

"Good point."

I kick at a stone that's in front of my shoe as we make a right turn and stand on a bridge that hovers over the lake. We lean our elbows on the railing and I shift over toward her so our arms are touching.

I see her grin when we make contact and it sends a jolt straight to my heart.

"You don't have to tell me if you don't want to," she adds, fidgeting with her fingers. "I guess it was more for my own sanity than anything else."

I take a deep breath and let my shoulders relax as I release it. "Well, I do have an internal battle. A few of them, actually." I look at what remains of the setting sun, shifting my eyes toward the dark purple sky above us. "I wasn't exactly truthful with you earlier when we spoke."

She turns toward me and I can practically see her building the barrier up between us.

"When I told you that my mom enjoys naps, it's not because it's her hobby. It's because she's battling cancer."

Giselle's face falls in a mix of sorrow and confusion. "Why aren't you home with her?"

"That's the thing," I continue. "My internal battles are keeping me far away. Being away from her when she's in this state is pulling my family farther and farther apart. My brother has been her sole caregiver since it all happened. There are nurses that go in and tend to her, administer her medications, draw her blood for testing, and ask her routine questions to make sure she's stable when they go to and from her chemo appointments."

"And she is?" she asks, looking almost frantic. "Stable, I mean?"

I nod. "For now. It's hard to say when things will take a turn for the worst."

"I'm sorry," she says, shaking her head slowly as though she can't imagine how I'm feeling. "For all of that. I can't imagine what you're battling, not being able to be there for her."

"Trust me when I say it's best that I keep my distance."

"Okay," she says, returning to her position against my arm. "I'm sorry I pried."

"Don't be sorry," I say. "I can't blame you for wanting to settle that feeling in your gut. It's never fun to have to fight those thoughts and try to calm your nerves. Especially with something you don't know much about."

She smiles and turns toward me. "Thank you for understanding. And for being so willing to share your past with us." She looks down at her hands and adds, "And thank you for not being an ax murderer."

"Only on Tuesday's," I tease.

Giselle just stares at me and I can't help when my gaze drops to her mouth. Her lips look so delicious and I want, more than anything, to feel mine brush against hers. I can feel myself leaning into her. She's not fighting me on this or telling me no, and I don't want her to second-guess it and push me away.

My hand reaches up behind her neck and I pull her into me. My mouth embraces her and I feel like a show of fireworks would be sufficient for this moment. I imagine the bright flashes of fire in the sky reflecting off the lake while two people are tangled up in each other.

But that's the kind of thing you only ever see in movies.

When I pull away from her and open my eyes, I notice that her eyes are wide and she appears to be frozen in place. I look behind me to make sure there's not a rabid creature waiting to devour us, or a real ax murderer waiting to make his move.

Nobody is behind us. Great. I scared her. I'm the one making her eyes do that weird crazy face.

"I'm so sorry," I say, not sure what to say to put her face back to normal. "I just... I don't know what came over me."

"It's okay," she says. She swallows hard and runs a hand through her hair. I notice she's avoiding eye contact and I feel about two inches tall.

"I'm sorry," I say again, feeling like a broken record. "I'm not after you for sex. I don't expect anything like that. I guess I just couldn't help myself."

She smiles nervously. "It's okay. Really. I didn't mean to look so freaked out when you kissed me. I just wasn't expecting it."

"Really?" I say. "I guess I got the wrong idea. I was giving you all my best moves."

She leans back and raises her eyebrows at me while tilting her head. "Those were your best moves?"

My jaw drops. "Give me a break! I went out on a limb just like you did, but guess what? Mine snapped under my feet."

She laughs and covers her mouth when she sees that my face is anything but amused. "I'm so sorry," she says. "I tend to laugh when I'm nervous."

Hearing her say that takes the edge off. "I do too," I admit. A squeak of amusement escapes my lips and it sends me into a fit of laughter, which makes her do the same. Her hysterics make mine intensify and now we're both standing on the bridge over a lake laughing like hyenas.

When we finally get ourselves together, she reaches for my arm and squeezes. "I'm sorry, Cal. I really am. But I have to say, that's the hardest I've laughed in a long time."

"I'm glad I could entertain you," I say, wiping a tear from my eye and realizing I too haven't laughed like that for years.

She straightens herself and sniffles. "I really didn't mean to react like that. It's just that I'm not looking for a relationship. Or anything of the sort, actually."

"Oh," I say, feeling like someone just squeezed my heart until it popped.

"It's not because of you," she says quickly. "I guess I should tell you that I'm married."

Now it's my turn to feel a bit shocked. I step back and put a hand to my mouth like I just got punched. "I kissed a married woman."

"No!" She says, reaching for me and grabbing my hand. She sounds panicked. "It's not like that. I'm in the middle of a divorce."

I let out a huge sigh of relief. "Well, that helps a little bit. I guess you could have started with that. Save a fella from having minor heart failure."

"Jade could have revived you," she says, waving it off.

"She's a doctor?"

"She's an author," Giselle says. "She's working on a series that takes place in a hospital and she's been doing medical research for forever. Her mom is also in the medical field, so I guess you could say she has a bit of a background."

"So, she knows enough to be dangerous," I conclude.

"Precisely."

"Well, I guess having a fictional doctor is better than none at all."

"Beggars can't be choosers."

I find myself staring into her eyes for a few seconds before I feel the need to break the tension so I don't ravish her here on this bridge.

"Well, anyway. I hope the divorce isn't an ugly one and that everything is working out for you. Separations aren't easy, for the adults or the children."

She gives a half smile. "It's going to work out the way it's supposed to. That's really all I know right now."

I look around. "Is he local? He's not gonna show up and try to kick my ass or anything, right?"

She snorts. "He's not local."

"Uhhhh, you didn't say no to the ass-kicking part."

"You could take him. He's worthless when it comes to sticking up for anyone, including himself. More talk than anything."

"Got ya," I say, immediately understanding his type. "Lazy?"

"Yep."

"Figures" I hear her sigh and it breaks my heart a little. "We should probably call it a night. Kiara and Jade are going to think I kidnapped you."

"Nah," she says. "They're actually coming around." I feel like I haven't blinked for a while when I notice her wave a hand in front of my face. "You okay?"

"I guess I'm not sure if my hearing is working properly."

I feel her punch my arm. "You act like they're terrible people."

"Do not! I just didn't really appreciate having a gun pointed at me, that's all."

"Listen," she says, her voice kicking up a notch in the serious category. "We have small children here. It was nothing personal, we just have to watch out for our own. We are all we have."

"I didn't say I didn't understand why you did it. I just said I didn't like it. Though I'm not sure I know many people who would."

She gives me a side glance. "Well, it was deserved."

I smirk. "I suppose."

She looks up toward the houses and I see her take a deep breath. "Anyway, I should head back up to the house and make sure my kids aren't giving them a hard time."

I give her a reassuring look. "Your kids are amazing."

"Thank you. I think so too, but I'm pretty biased."

"Thank you again for the opportunity to stay here. For however long you're offering, please know that I appreciate it more than you will ever understand."

She considers this for a bit and I catch her staring at my mouth. I want to kiss her again, but I don't want to freak her out. Especially now that I know why she's so stand-offish. Men suck sometimes.

I point a fist at her and she stares at it.

"You want to punch me?"

I reach down and grab her hand. I push her fingertips into her palm and touch our fists together.

"It's a fist bump," I explain. "I know that kissing you is out of the question, so I thought this was the next best thing."

"I always thought a chest bump was the next best thing."

I grab her hand and lead her away from the bridge. "Maybe tomorrow."

Chapter Eleven

GISELLE

T HE SUN IS PEEKING through my bedroom window, blinding me when I finally wake up. Tarot is curled up under my arm and he stretches his lengthy body when I move out from underneath the sheet. The comforter was just too much blanket for a scorching hot night, but I still need to be under a blanket so the boogie man doesn't get me.

Tarot's belly is exposed when he finishes his stretch and I can't help myself. I stick my face on his belly and rub my nose around, taking in his soft fur and kitty scent.

Tarot, however, is not a fan of that at all and inserts his claws into my skull.

"Ouch!" I yell, causing Abby and Owen to come running into my bedroom.

"Mom?" Owen asks, checking everywhere to make sure I'm okay.

"I'm alright," I say, twisting as much as I can to face the kids. "Can someone get the cat off my head?"

Owen giggles and removes Tarot, thankfully without taking any brain matter with him. He tucks the cat into his arm like a little baby and Abby walks over to scratch behind his ears, rubbing his belly while he purrs.

"Sure," I say to the demon feline. "But when I touch you like that, you become a phlebotomist and draw as much blood as you can."

The kids laugh and I walk out to the kitchen to brew a pot of coffee. I catch myself staring out the window toward the guest house. All I can see is the front door and part of the foyer window. Not sure what I was hoping to see, but I know the lack of view I'm getting right now isn't it.

I hear something shatter behind me and whirl around to see Tarot sitting on the counter. His butt is planted, his paws are tucked in between his feet, and his tail is wrapped around his bottom half while he sits tall and stares at me. Meanwhile, what used to be my favorite sugar bowl is now on the floor in pieces.

"Some days," I groan through gritted teeth. "I want to feed you to the wolves."

When my coffee is brewed and I've cleaned up Tarot's mess, I head outside to find Kiara and Jade. The kids dart past me and head for the playground.

Kiara is already in the garden, but this time she has Jade beside her.

"Well, hello there, my little veggie harvesters," I say with a smirk.

"Happy Lammas," Jade says.

"Happy Lammas," I reply. "Are we doing our bonfire tonight?"

Kiara sits back on her heels and runs a hand across her forehead, bumping the underside of her sun hat. "Yep," she says simply.

"Why on earth do you still wear that thing?" I ask. "If you went anywhere besides this commune, someone would turn you in as a UFO sighting and the press would be swarming the area."

Jade tries to muffle a laugh. "Giselle has a point."

"Shut up, both of you," Kiara snaps, straightening the monstrosity on her head. "I like it and that's all that matters."

"It's the little things that keep you happy," I breathe.

"Anyway," Kiara groans. "We'll do our bread baking and flower gathering after we pick all the veggies from the garden." She gets to her feet and brushes dirt off the knees of her pants. "The green beans are coming in nicely this year. So are the cukes and zukes."

"Any bell peppers?" I ask, stretching my neck to give the garden a once over.

"A few," Jade says. "But not as many as we wanted."

"Well, we'll make due with what we have," I say. "Let me grab my gloves and I'll help you finish up here."

I throw back the rest of my coffee like I'm doing shots at a college party, then rush to the small shed beside the garden to grab my gloves. It's a quaint little thing that Vince helped us build when we first got the garden put in. He painted it a deep red color to flow with the gray and white siding on our houses, but we covered it with art anyway, so the color didn't really matter.

Just like we told him in the first place.

We spend an hour picking the veggies and walk into Kiara's house to get them all washed off.

"So?" Jade says, giving me the eye.

"What?" I ask, knowing exactly what she's hinting at.

"How was last night?" Kiara says, reading Jade's mind.

I smile. "It was nice." I decide to leave out the kissing part, but tell them the rest. "It was a nice talk and I feel better about him staying here."

"That's a lot of nice," Jade says, mocking me.

"I didn't think you had a problem with him staying here," Kiara says, ignoring Jade and looking confused.

"Yeah," Jade agrees as she rubs the side of another bell pepper. "You seemed pretty eager to get us on board with him staying in the guest house."

I shrug. "I wasn't sure what I thought at first. He was a stranger and we do have kids here. But I also wanted to give him a chance since he looked like he needed a place to stay."

Kiara and Jade swap a look that says my concerns were what had them saying no. I ignore them.

"I got a glimpse of him as a person last night and it really made the bad feeling in my gut dissolve a little bit."

"I still have a bad feeling about something," Kiara admits.

"You think he's keeping something from us?" I ask.

Kiara nods. "I do."

"Well, he is," I say. The two of them slowly lower the veggies they're cleaning and stare at me. "Last night, I told him about the bad feeling I had. That I felt he was hiding something from us. And then he explained why I had that bad feeling." I tell the girls about his brother and how they lost contact. And I tell them about his mom and how he's not able to be there for her.

"Poor guy," Jade says. "First his dad, and now his mom?"

"He said she's stable for now," I tell them. "But they don't know how long that will last."

"What kind of cancer?" Kiara asks.

"I didn't ask. I figured he told me enough for one night."

"Well, I'm glad you got him to open up," Jade says, mindlessly rinsing the same pepper for the tenth time.

"Maybe it's your turn to open up," Kiara taunts. "Open up your lady bits! Bow-chicka-wow-wow!"

The three of us burst into laughter, but it's interrupted when there's a knock on the door. The three of us look at each other and I say, "Well, it's not me. I'm standing right here."

We look at the door and notice Cal on the other side of the glass, waving at us. I wave back and motion for him to come inside.

"Good morning, ladies," he says. His eyes move around the counters at all the veggies we have drying. "Looks like you've already finished a day's worth of work before I even got out of bed."

"It's a good possibility," Jade says. "We like to start our holidays early so we can make the best of them."

"Holiday?" Cal asks, looking at me. I can tell he's searching his internal calendar to see what he forgot.

"Lammas," I tell him. "It's a celebration of the harvest. Autumn is right around the corner."

"I see," he says. But by the look on his face, he certainly does not see.

"You don't have to understand," I say, offering him an easy smile. "Not everyone understands Wiccans."

His expression changes and I realize he didn't know that about us. I look at Kiara and Jade as a confirmation of us not telling him.

"Sorry," Kiara says, looking at him over her shoulder. "I guess we left that part out."

Cal holds his hands up and closes his eyes. "Let me get this straight," he begins. "You're all single moms. You're best selling authors. You've built your own commune. You live off the food you grow yourselves. And now you're telling me that you're witches?"

"Well, we don't grow the steak we eat," Jade says, drying her hands on a dish towel.

I bite into a green bean, unable to hide my amusement. "You make us sound pretty good," I tell him.

"I can't even tell you how impressed I am right now." His hands are now resting on his hips as he nods slowly, taking it all in.

"Are you sure?" Jade asks, folding her arms over her chest. "We sure do love to hear how amazing we are."

He laughs and shakes it off as he walks toward the counter.

"Is this your favorite holiday?" he asks all of us, examining a bell pepper.

I take it from him. "We don't have many of these, so let's just treat this like gold." I hand him a cucumber. "Play with this. We have tons."

Cal looks confused, but Kiara says, "She's a veggie snob." And he stares at me, considering.

"But no," Jade says to Cal. "It's not our favorite holiday."

"Mabon is our favorite," I tell him.

"And Samhain," Kiara adds.

Cal stares at us and I decide to elaborate. "Mabon is the celebration of the Autumn Equinox. You bake, decorate for fall, burn candles or incense or both, and basically just enjoy the season."

"Last year, we had simmer pots going all day in each of our houses," Kiara says, inhaling like she can smell the cinnamon. "And the kids picked leaves from the backyard for a craft we did later in the day."

Jade leans her elbows on the counter. "We made beef stew for dinner that day and baked a bunch of pies."

"It was a great day," I say.

"That does sound nice," Cal says. "And that was the llamas holiday?"

I chuckle. "That was Mabon," I say.

Cal winces. "Sorry. I knew that." He's tapping his fingers on the counter in deep thought. "And what was the other holiday you said?"

"Samhain," I repeat. "It's on October thirty-first."

"So it's just another word for Halloween?" Cal asks.

We shake our heads and I let Kiara explain this one. "Not exactly," she begins. "Samhain is the Gaelic festival that marks the end of the harvest season, and marks the beginning of the winter season. They call it the 'darker half' of the year."

"It's fitting for our dark souls," Jade tells him.

Cal looks at me and swallows like he's just been told a ghost hides under his bed at night and watches him sleep.

"She's not wrong," I add, and can't help but laugh when Cal starts fidgeting with his fingers.

"So, your religion is... witch?" he asks. It's so cute that he's trying to understand all of this. Most guys would just brush it all off and pretend that they're hearing us.

The three of us shake our heads again. "Being a Wiccan isn't a religion," Jade says. "It's a lifestyle. I guess you'd say that we're more spiritual than religious."

"Okay," Cal says. "That makes sense. Now I think I'm starting to understand this." He takes a seat on one of the barstools at the kitchen island and adjusts to get comfortable. "So you tend to go more toward how you feel than to follow a set of rules for a specific afterlife."

"Basically," I say. "To an extent."

Cal's eyes are scanning over all of us. "Are you going to bind me or something?"

Jade cackles. "We don't dabble in black magic," she says with a hand on her stomach.

"How do you know about binding?" I ask, unsure if I want to hear the answer.

"I saw it in a movie once," he admits sheepishly.

"For future reference," I say, rolling my eyes. "Don't believe the things you see in movies."

Cal hunches over in embarrassment.

"Don't worry," Kiara says, giving his shoulder a squeeze. "Most people think that everything they see in movies is what happens in real life."

"That's what turns people away from us," Jade adds. "They hear 'witch' or 'Wiccan' and they think we're these scary creatures that will turn you into a toad if you do us wrong."

I give Cal a wink when I add, "But I wouldn't recommend testing those waters."

Cal looks nervous as he rubs the back of his neck. "This is totally normal," he breathes. "Everything is fine. I'm fine."

All three of us break into laughter.

Owen and Lexie come racing into the house and see Cal on the stool.

"I told you he was here!" Owen says to Lexie in a tone that sounds like it should have 'nee-ner-nee-ner' somewhere in his sentence.

Lexie elbows him and looks at Cal. "Can we finish our lava monster competition?"

Kiara tilts her head at the kids. "How about we give Cal a bit of a break?"

Cal holds up a hand. "It's okay," he says. "Really." He gets off the stool and kneels down to the height of the kids. "I'll make you a deal. How about I get a cup of coffee and then I'll come out and play for a while?"

Lexie smiles her biggest smile. "Deal!"

The kids race back to the others and tell them the news about the play plans for later. I watch out the window and see them all jumping up and down, swapping high fives and fist bumps.

We give Cal a cup of coffee and watch as he downs it and disappears into the playground area. I watch for a few more minutes while Kiara and Jade work on getting some of the veggies packed up.

The more I watch Cal, the more I want him around. I want to relive the kiss from last night, but I also have a ping of fear when I think about kissing him or spending more time with him.

Maybe I just need him to be around a little bit longer before I can figure out what I want. Get to know him a little bit better before I'm comfortable kissing someone other than the man I'm technically still married to.

I sigh, thinking I should just dive in head first.

"I'll be right back," I tell Kiara and Jade as I walk out the door and head straight for the ruckus of laughter and playtime.

Cal sees me walking toward him and breaks away from the lava monster game, the look on his face transforming from excitement to concern.

"What's up?" he asks, taking deep breaths and resting his hands on his hips.

"What makes you think something's up?" I counter.

"The look on your face when you came out here. It's that of a woman on a mission." He looks over his shoulder toward the kids. "Everything okay?"

I nod. "Yeah. I just came out to tell you that you're more than welcome to stay here as long as you need."

I watch as he lifts his chin a little and narrows his eyes. "I'm waiting for the catch."

"There's no catch," I say. "Just a friendly offer." When I see the corners of his mouth turn up and his eyes drop to my mouth, I add, "But, you're still not allowed to kiss me."

He stares at me, considering. "I like a challenging woman," he says. "And I think you're just afraid of opening yourself up. Afraid of getting hurt."

My breath catches at how easily he's reading me.

"Am not," I lie. He smiles as he stares in my eyes and I can tell we both know I'm not being honest.

I winks at me before he turns away. "You'll come around to me, Giselle." And he starts to jog away.

I can't help but shake my head at him, being so cocky and so sure of himself. Though the butterflies in my stomach say that he may not be so wrong.

"Will not," I say to him, almost shouting as the distance between us grows bigger and bigger.

I see him stop jogging and look over his shoulder. He looks up to the sky and then back to me before he says, "Whatever you gotta tell yourself."

Chapter Twelve

Caleb

Slamming a hammer into things is a good way to counter the thoughts that are racing through my mind. Nail after nail, I work on hanging the new NO TRESPASSING sign on the property, and I'm picturing Evan's face with every swing.

There was no way he'd ever let me walk out of there alive. No way he would allow someone else the ability to live when it meant that he might not. And even if he had, I know for a fact he would have run right to JT and told him that I was still alive. He'd practically have written the coordinates down on a napkin and handed them over.

So why do I feel bad? Why does a small part of me feel guilty for leaving Evan for dead in the hideout?

I shake it off and focus on the sign, but the next swing of the hammer brings a whole other problem I've been facing internally.

I don't want to continue living my life afraid of taking the next turn and running into someone that's looking for me.

I close my eyes and take a deep breath as I swing the nail into the top of the sign, realizing I've probably overdone it with the security of the sign itself. So many nails. So many hits with the hammer, trying to calm myself.

I step back and give it a once over while I gather myself.

Evan is dead and JT thinks I am too. That's the best possible outcome for what happened.

I'll be fine.

"How is the sign coming along?" Jade asks, a bit perplexed as she walks up beside me.

I wipe a bead of sweat from my brow, happy that she's been warming up to me these last few days.

"I'm basically a professional sign hanger," I say as we both stare at the bright yellow and red sign. She doesn't comment on the nails and I'm glad I don't have to come up with a lie as to why there's so many. "Hopefully this does the trick and keeps people from wandering onto your property."

"People like you?" she asks, nudging me a bit.

I nod and grunt. "People like me."

She extends the beer she's been holding in her hand and I notice the top is already popped.

I take a long pull from the beer and feel the icy cold beverage slithering down my throat. It feels like Heaven and I let out a long sigh.

"How long until the poison sets in?" I ask, giving a dramatic look inside the bottle like I'm Inspector Gadget or something.

"I guess you'll know when your head starts to get a little fuzzy." She clears her throat. "But I wouldn't recommend operating any heavy machinery."

I stare at her. She has a way of saying things that makes me wonder if she's kidding or not.

Redheads scare me.

"I'm kidding," she finally says. Looking around the commune, she nods with approval. "We've been working you like a dog today. You've never turned down a chore that you've been asked to do."

"What can I say? I'm a regular Cinderella."

"You better not have a pile of mice in that guest house," she teases.

I finish off the beer. "I'm just grateful to be here," I say on a more serious note.

"We're grateful that you're not a serial killer," she says. Then, she reaches behind her and pulls out another bottle of beer, extending it to me. "The cap is still on this one."

I beam at her. "Where are you pulling these from?"

"I'm a witch," she says simply. As I take the top off and dive into the cold liquid, she says, "Thank you for being so great to Giselle. She really seems to be enjoying your company."

I swallow my mouthful and feel the butterflies in my stomach at the sound of her name. "It's mutual," I say, unable to control my immediate change in expression. I try to wipe away the giddy look on my face, but she gives me a wink before she heads back toward the houses. "Way to act like a schoolgirl," I grumble to myself.

Jade turns back toward me and shouts, "Lunch is in a few minutes if you want to take a break." Then, she looks skyward. "And the dark clouds seem to be rolling in a little earlier than expected. Maybe it's a good time to call it quits."

"Is it a passing storm?" I ask as the dark clouds roll into the white puffy ones, consuming them faster than they can escape.

She shrugs. "It's never for sure. I guess our witchy senses don't come close to that of a meteorologist."

"They lie half the time anyway," I say.

"You're not wrong."

Once she's halfway across the yard, I gather up my hammer and nails and enjoy the coolness of the stormy skies. I hope it clears up since I thought I heard one of them mention a bonfire tonight. That sounded like something I'd like to be invited to.

An hour later, I'm showered and heading up the path from the guest house to the commune when I feel a few raindrops on the top of my head. It makes me start humming as I finish my walk up the gentle hill.

"*Raindrops are fallin' on my head*," I sing, unable to stop myself.

I hear a giggle and look up to see Giselle covering her mouth as she stands on her front porch with a book in her hands.

"That's cute," she says as I get closer. "Who needs music when you have a walking jukebox on the property?"

"I didn't know anyone would be out here," I admit. "Otherwise, I would have added my mashup of *Barbie Girl* and *MMMBop*."

"Now that's a concert I'd pay tickets for."

My pulse goes jagged when she beams at me and it takes an effort to steady myself.

I point to the book in her hands. "What are you reading?"

She looks at the book as though she forgot she was holding anything. "It's the twelfth book in Kiara's series."

"Twelve?!" I practically shriek. "How the hell many books can a person put in a single series?"

"Well, according to Janet Evanovich, at least twenty-seven."

My eyes roll to the back of my head in shock. "Is she a friend of yours too?"

Giselle is practically wheezing at my question. "She's way out of our league," she finally tells me after a second.

Feeling a bit embarrassed, I gesture toward the book. "How many are in that series?"

"This is the last one," she says. "I read most of them as she was writing them. But I got a bit behind and promised to have my feedback to her by the end of today."

"It's nice that you read each other's work," I say. "And surprising that you find the time to do so." I step up onto the porch and out of the gradually heavier rain.

"Ever since we started writing, we've always read each other's work. It's nice to have an outsider's point of view on your story to make sure nothing gets missed. Each of us has a reading team, but we rely on each other more than anything else."

"Because you know that you'll be honest with each other," I conclude. "Y'all rip each other's work to shreds?"

"We don't leave anything untouched," she says with an evil look in her eyes.

There's a tapping on the glass door behind Giselle and we both look down to see Abby's toothy grin looking back at us.

"We'd better head in for lunch," she says. "Before my kid pushes her way through that glass door trying to get to you."

As soon as Giselle begins to slide the glass door open, Abby squeezes through the crack just big enough for her tiny body, and dives at me. Thankfully, the drug life left me with quick reflexes and I catch her in mid air, leaving Giselle grasping at her own chest.

She looks at me with a thankful gleam in her eye and stares at me for a second while I have my arms full of her youngest.

I hug her back when she wraps her little arms around my neck and I realize in this moment just how squishy kids are.

Weird observation.

We walk inside and I notice the rest of the kids are at the table eating their lunch.

"Are you hungry?" Owen asks with a noodle hanging from his lower lip. "It's chicken noodle soup."

"Starving!" I say, rubbing my stomach with my free hand. "Did you make it?"

All the kids erupt into laughter and Abby shouts, "No! Aunt K made it!"

I tickle her belly and she collapses into a ball of giggles against my chest.

"Oh, your Aunt K made it!" I say, exaggerating my words. "I guess I can have some then. I bet if *Owen* made it, he'd probably use frog seasoning."

All the kids groan with disgust. I put Abby down and she races to get her seat back at the table, diving into her bowl of noodles and broth.

Out of the corner of my eye, I see Giselle smiling at me, but I pretend I don't see her. When I look at Kiara who is standing near Giselle, I notice the streak of heat across Giselle's face.

And when our eyes finally meet, the heat in my face rises too.

"Food's ready," Jade shouts with a mouthful.

"Glad you waited for the rest of us," Kiara snorts, putting her dish towel on the handle of her oven.

"It's good soup," Jade says with her head tipped back so her very full mouth doesn't overflow while she talks.

"I know," Kiara says. "I kind of made it." As she's filling her bowl, she looks over her shoulder at me. "Thanks for hanging the sign. Even though you used a building's worth of nails to do the hanging."

"Yeah," I say with a forced laugh. I feel the corners of my mouth turn down, but say, "Jade and I decided it was best to get it hung as soon as possible so you don't have anymore Cal's wandering onto your property."

"We wouldn't want that," Giselle teases.

I lean in close and whisper, "Me either. I would hate to have to share you with anyone else."

I hear her hiccup or cough, and it leaves me feeling satisfied as I walk to the pot of soup to fill my rumbling stomach.

Bowls are filled with chicken noodle soup and we start passing around the wicker bowl that's filled with homemade bread. The fluffiness of the bread has my insides feeling cozy on this rainy summer day.

I follow the three adults out onto the covered porch as the kids sit at the kitchen table with the TV on beside them.

The rain is hitting the metal roof and crashing onto the ground in lines of water in front of us. The air, albeit a bit humid from the precipitation, smells like rain and makes me smile as I reach for my second piece of bread.

"This bread is to die for," I groan, cramming another bite into my mouth.

"Do you need to have a minute alone with it?" Jade asks.

I nod and continue to chew. "Give me about ten minutes. That's all I need."

"That's more than most men could ever hope for," Jade says under her breath.

I almost choke on my bread. These women sure have a way of getting a reaction out of me.

We eat in silence for a bit and enjoy the sound of the rain above us.

"I'm envious of you three," I say, heartbroken as I swallow the last bite of my bread, knowing I'd have to go inside for more.

They all look at me with chipmunk cheeks full of food and then swap a look with each other.

"Why?" Jade asks, wiping a drop of broth from her mouth after she swallows. "Because we have really nice asses?"

"That too," I say, tilting my head.

"Seriously," Giselle chimes in. "What are you so envious of?"

I hold my arms out and gesture to our surroundings with my bowl of soup. "You have all of this. Your own little world with the people you trust and the kids that you're going to raise to be amazing people. The proximity between your homes is enough to have a little privacy, but not so much that you actually have to put an effort into visiting each other. There's a guest house for," I clear my throat, "friends and family." The three of them chuckle. "And you have places for your kids to play outside." I sink into my chair and shake my head. "I'm just envious."

"Don't think it was given to us," Kiara says with her eyebrows lifted.

"We worked our fine asses off for this," Jade adds.

Giselle simply nods and spoons another bite of soup into her gorgeous mouth.

"I know you did," I say. "And I never understood how much work it was to be a writer. You women are seriously astonishing." I hold up a hand. "No. More than astonishing. There's not even a word for what you are."

"This is a fun game," Jade says, setting her empty bowl beside her. "Go ahead, Cal. Just keep telling us how great we are."

I give her a glazed look and continue. "And the best part of it all? You're great people."

Kiara and Giselle lower their soup bowls and stare at me. Jade's bowl is already down and I notice her picking at her fingernails as she listens to me. Their smiles all dissolve when they realize how serious I am.

"You're not these hoity toity, persnickety women who walk around with their chins in the air, acting like they're better than everyone else."

"Kiara does," Jade teases. Kiara punches her in the leg.

"I just want you to know that I notice all you do. I can see how hard you've worked and I'm glad that I've been allowed to be a part of your life for the time being. I've seen a lot of things since I've been here. And having each other is something you should cherish."

"Are you going to break out into song?" Jade asks, raising a brow at me.

I can't help but laugh. Especially when Giselle chimes in with *"Raindrops are fallin' on my heeaaaddd."*

Once lunch is done and we've spent some time chatting on the porch, the afternoon fades to evening. The rain has subsided but everything still seems to be a bit damp, so they decided to push the fire to another night. It bummed me out, but I figured it was going to happen when I saw how much rain we actually got.

I'm getting ready to head down to the guest house when I'm invited to hang around and play cards. I'm definitely not going to pass up time with Giselle. Especially if I get to let loose and have some fun for a while.

"The game is rummy," Jade explains as she shuffles the cards like a pro. "First one to hit five-hundred wins and the rest of you losers have to buy more beer."

"You're goin' down!" Giselle taunts.

"Puh-lease," I breathe. "You girls don't even know what you're up against."

Little do they know, I played rummy almost every night with Evan when we lived together. We tried to stay out of public as much as we could so we didn't become one of those guys that people recognize.

Stay invisible. That was the rule.

The three of them swap a look and create a scoreboard on a sheet of notebook paper. Everyone's first name is placed above a column, except mine which says 'Straggler'.

Beers are flowing and we're laughing as though we're in our teens. I can't remember the last time I had this much fun.

"You didn't even know what to say to him!" Jade howls as she taunts Giselle with a past relationship. "He showed up in a monkey suit and told you he was bananas over you!"

I'm laughing so hard I have tears running down my face. "Tell me you didn't send him away!"

"Oh, she sent him away without a second glance," Kiara says. "And then she used it in one of the books she wrote as a scenario for a drunken night."

"Wait," I say, pumping my hand in the air to calm everyone down. "The guy was drunk when he did this?"

The three of them are shaking their heads while they cover their mouths.

I hang my head, feeling sorry for the guy. "What spell did you put on the poor bastard?"

The three of them are looking at each other, their faces all beat red from hysteria.

"We don't dabble-,"

"In black magic," I say, finishing Jade's sentence.

"That's something we don't talk about in this house," Kiara adds.

I look at all three of them and they look so serious. Giselle says, "Just wow," and shakes her head at me, shocked that I would make a comment about putting a spell on someone.

"I'm sorry," I say, sitting back in my chair. "I... I didn't know... I'm sorry."

As I'm stumbling over my words, the three of them practically fall off their chairs in a fit of laughter.

"I can't believe I fell for that," I groan. "Especially when you have a cat named Hex," I add, pointing to Jade.

She shrugs and they continue to laugh at me. "So," I begin, tapping my cards on the table. "Are we going to continue to play rummy?"

For some reason, that only makes them laugh hard and all I can think to do... is grab another beer.

Chapter Thirteen

Giselle

THE KIDS ARE PRACTICALLY drooling on themselves as they lie sprawled across the couch in Kiara's living room. We finally wrap up the game of rummy and start to pack up the cards and beer cans.

Jade is grouchy because Cal actually beat her, but I think she's more mad that she only lost to him by ten lousy points.

It was a nice night and I'm glad it happened. It gave us all a chance to see Cal let loose and be himself.

"That was fun," Jade lies as she finishes off the beer in her hands.

"It really was," Cal agrees. "But I think I'm going to head down to the guest house and grab a shower."

Kiara waves a hand in front of her face and scrunches her nose. "Probably a good idea."

I watch as Cal does a smell test on his pits. Then, when he realizes he doesn't stink, narrows his eyes at Kiara. "It must be fun for you to know that I'll pretty much fall for anything."

Little do they know, it's a simple way of getting them to see me as more of an innocent man. Gullible and naive.

And it seems to be working.

"It is," Jade sings.

Cal walks toward the door, but as he grabs the doorknob, looks at Jade over his shoulder.

"And don't forget, Jade," he says. "Loser has to buy beer." He shoots a wink in my direction before he jumps to the other side of the door to dodge the empty beer can Jade hurls in his direction.

I'm wiping off the table when Kiara walks over to me and says, "You've got a good one on your hands."

"I have to agree," Jade says with a sigh. "Aside from the fact that he sucks at rummy."

"He sure found a way to kick your ass," Kiara muses.

"Beginners luck," Jade argues.

"It wasn't his first time playing," I say, shaking my head at their bickering.

"It was his first time playing with *us,*" Jade counters.

Kiara and I swap a look and continue cleaning up the kitchen and dining room area, trying not to wake the kids. Though as tired as they were, I don't think a hurricane could wake them.

The beer cans are piled up in the recycling bins, even though we live too far out to actually recycle anything, and the rest of the buffalo chicken dip that we made gets packed up and put in the fridge.

"You really need to go for it," Kiara says, leaning her elbow on the counter top.

"I second that," Jade says, cracking the top of yet another beer.

"Go for what?" I ask, playing stupid.

Kiara huffs at me. "Go down there and get some. He's cute. He's funny. And he seems like he has a good head on his shoulders."

"Hopefully a good head further down south too," Jade says into her beer bottle.

I fight the smirk, but quickly lose the battle. "He didn't come here to find a girlfriend," I tell them.

"You don't know what he came here for," Kiara says.

"And who said anything about being his girlfriend?" Jade adds. "Just get a little boink sesh and call it good."

I roll my eyes. "It's not in my best interest to sleep with him."

"Why?" Kiara asks, dropping the garbage bag at her feet to slam her hands onto her hips. "Because you're in the middle of a divorce that was put into play over a year ago?" Kiara looks at the ceiling and clicks her tongue. "Oh… that's right. I forgot that means you can't sleep with anyone else."

I plop down on the stool. "I wouldn't even know the first thing to say to him. I haven't been in the dating game for a long time. Mark was my high school sweetheart and he's all I've ever known." I swallow the lump in my throat. "Plus, it's not like I've let on that I'm into Cal."

"He's into you," Jade teases. "I'm sure all you'd have to do is knock on the door and he'd drop his pants right then and there."

"But what if-"

"You won't," Jade interrupts. "You've had an IUD for two years and it's good for five. You haven't had a period in almost six years. Pregnancy shouldn't be a concern."

"But what-"

"Who cares if you fall for him?" Kiara adds. "You act like it would be the end of the world if a guy came into your life. God forbid you're happy with another human beside you."

"Do you even need me for this conversation?" I ask the two of them.

They shake their heads in unison.

I look over my shoulder toward the door and wonder what he's doing. I'm assuming he's in the shower, water dripping down his amazing body. Or at least I'm under the impression he has an amazing body.

I doubt I'm wrong.

Then, I look toward the kids.

"They love him," Jade says, not even giving me a chance to say anything else.

"And he seems to love them," Kiara adds. "Now, go suck out his soul."

"Jump his bones!" Jade shouts. Then, clamps a hand over her mouth as her eyes dart toward the couch filled with sleeping kids.

"We've got it covered," Kiara says, watching as my eyes trail toward Abby and Owen. "They're asleep and will be easy to handle."

"And no," Jade adds. "We don't need you for that conversation either."

The two of them point toward the door and I nod as I walk outside and head for the guest house.

The night air is absolutely breathtaking on my skin. Such a change from the balmy days we've been having lately. Thankfully, fall is right around the corner and my favorite time of year will finally be here.

I put one foot in front of the other as I walk down the path, closing the gap between myself and the guest house. It's an internal battle not to turn around and go home.

The porch lights are on as I walk up to the door. I want to look inside and make sure he's not busy, but I'm afraid he'll think I'm a peeper.

Pacing the porch seems like a much better option.

"Knock on the door," I whisper to myself. "Just knock. It's better than you hitting your FitBit step goal outside."

I reach my arm out and knock twice on the door. It takes a while and I start to wonder if he didn't pack his things and leave.

But the door finally opens and Cal is standing in front of me wearing nothing but a towel.

Sweet Jesus, mother of Mary.

His dark hair is slicked back from the shower he obviously just stepped out of, and water is beading on his shoulders. I never realized how muscular he was until this very moment. And I'm sending a thank you out to the all the deities for allowing my eyes to land upon this magnificent creature.

"Hey," towel-wearing Cal says, stretching his glistening arm to lean against the doorframe. He looks behind me and around toward the lake area. His brows furrow when he sees nothing. "Everything okay?"

I realize he thinks I'm here with bad news. Awesome that I carry that vibe with me.

I nod. "Uh huh," is all I can manage to say as I continue to let my eyes trail over him. I want to touch my mouth to make sure I'm not drooling, but I'm afraid it would be too obvious.

"What can I do for you, my dear?" he says, crossing his arms.

Why can't he just know what I'm here for? Is he really going to make me say that I came down here for sex? That I'm curious to see what would happen if he kissed me and I didn't push away this time?

"Hi," I finally say. I point a thumb over my shoulders and look toward the houses. "They're watching the kids tonight."

His face brightens and he beams at me. "Is that so?"

"It is." I give myself a minute to clear my mind and try to focus on anything besides what might be under that very lucky towel. "I see you managed to take a shower."

Good job not focusing on his wet naked body, Giselle.

He looks down and I'm guessing he forgot he didn't have any clothes on. "I uh…" he stammers. "Yeah. Sorry about that." He runs a hand through his very wet hair. "I guess I wasn't thinking when I opened the door."

It makes me feel better that he's a little uncomfortable too. "Would you want to have a few beers or something?"

Cal looks toward the kitchen. "I don't know if you ladies keep this place stocked or not. I've honestly not looked around too much. Jade's kept me pretty hydrated lately."

I smile. "She's happy to have a drinking buddy."

"You don't drink?" he asks. The look on his face tells me he's trying to figure out if he imagined all the beer from rummy.

"It's not that I don't. I guess I'm generally more of a wine girl."

"And Kiara?"

"Not much of a drinker at all. She prefers the harder stuff."

"A liquor girl," Cal concludes.

I shake my head. "THC."

His eyes go wide and then he gives me a sideways glance like he's not sure if I'm kidding. Then he shakes his head. "I'm not falling for another one of your tricks. You three got me enough tonight."

"I'm serious," I say. "She gets it in the form of candy."

The look on his face tells me he's not a stranger to this. "I see."

"You've had it?"

He grins. "I have."

"Then, you and Kiara would have lots to talk about."

"I guess we would." We lock eyes for a few seconds before he looks down at his towel. "Come on in and I'll see what's here."

"It's not stocked," I tell him without walking inside.

He notices I'm not crossing the threshold and tilts his head in confusion. "It's safe in here. I promise."

I swallow hard. "I know."

I also know the minute I walk in there, I'm going to rip that towel off and have my way with him.

"How about you find something less slutty to wear and come up to my house," I offer.

Cal throws his head back and I can't help but smile to myself.

"I can definitely do that," he says. "But this is a high-class ensemble. Don't mock the towel."

"I'd never dream of it," I tease.

He waves before he closes the door and I head back up to my house. I make sure I have beer in my fridge like I promised, though I know I do because I always have some on hand for Jade.

There's at least one case in the garage, so I grab a few from there and toss them in, pulling the cold ones to the front.

I hardly have time to pour myself a glass of wine before he's knocking on the door. He's holding a six pack and smiling.

"Glad you found some," I say as I let him inside.

"You didn't have any?" he asks, opening the fridge to restock what he brought. "Nevermind. I guess I can answer my own question."

"They're not all cold," I admit. "But I did make the colder ones easier to access."

"I appreciate that," he says. "A woman who cares."

I flush and sip at my wine so my giant glass hides part of my face.

The sound of a beer cracking hits my ears and I feel guilty about already having chugged the first half of my glass.

His eyes glance at what's left of my wine and he looks at the beer in his hand. "I better catch up."

He tips the beer up and in three large gulps, half of it is gone. He walks over and holds his bottle up to my glass, leaning over to look at them side by side.

"Seems we're even now," he says, clinking his to mine before he looks around.

Jesus fuck. I hate that he keeps getting so close to me. I'm going to melt from the inside out.

"I can't get over how nice these houses are," Cal says, taking a sip from what's left of his beer.

"Thank you," I say, making sure my reply wasn't 'you too'. Kind of like when the waitress brings your food and tells you to enjoy your meal and you reply with, 'Thanks, you too'.

Makes me want to kick the corner of my bed with my pinky toe when I do that.

"Is the guest house alright?" I ask.

He nods frantically. "Oh, absolutely. I couldn't even begin to thank you for what you've done for me."

I can think of a few ways.

I finish my glass of wine and start to feel my nerves calming. I reach for the bottle, but Cal beats me to it.

"Allow me," he says. "I have to get you all loopy so I can take advantage of you."

The glass almost slips out of my hand, but Cal catches it and laughs.

"Sorry!" I say. "I guess I wasn't expecting that response."

He grins as though he's pleased with my discomfort and tops off my wine glass, handing it back to me.

"Thank you," I say.

I head for the couch, thinking it may be best to stay off my wobbly knees for a bit.

We settle down, not that far from each other, and without even thinking, I stretch my legs across his lap like we do this every day. I almost freeze when I realize I did it out of habit, but he settles his hand on my shin like this is normal for us.

That was always something I did in my past life. When I was happily married and wasn't with a guy who cheated on me.

"Tell me about your ex-husband," he says.

I almost choke on my wine. "Jesus! At least use some lube before you jam it in like that!"

His eyes widen at my reply. "You really do have such a way with words."

I smirk. "Sorry," I say. My hands are starting to warm up from the wine. "What is it you want to know about my ex-husband?"

"Anything you want to tell me," he says, staring into my eyes. It's such an intense look that I'm not sure if I should look away, or stare back.

I choose the latter.

"I'm just trying to figure out why you're so closed off," he says.

"I am not closed off," I snap.

"Okay," he says. "Maybe that wasn't the right word." He adjusts in his seat, but doesn't allow me to remove my legs from his lap. "I'm trying to figure out why you won't welcome another guy into your life right now."

"That's better," I say, giving him a nod of approval. "My ex-husband is an asshole." I rest my glass of wine on my lap. "He's lazy when it comes to doing anything, whether it be chores or even spending time with his family. But he sure as shit moved around a lot when he wasn't home."

I down the last little bit of wine from my glass. "I'll tell ya, if moving from one woman to another could be considered exercise, the man was an Olympian."

"I'm sorry to hear that." He looks at his hands. "Then, maybe your issue isn't with letting me in because you don't want a guy. Your issue with letting me in is because you can't trust anyone."

I see the look on his face and it makes me want to kiss him. It makes me want to run my fingers through his hair and stretch myself across his body. Show him how much I trust him, even though I don't even know him.

Prove him wrong.

But I realize it wouldn't be because I want to prove him wrong. It would be because I crave him. The taste of him. The feel of him.

I go to make another comment about how worthless Mark was, but instead, I hear myself say, "Kiss me."

Cal looks at me like I just sprouted another head. "What?"

I put my glass on the table beside us and look at him. I rest my hands on my lap, lacing my fingers like a woman with intent, and repeat myself. "Kiss me."

Chapter Fourteen

Caleb

I FEEL LIKE THE wine may be part of the reason Giselle is looking at me the way she is. And did she actually say what I think she said or are my ears deceiving me? She wants me to kiss her?

I want to obey that order in the worst way, but I don't want to be the guy that takes advantage of a liquored up woman. No matter how much she has my dick throbbing in my pants.

"Tell me again," I say, setting my beer on the table. "Because I don't want you to do something you're going to regret. I remember the last time and I... I just want to make sure you're being honest with yourself."

I don't, I want her to lie if she's not being honest. I just want to be greedy and devour every inch of this magnificent woman.

She sits up, grabs the collar of my shirt, and yanks me toward her. Her mouth finds mine in a split second like I'm a dish she's been craving for months.

Before I can get my thoughts straight, she's on top of me and there's no way I can say I'm taking advantage of her. She wants this.

And so do I.

My hands move to her back and I pull her closer to me as she straddles my lap. Her hips are already moving and I'm glad because now I won't seem like the one that's over eager.

Fuck it. I'll be the eager one.

I toss her onto her back and hear her *whoop* with surprise. Her hands race to the bottom of my shirt and pull it up over my head. She's fumbling with my belt when I get her shirt and bra off. Clothes are flying in all directions and we're finally down to nothing but skin.

My mouth finds hers again.

Her lips are sweet like wine and they part to welcome my tongue. I'm hard as a rock and I can feel my tip touching between her thighs. Her feet wrap around and pull me down, but I won't slide in just yet.

My hips raise enough for me to stretch a hand between us and feel her for the first time. She's soaking wet and moans as I explore her with my fingertips.

She's as soft as velvet and I can't wait to wrap myself up in her.

As soon as I find her sweet spot, her hands wrap behind my head and pull me in for a kiss that tells me she likes it rough. I keep rubbing, soaking my hand in her arousal and feeling her hips moving against me as I touch her.

"More," she moans into my mouth. Her eyes are clamped shut and her hands are above her head now, gripping the arm of the couch.

I push her legs up and move my mouth to her stomach. She smells like wildflowers and I wonder if she applied lotion before I got here or if that's just her natural smell.

Either way, it's intoxicating.

I move my mouth over her body, tasting her skin and feeling how soft she is against my lips. Her body is absolutely perfect. Curves in all the right places and the most beautiful breasts I've ever seen.

I move my mouth down farther until I hear a whimper escape her lips. My tongue is working her, moving in and out as I kiss and suck and tease.

When I notice she's about to lose it, I kiss the inside of each thigh and shift to my knees, positioning between her thighs.

"Don't stop!" she shouts, her nails scratching the surface of her couch.

Good thing it's not leather. For more reasons than her leaving marks behind.

Without warning, I slide inside her and she screams out as I fill her with my length. She's so tight and warm and it takes everything in me not to burst once I'm fully inside.

"Holy shit!" she yells, surprised that I gave her everything at once.

There's so much I want to do to this woman. My mind is racing with the idea of flipping her over, crawling up and sliding into her mouth, or even just having her use her hands while we makeout. I want to touch every part of her. I want to taste her again.

I lean down and kiss her mouth while I pump in and out of her. She's moaning and clawing at my back while her legs tighten around my waist.

She's so warm against me and I love how her body feels against mine.

"Cal!" she screams, arching her back and closing her eyes.

Her breathing quickens and the nails clawing my back are about to send me over the edge. I reach up and grab a handful of her hair, tugging it down and moving my mouth over her neck. I feel her muscles tighten around my shaft as she tips over the edge.

My knees go weak as I'm taken over by the complete feeling of relief and invincibility all at once.

I hold myself over her as her arms fall to her sides and her pulse pounds in her neck. Her chest is rising and falling, and I plant a kiss in the valley of her breasts.

She pulls me down to lay on top of her and the sweat between us is forming a puddle.

"Wow," she whispers underneath me.

"I know," I say, trying to catch my breath. "You feel absolutely amazing."

I press a kiss to her lips and her hands cup the sides of my face. She won't let me stop kissing her, even if we're both fighting for oxygen.

Dangerous. I like it.

When I go to pull myself out of her, she wraps her legs around me and keeps me inside, letting out a devious giggle.

"Not yet," she whispers. "One more minute."

I lie down on her, skin to skin, and stare into her eyes. She moans underneath me and I can feel myself coming down from the high of my climax. I want to touch her again. I want to kiss her again.

Her hips begin to move underneath me and I can see the look in her eyes.

She's not done with me yet.

"Again," She says.

The thrill of her request has the corners of my mouth turning up and I lean down to kiss her. She swirls her hips and the excitement is already pumping through me again.

"We can go another round," I groan. "But this time... I'm not going to be gentle."

Her teeth peek out over her lip and she bites down. "Music to my ears."

It takes three rounds of intense heat to finally satisfy ourselves. Our bodies are tired and Giselle's legs are shaking. We've managed to make it to the floor where we spread out a blanket for the last round, though I'm not sure we should still be lying on it after everything we just did.

"Maybe we should get ourselves cleaned up," I say, leaning over and nibbling at her ear.

She shifts her face toward me and I can see she's tired. "Probably." Her smile is weak, but it's definitely there. "Or, we can just lie here in our own filth and ignore it."

I laugh and lift her up off the floor. "Point me in the direction of the shower. I'll do the rest."

Giselle lifts her hand and I follow her finger movements that point to the hallway. I scoop her up in my arms and we head for the bathroom.

Even the bathroom in this house is gorgeous. Nothing like the Devil's bathroom that's in the guest house. It's elegant and modern. White walls, white tub, marble countertops. The vanity is black and there's a black rug at the base of the tub. The shower curtain is a swirl of white, gray, and black.

The entire bathroom is gorgeous. I love her taste in decor.

The room steams up pretty quickly once the hot water is running and I lead her into the standing shower stall.

It's this giant part of the bathroom that's stone with a waterfall shower head. The glass doors are gigantic and there's a ton of room for activities in here.

My list of things I want to do to Giselle just doubled.

The water streams over her sleepy face and she lifts her head to look at me. A grin appears on her face and she rests her head on my chest.

I reach toward the corner caddy, grabbing the container of body wash and the loofah that's on the hook below it. Lathering up the suds, I run the loofah over her skin.

She groans and sinks into me.

The smell of the body wash reminds me of the soap my mom used to use when we were kids. It has a fresh flower scent that reminds me of summer rain, much like the one we had today.

And now, I pinpoint the scent of wildflowers that I smelled on her skin earlier.

"Thank you," she whispers into me.

I kiss the top of her head and feel her smile against my skin.

Once we're both clean, I look out of the shower to try and find the towels.

"They're on the rack," she says as though she's reading my mind. Her voice is groggy, but she's at least standing upright.

"Why didn't you put the rack within reaching distance when you designed this bathroom?"

"Because I designed it knowing I'd have you in here naked at some point and wanted to watch your naked butt run across the floor to grab them."

She smirks at me despite the fatigue and I can't help but pull her in close to me and squeeze.

"But it's warm in here," I groan. "Use your witchy stuff and make one float over here."

She smacks my bare butt and I yelp like a dog. "Alright, alright."

I grab two towels and wrap them around us before I guide her down the hall to her bedroom, leading us into a linen closet on my first try.

Whoops.

When I finally find her bedroom, I gently let her unfold out of the towel and into the right side of her bed.

She looks so peaceful as she shoves her hands under the pillow and snuggles into her fluffy comforter. I notice an air conditioner in the window and shift the knob from *low* to *high*. It begins to hum and I slide under the blankets next to Giselle.

She feels me next to her and rolls over to rest her head on my shoulder before she starts to drift off.

We didn't discuss sleeping arrangements, but I just rode the woman raw and, as a gentleman, I must sleep here and make sure she's okay in the morning.

Or at least that's what I'm telling myself.

Chapter Fifteen

Giselle

I STILL FEEL GROGGY as I start to wake up and curse the makers of wine. I never drink sweet wine because it makes me feel like this when I wake up the next morning, but it's all I had.

I make a mental note to get more dry wine to avoid this feeling.

There's an arm wrapped around me and I turn my head to see Cal passed out in my bed. I forgot how great it feels to wake up beside someone.

Well, someone who isn't a child.

Then, it dawns on me why I'm so groggy. I was actually in a deep sleep all night, as opposed to my usual routine of waking up every hour and checking the clock. Part of the reason I sleep in so late, I suppose.

I'm staring at Cal, trying not to grimace at the fact that he's sleeping with his mouth hanging open. Or the fact that one of his eyes is practically staring at me.

"Cal," I say, super quietly.

Nothing. He's definitely sleeping with one eye almost open.

"Creepy," I whisper to myself.

Then, I notice that Tarot is curled up on the other side of him, completely asleep.

Weird cat. Bites me every damn chance he gets, but immediately warms up to the strange man in my bed.

Slowly, I slide out from under his grip and slip into the robe that hangs on my bedroom door before I head to the kitchen and brew a pot of coffee. The smell of it is heavenly and I'm dying to get it in my system.

I bought this coffee pot a year ago because it has the option to remove the pot before it's done brewing without continuing to drip all over my counter. It only starts dripping again once the pot is put back in its little home. Some kind of magic if you ask me.

Truth be told, I've never done it. I'm too scared that if I pull it out before it's done, it'll make a mess everywhere, and this time I can't blame Tarot for it.

But today, I'm a new woman. I had sex last night and I feel bullet proof.

I wait two minutes for the pot to fill to a respectable amount before I pull it out and pour myself a cup of coffee. I admit, I slid it back in after the first two tries of pulling it out because I was scared, but I did it!

Bullet proof.

An evil smile appears on my face and I'm glad my adventurous side has come out to play. Granted, it's just a cup of coffee, but this is what baby steps look like.

The sliding glass door opens and Kiara steps in. She looks around and finally sees me, which apparently means she needs to wiggle her eyebrows. "So? How was last night?"

"Last night was-"

"Good morning," a male voice says.

Kiara and I both look up to see Cal standing in the kitchen entryway wearing nothing but a pair of gym shorts. His abs are enticing and I bite my lip, but quickly stop when Kiara looks toward me.

"Last night is still going," I say, giving an apologetic shrug. I tug my robe tighter against me since I'm fairly certain I didn't tie it too tight.

"Afraid something's gonna pop out?" Kiara asks me as I continue to tug at my robe strings.

"This shit ain't free," I hiss. "You wanna see the goods? You gotta cough up some dough."

She lets out a howl and waves at us before she walks back outside. Cal is laughing at me too.

"Send my kids in!" I yell after Kiara, but I know she won't because they're already playing on the playground equipment out back.

"Did you enjoy snuggling up to Tarot last night?" I ask as I pull the cream and sugar from the cabinet.

"He's a nice little furball," Cal says, stretching to wake up his body.

A loud huff of laughter falls from my lips.

"What?" he asks. "He was such a purrbox all night. Just curled up in a ball under my arm."

"He's an asshole," I say. "Just wait."

He doesn't say anything, but I hear him grunt and look to see him stretching again. I know I'll have to do that at some point too. My whole body is sore.

I turn toward him. "Coffee?"

"Absolutely," he says as he walks over to me.

His hands find my waist and he pulls me into him. I put my coffee cup down on the counter and raise my arms to his shoulders while he kisses me. I smile against his lips and he pulls away from me.

"What's so funny?" he asks.

"Nothing," I say, grabbing my coffee cup from the counter. "It's just that you're the first guy I've ever let kiss me before either of us have brushed our teeth."

"Morning breath freaks you out?" he asks. I nod. "Me too. But lucky for you, I snuck into your master bath and swished some mouthwash before I came out." His lips find mine again and this time I notice the fresh scent on his breath. "But I love the way you taste. Regardless of the time of day."

My face flushes, but I like it. The way he talks to me has me feeling like I'm walking among the clouds. I've never had this before. A guy that treats me like a goddess.

"You're so good to me," I tell him.

"How good?" he asks.

I reach down and run a hand across the bulge in his shorts. My mouth finds his neck and I suck and nibble at him while my hand continues to caress him. My coffee cup lands on the counter again and my free hand slides under his shorts and touches skin. He moans and pulls on the band that holds my hair on top of my head. As my hair tumbles down over my shoulders, he buries his face in my neck and inhales.

"Bedroom?" he asks.

I don't even give him a chance to move away from me. "No," I say. "Right here."

He rushes over to the door and flips the lock before he pulls the curtains across the glass panes. It's like he can read my mind.

When he comes back over to me, he reaches around and grabs me by the ass, lifting me up onto the counter. I spread my legs and he leans into me, finding my mouth with his again. His hand reaches down the front of me and I feel his fingers slither from my breasts, all the way down to my center.

He slides a finger inside and I suck in a breath. I feel my eyes fluttering and I clamp them shut, focusing on the sensation he's creating between my legs.

Just as I'm getting into the moment, Cal jumps and scratches the inside of my thigh. I scream and we both look to find the cause of the crash that scared us both.

Tarot is perched on the counter and my cup of coffee is now a shattered mess at Cal's feet.

"Are you fucking kidding me?!" I shriek at the cat. Tarot licks his paw and ignores the fact that I'm about to rip his head off. When Cal takes a step toward him, he leaps from the counter and takes off running.

"You were right," Cal murmurs. "Your cat is an asshole."

I let out a frustrated sigh. "You're not lyin'."

After Cal finds his clothes and we make our way outside, the kids swarm and start hanging off his arms. They're chanting and calling for Cal to go play, and all Cal can do is smile at their enthusiasm.

"We want to have a picnic!" Abby shouts after she lets go of Cal.

"With peanut butter and jelly!" Wyatt adds.

"And a walk down the path!" Owen says with his arms in the air for an added level of excitement. "And Cal needs to come too!"

"Awe, I'm sorry, kids," Cal says. "But I promised I'd get a few things done around the grounds today." The kids groan with disappointment and Cal apologizes again.

"Then, Aunt Giselle needs to take us!" Lexie shouts, now yanking on my arm.

I laugh. "Alright, alright. I'll go pack up the basket and we will hit the trail."

The kids shout and cheer as they jump around. Cal looks at me and gives me a smile which makes me want to jump his bones again.

I won't though.

Still super sore.

"Enjoy your chores," I tell him.

"Enjoy your picnic," he replies.

The kids don't venture too far down the path before choosing a spot for our picnic. Owen and Lexie help spread out the blanket while Piper opens the basket and pulls out the sandwiches. Thankfully, I like salad because I had to use up all of my bread to make sandwiches for the kids.

I guess it's a good thing Cal wasn't able to come or he'd have to man up and eat a salad too. Not sure he would have cared though.

I wish I could get him out of my head.

That's a lie.

"These are super good!" Owen says as he bites into his sandwich. He really loves to boost my ego, even when it doesn't need to be boosted.

"Thank you, Sweetheart," I tell him, ruffling his already messy hair.

The rest of the kids join in with a chorus of 'Super good' and 'Thank you for lunch, Aunt Giselle'. I can honestly say that the three of us raised an amazing group of kids.

We spend some time on our giant blanket eating our lunches and enjoying the summer day. The breeze begins to pick up and I see a few dark clouds rolling in. I'm not sure if it's supposed to rain today or not, but by the angry clouds I'm seeing, we'd better pack up and head home.

Lunch gets cleaned up quick when I convince the kids that the rain is lava and we need to make it back before it gets us. Everything is easier when it is turned into a game of some sort.

The kids beat me back to the commune and I see them already monkeying around on the playground. Sprinkles of rain are dancing on my skin and I decide to herd the kids in until I figure out where the other three adults disappeared to.

I spend about fifteen minutes looking for them before I resort to calling one of their phones. It keeps ringing and I got voicemail for both Kiara and Jade. I need to ask Cal if he has a cell phone. I hate that I've never thought about that.

But what if he's the problem. I know I slept with him, but that doesn't rule him out as a serial killer. Maybe serial killers are really good in bed because they like to warm up their victims before they slit their throats.

I call out their names over and over but it gets me nowhere. The rain is really coming down now which has nothing to do with my friends going missing, only the fact that my hair and clothes are now sopping wet.

Panic is setting in. Would Cal actually hurt them? Would he kidnap them? Did he call someone to come help him finish the job on the three strange women he stumbled upon?

"Okay," I say to myself. "Calm down." I pace the porch for a few seconds while the kids run around inside like nothing is wrong.

I have to make the frantic call to the police. I have to report my friends missing. Normally, calling the authorities would make a person feel better, but in our case, the police are forty minutes away from our commune and my friends will be dead by the time they get here, if they're not already.

Should I grab his gun and go in search of my friends? Would I actually be able to shoot him if he was harming them?

"Hell yes," I say out loud. "Nobody hurts my friends." Now, my fear is dissolving into rage and I'm ready for a fight. I reach for the doorknob and just as I'm turning it, I hear my name being yelled from behind me.

I whirl around, ready to see my friends in distress, but I realize I've been overreacting when I see them. All three of them.

And I feel like such an idiot for thinking Cal would hurt my friends.

They're perfectly fine. Cal isn't a serial killer.

They're all three splashing around in the lake.

Chapter Sixteen

CALEB

The rain is pelting us as we jump off the dock into the lake. I'm grateful that the three of them have provided swimming lessons to all of the kids because kids who can't swim make me extremely nervous.

After another hour of playing around in the water, the rain clouds subside and the sun has finally made its appearance.

Owen yells, "Cal, watch me!" and jumps from the dock, making a huge cannon-ball splash. I clap with approval and his entire face lights up.

One by one, the kids jump from the dock, trying to outdo the last jump by adding a twist or turn as their feet leave the platform.

This is what summer days were intended for.

Giselle swims up to me and wraps her arms around my neck. I pull my knees up while I tread water and she settles her perfect little butt on my make-shift lap. She throws her head back when I refer to my lap as her throne.

"You two are sickening," Jade says.

Kiara agrees and begins splashing at Giselle and me. It turns into a huge water battle and the kids use their cannon-balls as weapon attacks on the adults. I grab Giselle by the hand and we swim under the dock, holding just our eyes above the water line to watch Kiara and Jade try to find us."

"Oh shit!" Jade yells in a panic as she stares into the lake water. "They're going to grab our legs!"

Bubbles float up from Giselle's mouth and I squeeze my eyes closed to keep myself quiet.

"Don't touch me!" Kiara is yelling at the water. "I don't want to go under!"

They look so ridiculous screaming at a body of water and I can't hold it in anymore. Giselle and I give away our position and everyone turns to look at us. Kiara isn't amused, but Jade begins howling when she realizes she was afraid of nothing.

"That was more effective than I thought it would be," I whisper to Giselle.

"Maybe they're more gullible than you are," she whispers back.

We drain the kids of their last drop of energy and head up to the house to get dried off and plan something for dinner. I offer to cook and Giselle gives me a studious look.

"What?" I ask her, jamming my hands onto my hips like a scolded housewife.

"Nothing," she says, averting her eyes. "I just didn't know you were Betty Crocker."

"You never gave me a chance to cook," I point out.

"Yeah," Kiara interjects. "You were too busy ripping his clothes off."

"Pipe down," Giselle snaps.

Kiara shrugs and she follows Jade into the house. I follow Giselle inside and pinch her butt, making her yelp and clasp a hand over her mouth. Kiara and Jade seem entertained by it, but Giselle doesn't seem to find it as funny.

"What are our options?" I ask once we're inside.

"For what?" Jade asks.

"Dinner," I say. "I'll cook. I just need to know if anything is off limits."

"Oh, you were serious?" Kiara asks, looking surprised.

I sigh. Kiara and Jade give me huge smiles, but I get the feeling Giselle is still unsure. I turn to her and put on my best convincing face. Like the one I used with JT when I wanted to join his team to get some cash.

"I can do this," I tell her. "Trust me."

It's almost as if it's the same exact speech as that day. I almost get chills up my spine.

"I trust him," Kiara says, raising her hand into the air as though we're voting.

"Same," Jade says. She pulls two beers from Giselle's fridge and pops the top on each, handing one of them to me as though this is our usual routine.

"Alright," Giselle says with her arms crossed. "I trust you too."

I brush my lips over hers and I feel her shoulders loosen. She smiles against my mouth and adds, "I already said I trusted you. You didn't need to sweeten the deal."

"That wasn't for you," I tell her. "It was for me." I pull away from her and give her hand a squeeze. "You ladies take the kids out to the playground and see if they have a second wind. If they say they're tired, tell them I have a five-dollar bill for the person who can play the longest. Sit on the patio and sip some wine while I take care of dinner."

"Can he stay here forever?" I hear Kiara ask the other two. It sends heat through my already warm body. Then, she starts barking orders. "Jade, grab the wine. Giselle, grab the glasses. I'll grab the kids."

Within minutes, I'm left in the kitchen to make a meal for four adults and five children. "I can do this," I coach myself. "I already convinced them I can. Now I have to prove it to myself."

After scoping out the contents of the massive kitchen, gigantic pantry, and deeper than deep freezer in the basement; I decide on a seafood and vegetable dinner with a trifle for dessert.

"They're gonna shit their pants," I say, feeling proud of myself already. "Now, let's get to work."

"Something smells like heaven," Giselle groans when she strolls into the kitchen.

I'm pulling a baking tray from the oven and wipe my hands on my apron when she stops dead in her tracks and looks at me.

Her eyes glaze over as though she's forcing herself to keep composure, and I put my oven-mitt-covered hands on my hips.

"Don't you dare..." I say, realizing I'm standing in a way that's only going to make her laugh even harder.

She's waving a hand as though nothing is wrong, but clearly that's not the case.

"You..." she says, clamping her lips and shaking her head like she can't even speak. "You look... like a..."

"Like a what?" I say, almost snapping at her.

"Like a professional," she finishes, ending it on a cackle.

I grin, unable to help myself and take off the oven mitts. "I had to wear the apron," I say. "I didn't want to get my clothes dirty. Limited supply."

She catches her breath. "No. You're right. And you look fantastic." Then, she wafts the smell of the food toward her nose. "That smells amazing."

I open a foil packet when she walks over to me and peeks over my shoulder.

"Thank you," I say. "Now that you're done making fun of me, you can tell me that you were wrong and shouldn't make snap judgements about people."

"I did no such thing," she says, placing her hand on her chest and dropping her jaw in mock horror. "I'm appalled."

"Oh, you quit." I give her a shove. "You were wrong and you know it. You decided that because I'm an overly sexy and brawny man, I can't cook. Whether or not you admit it is between you and your conscience."

She walks over, cups my face in her hands, and kisses me. "I'm sorry," she says. "It won't happen again. My sexy, brawny man."

"Thank you," I say, leaning over for another kiss. "You're supposed to be outside with your feet propped up. Can't a woman cook in her own kitchen without being interrupted?!"

She shakes her head at me. "I came in for more wine, ma'am."

"Well, that's an exception, I suppose." I walk over to the wine chiller and kneel to peer through the glass door. "What's your poison?"

"What will go best with dinner?" she asks.

"Red," I say. "Do you girls drink dry?"

"We're professionals," she counters. "We drink everything. No discrimination at this commune."

I grab the first bottle of red I see, read the label and give a slow nod as I hand it over. "If my Betty Crocker senses are right, dinner will be ready in fifteen. Drink fast."

"Are you trying to get me liquored up?" she asks, taking a step closer.

I grab her by the waist and pull her in. "I don't just try," I breathe. "I succeed."

She arches a brow and looks me up and down before she heads toward the door. "Feel free to bring the apron."

Sometimes I wonder if she's cast a spell on me to make me feel the things I feel about her. It's crazy how quickly I'm falling. Not to mention that I've never felt this way about anyone. Not even the girls I thought I was in love with back in high school.

I shake my head free of mushy thoughts and finish my meal prep. I pull the serving dishes from the cabinets and make the food look presentable. I fold napkins, distribute silverware, even grab clean wine glasses to put at the place settings.

It looks perfect.

"Dinner is ready," I say to the girls on the back patio.

I can tell by the way their cheeks are all flushed that they're feeling pretty good. They throw their hands up in celebration and stagger from their chairs to the door before piling themselves inside.

The kids race toward the door and Lexie starts shouting that I owe her five dollars.

I'll have to see if Giselle will loan me the money.

They flood inside and take their seats, commenting on how cool everything looks.

"What is it?" Owen asks as he stares at a plate of parmesan crusted shrimp.

Giselle looks at me and I go to speak, but she cuts me off. "You made this for everyone?" she asks, tilting her head in disappointment. "The kids won't eat this."

I go to speak again, but this time, Jade chimes in. "Way to think of the kids." She tips back the last of her wine and puts it on the table like the world is ending.

They're all ranting as I stand in the middle of the kitchen. Sad faces on the kids and frustrated faces on the moms. I walk over to the oven and pull out the second baking tray that has the kids' food on it.

All three of the women stop talking and the kids' eyes light up.

"Tiny pizzas!" Owen shouts with his hips moving in a happy dance.

"Thank you, Cal!" Lexie shouts.

"Oh my God, he's the best!" Piper yells, clapping her hands. With her being the oldest, I thought it would be tough to get her blessing. But it turns out, she's warming up to me faster than her mom did.

Giselle stands there and shakes her head in defeat. "I know, I know," she says. "I was too quick to judge the overly sexy, brawny man."

Chapter Seventeen

Giselle

Today I am happy. The rain is pelting the window beside my desk, my hair is up in a bun that doesn't need to be fixed, and the house is quiet because the kids are all over at Kiara's.

Life is good.

While Kiara is instructing the kids' craft with the flowers they've picked, I'm taking advantage of the alone time and working on my upcoming novel.

I'm so glad Kiara knows how to do flower pressing because they're absolutely gorgeous when they're done, and she promised me a bookmark. I love bookmarks.

I'm in the perfect sitting position on my chair. My favorite glasses are resting on my face. My chapstick is plentiful so I won't chew on my bottom lip and make it bleed. And my bra is somewhere on my bedroom floor, so the girls are living free.

Words are flowing.

I'm sitting at my desk focusing on my work-in-progress when Cal comes in through my front door. He has a smile on his face and I'm wondering what's going on. I take my glasses off and put them against my messy bun while I lean back in my chair, trying not to get frustrated at the fact that my alone time didn't last very long.

Don't get me wrong, I'm happy to see him. But when an author gets in the groove, getting interrupted is almost as bad as stubbing your baby toe on the corner of something.

I guess it won't hurt to give my eyes a break though. I feel like I've been squinting for a while.

"What's up?" I ask him.

I swear, it's hard not to match the excitement on someone's face when they look this thrilled about something. It's like when someone starts laughing because of something they're about to tell you, and you can't help but laugh too, even though you have no idea what they're going to say.

"Nothing," he replies, jamming his hands in his pockets. "I feel like I've interrupted your work."

"You did," I say simply. "And you should be ashamed. Interrupting a best-selling author when she's trying to provide food for her family."

Cal swallows a giant lump in his throat as his eyes go wide. "I... I..." he stammers over the right words, but when he sees the look on my face, his head falls forward. "Alright, you have got to stop doing that." He sighs. "I actually felt bad."

"I know you did," I chuckle. "It's almost my break time anyway. What's going on?"

He rocks back on his heels while he looks around my work area, his excitement returning. "I just can't stop smiling today for some reason. That's all."

"Is that so?"

He nods. "Yep."

I get to my feet and walk to the kitchen. "Well, Smiley, I'm going to make some moon water tea if you'd like some. Not sure you really need any more positive energy, but it's up for grabs if you'd like some."

"What's moon water tea?" he asks, following me into the kitchen and stopping to rest his elbows on the island.

"It's tea… made with moon water." I say it as though the name of it is fairly self-explanatory.

"Okay," he says slowly. "Let's do this one step at a time. What's moon water?"

I hold up the small vial I have sitting in my windowsill. "It's water that's been charged by a full moon."

"So, you have a direct plug that runs from your kitchen to the moon? How long is the extension cord?"

I glare at him. "Are you making fun of my beliefs?"

He straightens himself. "Oh, heavens no!" he says in the voice of a television diva.

"I'm going to pop you one," I threaten. "Moon water is a powerful thing."

His cockiness fades and is replaced with a hint of concern. "What does it do?"

I wait for the kettle to whistle, knowing that if I stare at Cal long enough, I'll get the reaction I want. And sure enough, the kettle whistle startles the shit out of him and I smirk.

"You did that on purpose," he accuses. "You've had that kettle going before I even got here."

"Maybe I did."

The look on his face is one of annoyance, left over from my accusations of being interrupted earlier. But he seems to move past it pretty quickly.

I move the moon water vial over and put it in front of him. He almost leans back like it's going to bite him.

"Moon water can be used for all kinds of things," I explain. "You can cleanse crystals, wash your hair, spray it in a room, use it in a spell, pour it into a bubble bath, water your plants with it, or even drink it. Like we're about to now."

"Moon water isn't just another name for poison, right?"

I give him a mischievous look. "Wanna find out?"

He straightens and stares at the vial. "Absolutely."

I hold the moon water in my hands and realize that I've been so wrapped up in Cal being here, that I haven't really had much time to myself. Much time at all to practice my craft or focus on my writing.

Is this what it's like to be back in a relationship? To lose who I am as a person?

Would he cheat on me if he got the chance?

My mind is now racing and I can't seem to settle it, but I hear a snapping sound and refocus my eyes. Cal is waving his hand in front of my face with a concerned expression.

"You okay?" he asks, sitting back down on the stool at the island.

I nod and force a smile. "Yeah. Just a lot on my mind I guess."

"Do you want to talk about it?"

I shake my head, "Nah. It's really not important."

He nods slowly, considering, but refocuses his attention on the moon water. I grab two mugs and put them on the counter before walking toward the tea selection I have in my cabinets.

"Do you have a preference on flavor?" I ask, thumbing through the options. I was going to go with a loose leaf tea, but didn't want to wait for it to steep in another pot.

"Whatever you recommend," he says. "I trust your judgment."

I purse my lips and tap my chin while I think. "Maybe a calming tea," I conclude. "It's raining and I like to match my mood with the weather."

He leans back on the stool and cranes his neck to see outside. "Calming? I don't need calming."

"You came into my house with a smile that only a killer clown would wear. I think calming is the way to go."

He laughs. "I thought it was good to be high on life. Happy as a clam. All those stupid sayings."

"It is," I agree. "But not when you enter the house of a stressed woman."

His head bobs in thought while he watches me pour the tea. "What's in the calming tea?" he asks, letting his voice fall to a soothing tone.

"Hibiscus, orange peel, lemongrass, chamomile, gotu kola, and lavender."

"I'll pretend like I understand what you just said and skip ahead to, 'Sounds great!'."

"You'll like it," I tell him.

He accepts his mug of tea and takes a sip. He considers the flavors in his mouth for a minute before giving me a surprised look. "I must admit, I was skeptical. But this is pretty good tea."

"I didn't know you were a tea connoisseur."

He takes another sip. "Well now you do."

I take a long sip of my tea and let the warmth move down my throat.

Cal adjusts himself on the stool and settles his mug between both hands as someone would on a cold winter day.

"So," he begins, staring into the deep yellow liquid in his mug. "Why are you so stressed?"

"I said we didn't have to talk about it," I tell him, lowering my cup to the counter.

"I know," he says. "But let's talk about it anyway."

"You don't need to hear about my problems."

"Sure I do. Make your problems my problems. Maybe I can help."

I consider this for a second before I lean against the island. "It's my ex-husband," I say, jumping to the point. "I sent out the signed divorce papers a week ago and I'm just waiting to see when this feeling in my stomach will go away."

"What feeling?"

"The feeling that I did something wrong," I admit. "Or maybe that something bad is coming my way."

Cal gestures toward our mugs. "Is that why we're drinking long-ass extension cord tea? Does it have some protection abilities or something?"

I smirk at his description but let it go. "It has a lot of abilities when used in certain ways, but by itself, not really. I'll most likely use it in a ritual later today to make myself feel better. Right now, I'm drinking it to focus my energy in other ways. Worrying is too exhausting to keep going like this."

"I'm sure it is," he says softly. "Stress isn't something to mess with. And if you need someone to talk to, you know I won't repeat anything you say to me."

I smile at him and place my hand on his arm. "I know. And I'm grateful for that." I place a gentle kiss on his tea-warmed lips. "Now, I need to get some work done on my book."

Cal looks toward my desk. "Are you almost done with it?"

"Not even close."

"How long does it take to write a book?"

"It varies," I say. "Sometimes I can write a book in twenty-four days, and sometimes it takes me a full year. Each story is different. If I'm not connected to what I'm writing, that's when I tack on the extra days."

"I get that," he says.

Just as I'm getting ready to switch the topic to his job, my phone rings. "That's probably my mom," I sigh.

"Everything okay?"

I nod. "She just does a weekly check-in to see how things are going with me and the kids." I glance over my shoulder at him as I walk to pick up my phone from the counter. "You really should call your mom and check in with her."

"I meant what I said before. I can't go back there."

My lips curl down and I drop the topic of his mother.

The screen is lit up on my phone, but when I look at the number I don't recognize it. "Not my mom," I say. I press the green button and answer the call. "Hello?"

Hello. May I please speak with Giselle Palmer?

"Speaking."

Mrs. Palmer, this is Jace Binder calling you from Binder and Associates. I'm calling on behalf of your husband, Mark. I was hoping you could put me in touch with your lawyer so we could discuss a few things regarding your court hearing.

"What court hearing?" I ask. "Our divorce is being done between the two of us. We agreed we weren't getting lawyers involved."

Ma'am, did you not have a lawyer write up your divorce agreement? It seems very thorough.

"Look, Mister. I don't know what kind of scam you're pulling, but Mark and I had an agreement. I wrote up the damn papers and sent them to him for approval before we even signed anything. This was supposed to be a simple divorce where we both sign on the dotted line and go our separate ways."

I can feel the knot in my stomach winding tighter and tighter the more this guy talks to me. The look on Cal's face tells me that he hasn't missed a word of what I've said. I know for a fact I'll be unloading my problems on him after this phone call. I hope he means what he said.

Mrs. Palmer, I'm your husband's attorney. This is not a scam, and we need to get some things taken care of sooner, rather than later.

"What exactly is this urgent matter that needs to be discussed with my so-called lawyer?" I hiss.

Well, ma'am. I don't want to throw a stick in the bike spokes, so I'm going to need to speak with your lawyer.

I feel the rage starting to boil in my gut. "Just tell me what the fuck your issue is!"

Cal gets to his feet and I hold up a hand to make him stop, feeling like a fool for the way I'm acting.

I hear the lawyer clear his throat on the other end of the line. Part of me wants to apologize for swearing at him, but he's really pushing me to my limits here and I don't like the way I'm feeling.

Ma'am. Your soon-to-be ex-husband is requesting a court hearing.

"What?" Why? The divorce papers were mailed a week ago."

We're aware of that, ma'am. I have a copy of them in my hands right now.

"Then, what's the issue?"

I hear him hesitate and I know it's a proper procedure to work through the attorney, but I don't have mine on the phone at the moment and I'm not sure I'm willing to let this guy hang up without giving me information.

He's claiming that he wants full custody of the children.

My whole body goes numb. I feel my throat close, forcing me to swallow nothing by air. My stomach does a twist that makes me cover my mouth so I don't throw up all over my floor.

My chin quivers and I try to keep my tone steady. "On what grounds?" is all I'm able to manage. Three words. Three words asking why my cheating ex-husband thinks it's okay to take my children away from me. The children that I carried for nine months and raised while he was out screwing other women.

On the grounds that you're unstable.

"Unstable?!" I echo. My breathing quickens and I don't even know how to reply to that. "How the hell does he think he can prove I'm unstable?!"

He has no case. Anyone that knows me knows that I may be ditzy from time to time, but I'm anything but unstable.

And on the grounds that you fled the state with your children.

I've lost my ability to speak. He knew that I was leaving the state. I told him where I was once we were gone.

I'll try back another time. I recommend getting a lawyer. Have a nice day.

And the line goes dead.

It takes less than fifteen minutes for Cal to have Jade and Kiara in the kitchen with us. I'm being handed glasses of wine from Kiara while Jade paces and curses out Mark to anyone that will listen.

"Are they coming to take the kids?" Kiara asks.

I shrug. "No idea. He didn't really say much."

"What did you write for your custody agreement in the divorce papers?" Cal asks.

"That I would have full custody and that Mark would get the kids for two weeks during the summer, and every other Christmas and Thanksgiving," I say, trying to remember the agreement despite the wine haze.

"Then, they shouldn't be able to take the kids," Kiara says, her voice rising.

"As long as he signed the papers," Cal adds.

"They were signed when I got them in the mail," I say.

"And he didn't change anything on the forms, right?" Jade asks.

I shake my head. "I read them over just to double check."

"Still. Who the hell does he think he is?!" Jade yells to the ceiling. "Having an attorney call you? I'm gonna hex that sonofabitch!"

"We don't-"

"Don't tell me I can't do black magic," Jade shouts, cutting off Kiara. "This asshole deserves everything that comes his way."

Cal looks at me while I sit on the stool at the island with a straw in the wine bottle. He seems worried for me and I appreciate his concern, but I don't want to bring him down when he seemed so happy earlier.

"Maybe we just need to focus on something else for a while," I say as I chew on my fingernails. "I don't want to bum everyone out. This is my issue and I'll come up with a way to handle it."

"I say we crush him," Kiara says. "We have enough money to make that asshole disappear."

Jade hitches a thumb toward Kiara. "She has a point."

"We're not crushing him with money," I say. "That won't do much. He needs to be hit where it hurts."

"Where do you think it'll hurt?" Cal asks. Kiara, Jade and I all look at Cal. His eyes scan the room like there's a hint hidden somewhere. "What?"

I roll my glossy eyes and move on. "Just let me handle this."

Kiara is frantically shaking her head. "No. I'm calling Trina."

"You don't need to do that!" I shout. "Don't put yourself through anything just because I have shit hitting the fan."

"You need a lawyer, right?" Kiara says. I nod helplessly and my eyes drop to the bottle in my hand. "Then, I can handle a quick phone call with my ex sister-in-law in order to help you."

"At least you're on good terms with the family," Jade says.

"So true," Kiara agrees. Then, points a finger at me. "You need to get your thoughts straight. You're going to win this case, but you need to be strong. This may take a bit since there are children involved."

"I'll be fine," I say. "And thank you."

Kiara grabs her phone out of her pocket and disappears down the hall. Jade storms out the front door, but I have no idea why.

"What are the kids doing?" I ask Cal to try and refocus my mind.

He looks out the window and smiles. "They're playing on the playground equipment. Probably lava monster or some variation of the game since they love to make up rules."

"That they do," I say with a pathetic excuse for a grin.

After a moment, he turns back away from the window and looks at me. I can't imagine what he must think. My makeup is running, my hair is wrecked, my cheeks are soaked with emotion. And I'm sure my eyes are bloodshot from all the wine and crying.

"I'm sorry," I say, wiping snot from my nose.

"You have no reason to be sorry," he says. He walks over to me and takes one of my hands in his. "I'll help you get through this."

"There's no reason you should have been dragged into this. It's not your problem to deal with."

He leans down and gently kisses my tear-soaked cheek. "I'm making it my problem." He stares at me and I watch his eyes move from my mouth to my eyes. "I'm making you mine, Giselle. And by default, that makes this my problem. Unless you object to any of that." I swallow hard and shake my head, making a mental note to have him repeat all of this when I'm sober so I know it really happened.

"Alright then," he says with a nod. His lips find mine and I sink into his kiss. "Now, let's get this taken care of."

Chapter Eighteen

CALEB

My heart hurts for Giselle.

After all the time I've spent here and watched her; not in a creepy way, but more like observed, I've come to find that she's more pure than her friends. She's naive, she's sensitive, she cares about what other people think of her.

Watching her try to handle the attorney was gut wrenching. I felt so helpless. I wanted to knock his damn teeth in.

"I feel like I should be doing something more than sitting here on my ass, watching her go through all of this," I say to Jade and Kiara as we sit on the back patio. "She looked so fragile when she left to go meet with Trina."

They nod slowly, but keep staring off into the distance.

"What can her ex husband do?" I ask, leaning my elbows onto my knees. "Can he actually take the kids?"

Jade shakes her head. "I hope not. Though, I think Trina will know that Giselle doesn't have a bad past."

"And that Mark's accusations are a bunch of bullshit?" I ask.

My fist clenches and Kiara puts a hand on my arm. "She's going to be okay."

"She has an army behind her," Jade says reassuring me. "We won't let anything happen to her or those kids."

"Neither will I," I say. I let my fist unclench and Jade reaches into the cooler beside her to hand me a beer. I laugh and stare at the bottle in my hands. "Ya know, I never thought you ladies would actually warm up to me."

Jade laughs. "We aren't ladies."

This makes me laugh harder, even though my insides are wound so tight it almost hurts. Even the corners of Kiara's mouth twitch. "Sorry," I say. "You *women*."

"Better," Kiara nods. She is looking at me funny and I can't figure out why.

"Everything okay?" I ask her.

"I have to ask," she begins, leaning forward. "Is that the only outfit you have? I've seen you wear that multiple times this week."

"That outfit, and maybe one other," Jade says. "Now that you mention it."

I lower my eyes. "I only have what was on my back," I admit. "I lost everything on the trail."

Jade's eyes go wide. "Holy shit. Did you get mugged?!"

"Something like that," I say, remembering Evan's knife against my skin.

Kiara scoots to the edge of her seat. "And you're just now telling us this? What if they followed you? What if they show up here?!"

I hold up my hands. "Easy now," I say gently. "They're long gone. Went in the complete opposite direction after my things were all taken. I was on that trail for a few days after it happened. They have no trace of me, nor would they want to for fear of being turned in."

Jade considers this and settles back into her chair. "That's true."

"I guess," Kiara says. Then, she clears her throat. "Have you told Giselle that you were mugged?"

I shake my head.

"Why not?" Jade asks. "I thought you two told each other everything?"

"I guess that was left out of the conversation." Among forty other small details about my life.

Jade claps her hands, scaring the crap out of me. "I think we should take you shopping."

I look at her and my face twists with confusion. "Shopping? Why would you want to do that?"

"Helllooo," Kiara says, her face warming at the idea. "We're women. We love shopping."

"And you've done so much around this place without a complaint," Jade adds.

"Well, you've given me a place to stay," I say. "And I can't tell you how grateful I am to still be here. To be able to prove that I'm not a bad guy. And that I really do care for Giselle."

"We know you do," Jade says.

"And you're great with the kids," Kiara adds. "I think that may have been the winning point for me. Free babysitter."

"Same," Jade says, tipping her bottle to her lips.

I sigh and look past Kiara and Jade to see the kids playing. "I'll babysit any time. They're great kids."

"That they are," Kiara agrees, following my gaze toward the laughter on the jungle gym. "You never had any?"

"You think I'd be in the middle of the woods with three women if I did?" I ask.

Kiara shrugs. "Sometimes men suck."

"Fair," I say, my head tilting to the side. "But no. I don't have kids. I never found anyone that I was willing to tolerate long enough to procreate. Have you seen some of the crazy women out there? Like, literally threaten you with your life, kind of crazy."

"I have," Jade says. "I've dated a few."

My jaw drops. I don't even mean to let my facial expression use its outside voice.

"Okay," I say. "What?"

Jade laughs. "I've dated women."

I look at Kiara who holds her hands up in surrender. "She didn't date me!"

This makes me laugh. "I'm sorry," I say. "I guess I'm just not sure how to respond to that."

"You don't," Jade says. "You take a swig of your beer and know that we understand you when you say that women are crazy."

"You sure do like throwing curve balls, don't you?" I ask.

"Gotta keep you on your toes," Kiara says.

"Yep," Jade adds. "Because it's Giselle's job to keep you on your back." She extends her beer to mine and clinks the bottlenecks together. "I don't care who you are, that one was funny."

Kiara covers her mouth and looks away.

"You women," I say, clicking my tongue. "Always assuming the guy likes to be on the bottom."

I watch Jade look at Kiara and they swap a look that says they're sharing a thought.

"Actually," Kiara says. "Giselle's hair was pretty messed up that morning when I showed up."

"So, she is a bottom girl," Jade concludes. She scoots toward the edge of her chair toward me and looks around like she's about to tell me a secret. "Do you need us to have a talk with her? Show her how to ride the pole?"

"Yeah," Kiara says, crossing one leg over the other. "We can't have our girl being a dead fish in bed."

Beer almost sprays out of my nose. "Oh, wow," I say. Jade hands me a napkin and I wipe my face. "I ummm... I don't really know how much of our sex life we really need to be sharing."

Should I be telling them that she does moves I've never seen before?

I get these three are super tight-knit and probably tell each other everything. But Giselle is the quietest and sweetest one in the bunch, so I don't think I should be the one to correct their thoughts of her in bed.

"You started it," Jade says, slumping in her chair like a kid who just got told they can't have a cookie.

"I was making a joke," I say. "I'd much rather not have Giselle thinking I'm going to tell her friends how she is in bed."

"Why not?" Jade asks.

"She's told us about you," Kiara adds as she wiggles her eyebrows at me.

I sigh and take a pull from my beer. "I'm just going to pretend you didn't say that."

"That's okay," Jade says, smacking her lips as she finishes her beer. "We'll revisit that topic when we all go shopping later."

The stillness of the water in front me is exactly what I need to try and clear my mind. I don't know what's been going on with me today, but I just have a weird feeling in the pit of my stomach. I thought talking to Jade and Kiara would ease my discomfort, but that conversation only ended with a shopping trip and my abilities between the sheets.

After that talk was over, I finished my beer and scurried down here.

I can't shake the feeling that something bad is coming. Giselle shouldn't have to go through all of this alone, but she keeps fighting my offer to support her. The minute she took off with Kiara's ex-boyfriend's sister - yikes - Giselle was practically paper white. She was so nervous and I felt like someone pressed a taser to my heart as I stood on the porch and watched her disappear down the stone drive.

"She's going to be fine," I whisper to myself. "Everything is going to be fine. It has to be. She can't lose her kids just as things with us are taking off. Not that she should ever lose her kids, but I don't want her to tie this incident in with my arrival."

I jam my hands in my hair. "Quit being so selfish. This isn't about you. This is about her."

"You okay?" I hear a voice ask me. I look up to see Giselle standing in front of me, wearing the business suit she had on before she left.

I get to my feet and walk to her, grabbing her hands in mine and pulling them to my chest.

I sigh. "Aside from getting conned into a shopping trip later? Yeah, I'm okay." I kiss her cheek and she looks at me like she needs more context. I save that discussion for later because I'm too antsy. "What did Trisha say?"

"Trina," she corrects.

"Sorry."

"No big deal," she says, offering a gentle smile. She walks us away from the bridge and heads to the pavilion picnic table before she sits us down. "She told me that it's going to be a fight in court. But she doesn't think he has much of a case."

"What exactly did she say?" I ask.

Giselle shakes her head, her eyes darting back and forth as she tries to think back on their conversation.

"We didn't really get into much. She just wanted to let me know what the attorney was saying and tell me that she did a dig on my history. She thought it was a good idea to have a formal meeting before the court hearing."

"When is the court hearing?"

"Next week," she sighs. I can tell by the look on her face that this whole ordeal is bothering her. "They said they couldn't get me in any sooner, but in reality, that's hella fast. Most family court cases take a month or two to get in front of a judge."

"Trina pull some strings?" I ask.

Giselle nodded. "Like you wouldn't believe."

I squeeze her hands. "Everything is going to work out. You have an army behind you," I say, almost shuddering at the realization I'm quoting Jade.

Giselle leans in and wraps her arms around me. The scent of her has my eyes closing as I inhale deeply and pull her closer.

"I'm so glad you're here," she whispers. I swear she's crying, but I won't point it out. I've come to learn that these three women don't like to show weakness when it comes to anything.

I learned that when they pulled a Charlie's Angels and had me at gunpoint before I even realized what had happened.

I kiss the top of her head, and when she pulls away, I see a tear sitting on her cheek. With a quick swipe of my thumb, I wipe it away and try my best to smile.

"We're going to get through this," I tell her. "Everything will work out the way it's supposed to. Your kids will be safe here with us and I'll be here to keep all of you out of harm's way."

I don't know what part of that made things worse, but she begins sobbing and buries her face in her hands. After a few hiccups of emotion, she lets herself fall into me, soaking my shirt in tears.

"I'm sorry," I say, stroking her hair as my heart rate kicks up a few notches. What the hell did I say that made her upset? Does she not want me to stay? I thought she just said she was glad I'm here. "I didn't mean... I-,"

"You're amazing," she says as she lifts her head. She sniffles and wipes her nose on her jacket sleeve before she leans in and kisses me. She pulls away slowly, but leaves her eyes closed. Tears have become a paste in her mascara coated eyelashes. "I'm sorry I'm snotty and wet with tears, but I need you to know how happy you make me."

I laugh and wipe another tear from her cheek. "Not as happy as you make me," I say.

Her eyelids flutter open and the redness of her face makes the green in her eyes jump to a notch below neon. I smile at her and tuck a lock of tear-soaked hair behind her ear.

"You are absolutely beautiful," I whisper. I brush a kiss over her mouth and feel the sadness on her lips. "And I don't care how snotty or soaked you are." I kiss her again. "I'm going to be here for you to kiss and cry on and vent to..."

I let my words trail off, not sure if I should continue on the path that this conversation is heading. My head is telling me to shut up, but I can't seem to portray the message to my mouth. Before I can stop myself, I hear the words fall from my lips.

"I love you, Giselle."

The trip to the mall was fairly quick, surprisingly, considering Jade had me try on every pair of cargo shorts she could find.

"They seem to be your favorite," she'd said.

"And make sure you try on some jeans," Kiara added. "Fall is right around the corner."

After all was said and done, I'd left the mall with six new pairs of shorts, three pairs of jeans, a new belt, ten t-shirts, one button-up shirt, two hoodies, and three new pairs of shoes.

I can't tell if they were spending money on me because they were enjoying themselves, or because they just needed a mental break from everything that was happening.

Even though I'm grateful for everything they've done for me, the trip to and from the mall isn't exactly comfortable since I'm squished between the carseats, despite the fact this has a third row. It wasn't made for this many people.

If this turns into something serious, I need to make a mental note to suggest multiple vehicles for future trips.

"Thank you," I say from the back seat of Kiara's SUV. "For everything you did for me today. I don't know how to repay you."

"Lawn will need to be mowed again," Kiara says from the driver's seat.

"And our outdoor decorations will need to be put away for the winter," Jade adds. "Not all of them, but some of them will rust or crack if they have to stay out in the snow."

I grin, knowing I should have expected that.

Giselle stares at me, wearing a giant smile on her face as she keeps her fingers laced with mine. Granted, it's over the carseat that's sitting between us, but it's still nice to be holding her in some fashion.

She didn't say anything after I told her I loved her. She simply leaned into me and let me hold her for a while before we had to get back up to the houses so she could change clothes. She didn't tell Jade or Kiara when we got up there, and she didn't bring it back up to me, even when we were left alone for a few minutes while Kiara and Jade took the kids to the bathroom.

Maybe I made a mistake. Maybe I shouldn't have said anything.

Sometimes I'm an idiot.

I have everything spread out on the guest house bed after we get back and I'm examining everything when Giselle walks into the bedroom.

She knocks gently and I turn to see her, arms crossed, leaning against the doorframe.

"Knock, knock," she says, before letting herself in.

I have my hands on my hips as I examine everything. "I don't know what to do with myself," I admit. "I don't even think I had this much of a wardrobe before I hit the trail in the first place."

Giselle looks down at her feet, unable to make eye contact with me on that topic. When we were in the SUV, I blurted out the fake story to Giselle so she wasn't left out. It was easy to admit all of that since it never actually happened.

Another lie in the weave of our relationship.

"You're going to be living in style," she says, amused at the massive pile. "And I can't wait to see you in that button-up shirt."

I turn and look at her, putting my hands on her hips and pulling her into me. Her arms go over my shoulders and I lean down to kiss her.

"If you think I'm going to look good *in* that shirt, just imagine how you're going to feel with it laying on your bedroom floor."

Chapter Nineteen

Giselle

The warmth of the rising sun is nothing compared to the warmth of Cal's body against my back. It's so nice to feel him wrapped around me each night. And even better to wake up to each morning.

Ever since he told me he loved me down at the lake eight days ago, I haven't allowed him to sleep in the guest house. He deserves more than that. Especially since he doesn't come off as the kind of guy to spill his emotions.

Owen and Abby have also been excited that Cal's been staying here. They love having their lava monster buddy right down the hall. Even Jade has been stopping by more often because she has a drinking buddy to share her beer with.

"Good morning," he groans when he feels me turn toward him. His eyes are still closed and his voice is husky.

"Good morning," I tell him in a chipper tone. "I'm going to make some coffee."

He pulls me in tighter and I see his eyes squeeze hard. "No," he whines. "Stay here. In bed."

I giggle and kiss his sleepy face. "I can't. I have to get up and around to go meet Trina before the hearing."

His eyes jolt open and he sits straight up like those freaky people do in horror movies. "Shit. That's today," he says in a panic.

"Yes, it is." I nod.

Cal rips the blankets from the top of both of us and jumps out of bed. "I'll go make the coffee. You get yourself ready and DON'T fret over anything. I'm going to do everything."

Watching him match my level of anxiousness has me feeling better about the day already. "You don't need to be worried," I tell him as I climb out of bed and slide into my slippers. "I will make the coffee. You go get a shower and wake yourself up."

He stops in his tracks and stares at me as I stand naked by the bedside. He comes over and wraps his arms around me, pulling me into him and kissing my neck. I can feel the tension melting from him as his hands glide over my exposed skin.

"I'm not worried," he whispers into my hair. "And if you're worried, I can help relieve some of that built up tension."

I laugh. "Two seconds ago you were panicking. Now you want to have your way with me before you send me off to the judge?"

Shame floods his face. He shakes his head. "Sorry," he says. "I guess I've just never been through something like this. I don't want to be nervous because I don't want to make you nervous, but I also don't want to act like it's nothing because it's everything." He brushes his mouth over mine and takes a slow, deep breath.

"Everything is going to be okay," I assure him, despite the feeling in my gut that's telling me otherwise. "She told me last week not to worry. So I'm not worrying."

"All you've done this past week is worry. That's why my brand new pants are already getting tight. I've been eating everything you've been baking and my clothes can't handle the weight gain."

I tap his belly. "We'll buy you new clothes."

"Not the solution I was hoping for," he says. He puts his hands on my shoulders and looks at me with pity in his eyes.

"Don't do that," I say, putting a hand on his bare chest and pushing him away.

"Do what?" he asks.

My eyes trail down the front of him even though I just scolded him for sexy talk. His hand covers his dick and he wags a finger at me.

"No, ma'am," he says. "Not going to feel you up and send you off to the judge."

I walk up to him and press my naked body to his. "I'd rather have that than you giving me puppy eyes because you're worried about me."

His head falls back. "I'm sorry." He gives me a quick peck on the cheek. "I'll go get a shower and meet you in the kitchen for a cup of coffee."

"Deal," I tell him. And watch as his naked butt heads toward the bathroom. I give him cat calls and laugh hysterically when he wiggles his ass in response, snapping his fingers in the air like he's doing the cha-cha. "And that right there," I say. "Is why I love you too."

Trina is waiting on the steps of the courthouse when I pull up and park my car. My palms are damp with nerves and I can't help but want to vomit on my steering wheel.

I step out of the car and head toward Trina who is waving for me to hurry.

"I don't think we're going to have too much trouble," she says as she hurries me toward a private conference room inside. "I only have a few questions to ask you about Mark's past and then we can head in to meet with the judge."

My breathing quickens and I begin to fan myself with my file folder that I brought along. Trina grabs my hand. "You're going to be okay," she says. "There's no way the judge will side with him."

I let out the breath I've been holding. "Okay. Let's go do this."

The conversation lasts ten minutes, and I'm grateful because this place is beyond intimidating.

The courthouse is massive. Giant peaks on the outside of the building with a huge clock in the center. The pillars that lead to the front doors look like something that would be on a mansion of a loving home, not a place that was made to break families apart.

Inside, the carpet is a deep red that leads to gray walls which are lined with pictures and plaques of all sorts. Recessed lighting in the ceiling leads the way from the private room we were in for our quick conversation about Mark, to the massive courtroom that threatens to rip my life apart.

Once we reach the end of the hall, we are ushered into the courtroom and I sit in the chair to the left of Trina. I reluctantly look to my right when Mark and his attorney stroll in and take their seats.

My heart leaps in my chest, but not in a good way. It's the first time I've seen him since I left.

Trying to control the urge to puke is getting more and more difficult.

The bailiff that was standing by the side entrance door walks in front of the stand and says, "All rise." The courtroom obeys. I look over my shoulder and realize I don't recognize anyone here. "Court is now in session. The Honorable Judge James Thompson now presiding. Please be seated."

The judge gracefully enters the room and ascends the stairs behind his stand. He doesn't look mean or untrustworthy. I always hear horror stories of judges who are old and grumpy and will only take the side of someone they know.

This guy is a bit on the older side with dark hair that fades to gray toward his scalp. He has small square glasses on his face, and smile lines around his mouth. He nods to the bailiff and the bailiff nods back.

The judge sits in his chair and opens a file before lacing his fingers in front of him and looking down at us.

I gulp at the dry ball in my throat.

"Thank you," Judge Thompson says. "Mr. Odell." Mark looks up at the judge. "You are suing the defendant for custody of your children, on the ground that she is unstable and fled the state of Idaho without consent from both parties prior to departure. Is that correct?"

My stomach jumps into my throat when Mark confirms the accusations.

"Yes," is all he says, and that's all it takes for my breath to hitch. His voice. That voice that came home angry on so many occasions.

Judge Thompson looks at Mark's attorney, the old twat that had the audacity to call my phone and tell me that I was being taken to court. "Mr. Binder," Judge Thompson says to the attorney. "Please state the case details."

"Mr. Odell was at their residence when he woke up to an empty home. No note from Ms. Palmer explaining that they were leaving, or any indication of a return date. Her phone was turned off during their trip and he was called a few days later from a new number, explaining that they had left the state and would not be returning."

"What was the date of the departure?" Judge Thompson asks.

"April seventeenth of this year, Your Honor," Jace Binder says.

Judge Thompson makes a note in his file. "And what was the first date of contact between Ms. Palmer and Mr. Odell?"

"April twentieth, Your Honor," Jace replies.

I wince. Four days? Was it really that long? I guess it didn't seem so bad when I was leaving him behind. But now that I'm sitting in front of a judge who is looking for a direction to sway the case, it seems like I may as well have waited a year.

Shit.

Judge Thompson makes another note. He ruffles through a few pages and nods slowly before looking back toward Mark and Jace. "What is the justification for Ms. Palmer's instability?"

Jace leaves through a few documents in his green folder before adjusting his tie and speaking. "She kidnapped his children, Your Honor. That can't say much about the mental stability of a person."

I can see Trina wants to say something about him mentioning my mental stability, but she remains silent.

"I see," says Judge Thompson. This time, he looks toward Trina and me. "Ms. Palmer has noted that she is counter-suing for full custody of the children without visitation against Mr. Odell. Please state your case."

Unable to handle it anymore, I reach forward and pour myself a glass of water, drinking it fast. When I notice everyone is watching me, I go to place the water on the table, but miss the table, causing the glass to land in my lap, soaking myself and my perfect suit.

"Sorry," is all I'm able to say. Mark is smirking, Trina slowly shakes her head, Judge Thompson pulls his glasses off to rub his eyes before returning them to his face, and Jace Binder laughs.

The bastard actually laughs.

Trina rises and presses her palms against the table to keep the hearing moving forward. I'm grateful for that.

"Your Honor," Trina begins. "The information given to you by Mr. Binder is false. I have the phone records here that prove Ms. Palmer was in contact with Mr. Odell the day she left the state."

A sense of relief washes over me as I remember the call. It didn't go well. But I definitely called the day we left.

I remember now.

"Please hand those documents to Gordon," Judge Thompson says as the bailiff walks toward us with his outstretched hand.

He takes the documents and hands them to the judge. I feel beads of sweat forming on my forehead, but I ignore them. I've already made a fool of myself.

"Mr. Binder," Judge Thompson begins again. "Explain to me why I'm seeing calls received by Ms. Palmer on the days you claimed she was inaccessible."

"Those calls weren't answered, Your Honor," Binder says.

Judge Thompson pulls the glasses from the bridge of his nose and places them on the stand in front of him. "Then, how is it that there on numbers on this document, noting the call durations each time?"

I look at Trina and she looks at Binder. I had no idea how much of this case they were prepared to lie about. The knot in the pit of my stomach starts to loosen, but the embarrassment from wearing my water remains the same.

I take a deep breath.

When Jace Binder doesn't say anything, the judge looks back toward Trina and me.

"Ms. Olson, please continue," Judge Thompson says.

"Your Honor, my client was trying to get her children out of a toxic environment," Trina begins. "She removed those children from a home where the parents were unhappy. Where the father was constantly under the influence of drugs and alcohol. And the deciding factor on my client leaving was when Mr. Odell was detailed for hospitalizing another man during a bar room brawl." I watch as Trina takes a deep breath. "Your Honor, Ms. Palmer is a good mother. She is living on a piece of land with two of her best friends. A commune, if you will. There are other children nearby and they're in a safe location."

"Your Hono-,"

Judge Thompson holds up a hand, shutting up Jace before he can speak. "Ms. Palmer, what is the education system for your children?"

I clear my throat, suddenly aware that I spilled more water than I consumed. "We homeschool our children, Your Honor."

"Do any of you in this," he waves a hand in a circular motion, "commune have any background in education?"

I shake my head. "No, Your Honor." And the anxiety sinks back into my stomach.

He laces his fingers in front of him again. "What is it that you do for a living, Ms. Palmer?"

"I make a living writing and selling books, Your Honor."

The judge's eyebrows raise in a way that tells me it wasn't the answer he was expecting. "How many books do you publish in a year?"

"It depends on the year. Last year I published eleven. This year, I'm already at nine."

"How is this relevant?" Jace Binder mumbles.

"I recommend you hold your tongue," Judge Thompson snaps at Jace.

"I'm sorry, Your Honor," Jace continues. "I just don't see how her ability to write a book is relevant to this case."

Judge Thompson looks at Jace. "And what is it your client does for a living?"

He asks the question as though he already knows the answer.

Jace clears his throat. "He's between jobs right now, Your Honor."

I look over at Mark and notice a grin on his face. I know what he's going to say, and I know he thinks it's a win in his book. What he doesn't know, is that the judge already thinks he's worthless. My nerves are starting to settle, aside from worrying about the question regarding their education. I'm now focused on how much of a fool Mark can make of himself.

Even though I'm the one with a puddle on my skirt.

"Giselle left me everything," Mark blurts out.

The judge raises his eyebrows and pulls his glasses from his face. "So, you mean to tell me that you don't work and you're now living in a house that was provided to you by your..." he pauses and looks at the documents in front of him. "Ex wife?"

"Yes, Your Honor," Jace Binder says with a glare toward Mark.

Judge Thompson rubs his temples and places his glasses back on his face before taking a deep breath and looking at me.

"Well, Ms. Palmer, I can honestly say that I commend you. I commend you for being a successful writer. I commend you for looking out for your children." His eyes slide to Jace and Mark. "I commend you, Ms. Palmer, for staying with this imbecile for as long as you did. And I commend you for not ending up in prison for homicide."

He gives me a nod and I can't believe what I'm feeling in my stomach. Not anger or fear or nerves, but sympathy.

There can't be any possible way that I could feel bad for a man that threatened to take my kids away from me.

But there he sits. Miserable with the life he chose for himself. Now having to deal with the consequences and losing a game that he dealt himself.

That's what lying will get you. It will get you called an 'imbecile' by a judge in a courtroom full of people. I didn't even get called an imbecile when I dumped a glass of water on myself because I was unable to return a glass to a table that was inches away from me.

"Mr. Odell," Judge Thompson boasts. "You need to get your life together. You need to know that coming into a courtroom and basing your case off a mound of lies is not in your best interest. You wasted my time. You wasted your time. And you wasted the time of your lovely ex wife, who by the way, is far from unstable." Judge Thompson picks up his files and taps them on the desk in front of him before grabbing his gavel.

"This court rules in favor of Ms. Palmer for full custody of her two children with no visitation rights granted to Mr. Odell. Case closed."

The sound of the gavel slamming on the stand makes my heart jump in my chest.

But in a good way this time.

I won.

Chapter Twenty

Caleb

My stomach is in knots when I see Giselle's car coming up the driveway. Jade and Kiara are standing next to me in the same state of panic that I'm in. We were hoping she'd at least call us to let us know how things went, but all we got was a text that said '*grab the wine glasses, we're gonna need them.*' She didn't say if we needed them for a cry session or celebration.

So, we've been waiting.

These two women to my left have never looked so scared. Not even when a stranger walked onto their property, which goes to show just how close these three friends are.

More like sisters, I'd say. Kiara and Jade being the overprotective big sisters who are willing to throw down if someone steps out of line or comes after someone they love.

Giselle has such a soft heart. I need her to be okay.

I'm swaying back and forth as I watch the car get closer and closer to us.

"Can you tell if she's smiling?" Jade asks, squinting toward the gun metal gray car.

"Can she drive any fucking slower?" Kiara snaps, clasping her hands at her chest.

I let out a breath and just stare.

Giselle puts the car in park and gets out, I swear it takes a lifetime for her to do these two small tasks. She closes the door and holds three bottles of champagne in the air, her face flushed, but in a good way.

"I think we're about to celebrate," I say as a huge smile consumes my face.

I race to Giselle and wrap her up in my arms. She laughs and cries and I spin her around and bury my face in her neck. A tear forms in the corner of my eye, but I wipe it away before anyone can see it.

"I won!" Giselle shrieks. "I won!"

Kiara and Jade are already at her side, wrapping around us as I continue to hold Giselle tight in my arms. I'm so grateful that she won that case. I had no idea what my next moves would have been had Giselle lost her children. How do you help a mother cope with something like that?

I shake away the thought of what my own mother must have felt when I stopped coming around.

Giselle wipes away a tear and smiles up at me. "It's time to celebrate! Let's go inside so I can change into some jeans. We're having a cooler night and I'm so thrilled for fall to be peaking it's head around the corner." She acts like she's clapping her hands even though they're filled with giant bottles of bubbly. "Jade, we need a fire going. Kiara, grab the steaks from the fridge. Cal, meet me in my room in five minutes. We have a bit of time before the food and fire will be ready."

She stands on her tippy toes and crushes her mouth to mine. "Yes ma'am," I groan. Her kiss is loaded with a variety of emotions and I can't wait to help her relieve some of it.

I look at Kiara and Jade who are smiling at Giselle and I. I give them a wink and say, "You heard the lady."

Kiara laughs and says, "Yes, we did hear the lady. You're gonna get some while Jade and I get to do the hard work."

Jade looks at Giselle and laughs. "Can you at least ride on top this time?"

Giselle's jaw drops and she looks at me. I hold my hands up in surrender before Kiara says, "Your just-got-fucked hair kind of gives things away. Don't blame Cal. He was a vault with your bedroom secrets."

I feel Giselle pat me on the shoulder now that she's handed off the bottles to Kiara and Jade. "Good boy," she says.

"I don't need to wag my tail or anything. Do I?" I smirk.

Giselle rolls her eyes. "Can we just get back to celebration mode?"

I dip Giselle in my arms and give her one hell of a kiss so she knows what's to come. "Absolutely."

Later in the evening as we're gathered around the fire, the laughter of the kids running around and playing is dancing through the air. Beer and champagne are flowing faster than a creek after a summer storm, and I'm surrounded by an amazing group of women.

Music is playing as I wrap my arms around Giselle and sway back and forth. Kiara and Jade are shaking their butts and we're all enjoying the celebration of Mark getting his ass handed to him.

"Cheers," I say, raising my beer bottle in the air. "To a wonderful commune, filled with amazing people, and a great outcoming from an almost shitty situation."

"And good sex," Giselle adds with a wink.

"Good sex when we can get it," Jade adds, laughing.

"Cheers to that!" Kiara shouts.

We clink bottles as the fire crackles in the background. It's icy cold as it trickles down my throat and I moan after I swallow.

"That was quite an eventful day," I say.

"It sure was," Giselle breathes. "And I'm glad it's over."

"Me too," Jade says. But her voice has all of us looking in her direction. She sounds sad or upset.

"You okay?" Kiara asks.

Jade nods. "I think so."

"What's wrong?" I ask her, leaning forward and resting my elbows on my knees after we all take a seat. The feeling of the celebratory toast is fading quickly and I don't like the jitters in my stomach as a result.

Jade shrugs. "I can't shake the feeling that something else is wrong."

Out of the corner of my eye, I see Kiara and Giselle nodding.

I look at all three of them.

"Like what?" I ask, feeling my stomach clenching tighter as I ask.

Am I the reason they have this bad feeling? Can they sense I've been lying about who I am or what I've done?

"I can't put my finger on it," Giselle says, shaking her head. "It's something. I thought it was the court hearing, but I was feeling this way before those papers were even mailed out."

"I know," Kiara says. "Like something or someone is coming. Maybe it's not a bad thing. I can't really tell."

"Same," Jade adds.

I can't quite tell if they're screwing with me again.

"So, you three all share the same bad feeling? I ask. "Visions or something?"

"Not visions," Jade says. "But we do get inklings or suspicions every once in a while."

"How accurate are they?" I ask.

"Usually pretty spot on," Kiara says.

I feel my pulse speed up and a cold sweat start to form. There's no way they found me. There's no way they know I'm still alive. I haven't even been in contact with Ash or my mom.

I need to calm myself down. I know it's not possible.

"Are you okay?" Giselle asks. I look up when nobody answers and realize she's talking to me.

"Yeah," I lie. "I'm fine. I guess I'm just curious about the way things work between you girls. It's all very new to me."

"We still surprise ourselves sometimes," Jade says.

I jump to my feet when I hear a high pitched scream coming from the playground. Without thinking, I drop my beer bottle at my feet and take off in a full sprint with three scared women behind me.

When I reach the playground, I slow my pace as I realize this isn't a job for me. It's a job for Giselle.

"Looks like it will be an early night tonight," Giselle says as she races to Abby's side and holds her hair back. She runs a hand over the back of Abby's neck and says, "Honey, why didn't you tell me your belly hurt?"

Abby whines as she heaves and her little voice coos, "I don't know, Mommy."

"It's okay, baby," Giselle says, trying to soothe her. "We'll get you all cleaned up."

"Definitely an early night," Jade agrees as she takes another pull from her bottle.

I look at her, impressed that she never even put her drink down when she sprinted the distance to the playground.

These women.

"It's time to call it," Kiara says. "Early night for sure. It's not even eight."

"The joys of having kids," I say.

I watch Giselle hoist Abby up into her arms and realize I should be doing something. Just as I'm getting ready to take a step over toward Giselle, I hear Jade say, "Well, now we know what that bad feeling was that we all had."

"A little bit of puke set us all off," Kiara adds. "Way to go, kid."

I see Abby give the slightest hint of a smile to her Aunt K as Giselle walks her toward the house. Giselle glances over her shoulder at me like she's waiting for me to follow.

"I'll be right there," I tell her.

Once she's inside the house, I look toward Kiara and Jade and let out a long hard breath.

Kiara draws her brows together and says, "That's a mighty big sigh."

"I know," I say. "I dropped my beer by the fire."

Kiara and Jade break into a laughing fit and I follow them back to the patio area. Jade pops the top on a new bottle and hands it to me. I take a big swig and I feel a smile creep across my face.

Kiara plops down on her chair and says, "I don't know if it's the beer or the fact that Abby puked her guts up, but that feeling in my gut went away."

Jade jams her hands in her pockets. "Mine too."

I grin. "Well, not that I'm glad Abby doesn't feel good, but I'm glad you two are doing better." I look toward the house. "I should probably head in there and check on them. Not sure how much help I'll be with a pukey kid, but I think my being there is better than not."

"Probably a good idea," Jade smiles.

"Either of you want to come lend a hand?" I ask.

Both of them start frantically shaking their heads.

"I don't do vomit," Jade says.

"I see puke and I puke," Kiara admits.

I chuckle.

The knot in my stomach loosens as I throw back the rest of my beer and toss the bottle into the basket beside Jade. She holds up a hand and I high-five her on my way off the patio. Before I hit the house, I hear Kiara tell Jade, "Maybe we better do a ritual tomorrow. Just to be sure."

Jade smacks her lips after finishing off her drink. "Amen to that."

The second bath seemed to do the trick in getting the last chunk of vomit off Abby.

Poor kid, I don't think I've ever seen a tiny human so sick. She spiked a fever shortly after we brought her home and Giselle knew just the thing to give her.

Popsicles.

What kid wouldn't feel better after being told they HAVE to eat a popsicle?

When I was a kid, and I don't mean to sound like an old grouch who yells at whippersnappers, I got nothing more than a good old-fashioned 'Stay your ass in bed'.

Ah, the good ol' days.

Giselle slowly pulls Abby's bedroom door closed and we tip toe out to the kitchen after telling Owen he can stay up a little bit later if he's careful not to wake his sister.

He's such a grown up little kid. I don't remember ever feeling like I needed to take care of Ash. Granted, Ash is older than me, but still.

Owen's neck is constantly craning toward the hallway like he needs to check on Abby every two minutes. It's definitely a warming feeling to see how much he cares.

"How are you doing?" I ask Giselle as she saunters toward the fridge.

She shrugs. "About as good as any mom can be after bathing her child that many times to get rid of the puke smell." She smirks when she hears herself.

"These kids are lucky," I tell her. "You're a great mom."

She sighs and looks at me. I can see that she's deep in thought so I remain quiet for a few minutes.

"I almost lost them," she says, her eyes growing wet with emotion.

I all but race across the room to be next to her. Looking over my shoulder, I make sure Owen is still absorbed in his show before I say, "But you didn't. That's all in the past now and you can move forward and forget about him."

She's nodding while she tries to gather herself. "You're right."

"I'm always right," I say, pressing a kiss to her temple. "Now, let's go join Owen on the couch before it's time to get ourselves to be-,"

"Mommy," a tiny little voice says from the hallway.

Giselle takes off at a sprint and Owen is right on her heels.

I walk slowly toward the hall even though I don't want to be in the way.

"Can I sleep in your bed?" she asks.

Giselle sighs and I watch her brush hair from Abby's face. "Of course you can."

"I'll sleep in the hall outside your door," Owen says, his voice sounding drastically deeper than normal. "Just to make sure you're okay."

Abby gives her big brother a hug but shakes her head. "You need to sleep in your bed," she says. "The hall isn't comfy."

Owen smiles at her and nods. "Alright. I'll sleep in my bed. But if you need me, you just come find me."

"Deal," Abby says. Owen holds up a fist and gives her a fist bump before he looks at me. "Can you turn off the TV so I can get to bed? I need to make sure I have the energy in case she needs me."

I give him a big smile and nod. "I'm on it."

"Thank you, Cal," Owen says. Then, he walks into his bedroom and goes to close his door, but leaves it open just a crack so he can hear anything happening outside his bedroom.

I'm looking at the hallway walls and notice a bunch of pictures on them. I never really stopped to look at them before which makes me feel like I've only used this hallway as a path to the bedroom.

Smiles and laughs and memories scatter the walls in frames of various shapes and sizes. It's a cozy place to be when you look at the photos, wondering what was happening in each of them.

There's one in particular that makes me stop and stare. Giselle with her arm around an older woman who looks just like her. It's not hard to figure out that it's her mother. The joy on Giselle's face is radiating through the glass of the frame and I find myself smiling back at the two of them.

This is the woman that does weekly phone call check-ins with her daughter to make sure she's okay. Checks on her grandchildren, and I'm sure, makes an appearance around the holidays.

What I would give to be a part of that family.

Giselle takes Abby into the bedroom and after a minute, comes back out and walks up to me.

She sighs. "I'm sorry about all this."

"You have absolutely nothing to be sorry about," I say. "I'm sorry she doesn't feel good. She looks so little when she's curled up in a ball feeling like that."

Giselle looks down the hall like she can see her through the hallway walls. "She really does."

"You go in there and snuggle up with your little girl," I say. "I'll be right here waiting when you all wake up to make sure you don't need anything."

She smiles at me and stands on her tippy toes to press a kiss to my lips. "You're amazing," she says. "And I love you so much."

"I love you too."

She goes to walk down the hall and stops to turn back to me. "Just so you know, Owen learned that fist bump from you."

I draw my brows together and look at her, confused. "How?"

"He saw us that day," she tells me. "Down at the lake. They were playing hide and seek, and he picked a spot closer to the lake to hide. He saw us fist bump and he started doing that with the other kids."

I make her laugh nervously when I say, "Let's hope that's all he's witnessed."

And honestly, it makes me a bit nervous too.

Chapter Twenty-One

Giselle

I feel like I pulled an all-nighter, which is a lot different in your early thirties than back when I was a teen. When I was a teenager, I could bounce right back after downing enough alcohol to kill me, and after not having slept for almost forty-eight hours to boot. Now that I'm what they call a grown-up; I feel like I've died twice and only my shell remains to roam the earth.

I spent all night up with Abby since she couldn't seem to kick the stomach bug. Red popsicle was regurgitated onto my bed, which was awesome, but I'm glad it was all contained in one spot.

Around three o'clock this morning was when the exorcism side of Abby finally subsided and she was able to fall asleep without dry heaving. Her temp went down and after an hour, she looked like my perfect little girl again.

My eyes feel like they are cemented shut when I try to open them. The smell of coffee tickles my senses as Cal comes into the bedroom with two mugs in his hands. He looks at Abby who is still curled up beside me and nods toward the bedroom door. I give her a quick look to make sure she's still sound asleep, and I get up out of bed, slide on my slippers, and follow Cal out to the kitchen.

"You didn't need to sleep on the couch," I tell him as I accept the steaming mug from him.

"Abby needed her mommy," Cal says. "Of course I needed to sleep on the couch."

I'm so grateful for everything he does for us.

He walks over and brushes a soft kiss across my hips, just as something crashes behind us. I jump and spill scalding coffee on my leg before looking to see what the hell just happened.

"Dammit, Tarot!" I yell as the cat scatters from the counter when I reach for a spatula. Cal muffles a laugh beneath his hand and I glare at him with the spatula now pointing in his direction. "You think this is funny?"

He shakes his head. "Not the fact that he broke your mug," he says. "But maybe it's a bit comical that Tarot won't let me get close to you."

I smirk, realizing he's right. "He may be an asshole sometimes, but I guess he can be a bit protective." I put the spatula back in the drawer and clean up the sugar bowl that replaced the last one he broke. "Jade is going to go nuts when she finds out that Tarot broke the one she gave me as a replacement."

"I won't tell if you don't tell," Cal says with an innocent face.

"Deal." I check the clock and put my coffee down. "We have to go," I say.

"Where?" Cal asks.

"We're doing a ritual this morning to ward off the bad feelings we've been having," I tell him.

Cal puts his mug down next to mine. "Kiara and Jade said last night that their bad feelings went away. You still think something is going to happen?"

I shrug. "It's better to be safe than sorry, as the saying goes."

"What about Abby?" he asks.

"She'll stay here sleeping until Owen comes and gets me if something is wrong," I say. "Her fever broke and she stopped throwing up hours ago. If he comes and tells me she's better, then she has my approval to go play. Otherwise, we'll cut the ritual short and I'll go back to snuggle my sick baby girl."

He nods. "Sounds like a solid plan. After you, my dear."

We get ourselves around and head over to Kiara's, where she and Jade are waiting for us. They both look at Cal and smile.

"Do we have ourselves a warlock this morning?" Kiara teases.

Cal swallows and looks at me like he's not sure what to say. "We will see what he brings to table," I tell them.

Jade has the altar already set up and smoke is rising from the incense sticks. Blue, white, and black candles are lining the patio while their flames dance against the movement of the air. Kiara is anointing her crystals in drops of various oils, and I notice Cal watching it all unravel.

His face says it all when Jade begins to take a few deep breaths as she pulls her amethyst from her bra. When she reached under her shirt, his face was absolutely priceless.

I put a hand on his arm. "We aren't getting naked," I assure him. I reach into my own bra and remove a matching crystal. "See?"

Cal reaches under his shirt and I try not to laugh when he comes up empty.

"We carry these for good energy," I tell him. "Protection and peace. Sometimes even encouragement or luck. It's all about the type of crystal and what our intentions are."

"I see," Cal says. He stands quietly while I work with Kiara and Jade to get everything in place.

The smell of our altar causes my heart to lighten and I can instantly feel a change in my mood. It's amazing what being surrounded by your people can do to a person.

"Let's cast the circle," Kiara whispers. She looks at Cal and extends a hand. Cal quietly accepts.

Jade and I link hands with Kiara and Cal, and we take a deep breath. Cal does as we do.

"Just focus on your breathing and listen to what we say," I whisper to him. "You don't need to do anything but breathe."

"I'm pretty good at breathing," he says from the corner of his mouth.

Kiara's words begin to flow as we close our eyes and exhale. "By the Earth that is her body. By the Air that is her breath. By the Fire that is her spirit. By the Water of her womb. As above, so below. The circle is cast. As we will, so mote it be."

Cal looks at me as we release hands. Then, his eyes look away from me and start analyzing the ground around him as if something is going to happen.

I chuckle, which gets Kiara and Jade's attention. We all find entertainment in Cal's curiosity.

"You're not supposed to be laughing during the ritual," Cal snaps as his cheeks blush with embarrassment.

"Actually, it's a free space," Jade counters. "A safe space. We can do anything we feel is necessary to help our session."

"Laughter is positive energy," Kiara explains. "Since that's our purpose today, it's encouraged."

I can tell Cal wants to glare at all of us, but he won't because we're a group of witches and he's beyond intimidated right now.

"Well, now the laughing is out of the way," Cal says. "What's next?"

"Now, the fun begins," I tell him.

Part of me wants to assure him that nothing is going to happen, but I'm starting to enjoy the fact that I scare him a bit. I guess it's only fair since he had the three of us on edge when he first arrived.

I grab the incense stick and the glass jar that Kiara brought from our stash. Cal watches as I lower the burning end of the incense into the jar and let it fill with smoke.

"What's that for?" Cal asks.

"We're going to make a spell jar," I tell him. "But we need to cleanse the jar before we use it."

He looks over his shoulder at Kiara and Jade. "Are they doing the same thing?"

"No," I tell him. "They'll do jars that feel right to them. Whether it be for clarity, peace, or sex."

His eyes widen. "You can make a jar to get laid?"

I nod. "Sure can."

He clears his throat. "What's your jar for?"

I smirk at him as a way of saying it's not for sex. Then, I remove the stick from the jar and watch the smoke roll over the rim. After I place the stick back in it's holder, I whisper, "It's for protection."

"Can you tell me what you're going to do with it?" he asks.

I nod and smile, "You're actually curious about this stuff."

"Maybe a little."

"Alright." I reach for the flowers and herbs that are scattered on the table next to me. "First, we need to line the bottom of the jar with salt."

"For protection," he says.

"For protection," I echo. I grab the small crystal on the tray next to us and drop it in the jar. "This is amethyst."

"From your bra," he concludes.

I chuckle. "Yes. We put it in our jar because it will help reduce the anxiety that we're feeling about the threat we can't seem to shake. And this," I say as I drop a small black stone inside, "Is black obsidian. It-,"

"Absorbs negative energy," Cal interrupts.

I look at him and notice he also got the attention of Kiara and Jade. "How did you know that?" I ask.

I watch as he looks toward Jade and swallows a lump in his throat. "Piper has one in her bedroom. She was carrying it one day and she corrected me when I asked if it was a mood stone."

"Piper has black obsidian in her bedroom?" Jade asks.

Cal nods. "It was just a small one. She really didn't explain why she had it. More what it was for than anything."

Jade looks at me, then goes back to work. I'm not really sure what to say to Cal right now, so I go back to my jar in hopes of changing the subject.

I can't believe Piper is carrying that around. I wonder why she didn't tell anyone. She has been opening up to Jade more and more lately, but I'm wondering if maybe Piper is feeling the bad feeling too.

Wouldn't that be something?

I drop the black obsidian into the jar and top it with a bay leaf. "The bay leaf is known to reverse bad luck and bestow healing on those who use it. And this," I say, stuffing dandelion flowers into the jar, "is for strength and balance. Hopefully this can set us all straight and put our minds at ease. The cinnamon and rosemary I sprinkled in are for added protection benefits."

I push the cork into the top of the jar, setting it in front of Cal before I walk over to the altar. I grab the black candle and do a quick scan to make sure I didn't forget anything before I walk back to sit beside Cal who is staring at the jar.

"And this is to seal the jar." I tilt the lit candle and allow the melted wax to pour over the top of the cork and down the sides of the glass.

"I always thought black candles were for dark magic," Cal says as he gets his face close to the wax. "Why are you using black wax for this? I thought you didn't use that kind of magic."

"Black candle wax on a spell jar is used to hex any individual within ten feet of it. It was used a lot in the olden times when a witch didn't feel comfortable with those around them. Within days, bad things flooded the lives of whoever they were trying to protect themselves from."

Cal goes to get up from the table, but I grab his arm and pull him back down. Jade and Kiara are giggling behind us.

"That was a dick move," Cal says to me, sitting back down.

I lean in and give him a playful kiss. "I know." I put the candle back on the altar and grab my spell jar once the wax is set. "Are you ladies done?"

Kiara nods and Jade finishes sealing her jar. "All done," Jade says.

"I think we need a trip to Wren's store," Kiara says. "I used the last of the bergamot."

"I need a few things too," Jade says.

"Me too," I add. "Our black candle is withering and we'll need a few more if we're going to do any more jars. I say we pack up the kids and head out."

"Maybe hit the mall and see what kind of decorations they have left before Samhain arrives," Jade says.

"Sounds like a plan to me," I agree. "Cal? Are you up for a trip to the witchy store?"

"Sure," he says, jamming his hands in his pockets. "But can I ask what you do with these little jars after you make them?"

I examine the jar in my hands and say, "I'll put mine on my altar. It feels like the best place for this one."

Jade and Kiara both echo my reply.

"So, I need an altar to be in your group?" Cal asks.

This makes us laugh. I wrap my arms around his neck and pull his mouth to mine. "You're already in our group."

Chapter Twenty-Two

CALEB

I FIGHT THE URGE to plug my nose when we walk into the small store that's sandwiched between two larger buildings on one of the main streets in the local neighborhood. Aside from the smell, you'd never know what was on the other side of that front door if you were standing on the sidewalk.

The store front is all glass with a large pink banner hanging over the top that reads GET WICKED. There is jewelry in the display cases, and aside from the occasional amethyst crystal - yeah, I'm basically a professional now and can tell the difference - it would come off as someplace you'd go to buy the perfect proposal ring.

But once you're inside, that wicked nose-burning smell smacks you in the face and you're faced with black walls that are filled with jars, skulls dangling from the ceiling, and if I'm not mistaken - a cabinet filled with wands.

"You make one crack about Harry Potter," Jade whispers to me, "And I'll make sure you don't have sex for a week."

"Wasn't gonna," I lie, walking away from her and heading deeper into the store.

The smell that's melting my insides is getting stronger as I approach one of the walls filled with boxes. Each of them are labeled with things like 'lavender' and 'frankincense'. I read over the boxes and come to the conclusion that the one I don't like is patchouli. I scrunch my nose at the box and see the kids walking toward me. Their hands are in their pockets with orders not to touch anything as we all walk through the store.

I lean down to them and whisper, "Don't worry. I'm not allowed to touch anything either." They giggle and we all make faces at some of the weird stuff that's hanging on the walls. This gets me a look from Giselle and I straighten myself, nudging the kids to do the same.

They follow my lead.

I walk to another wall which is filled with glass jars and trinkets. The jars resemble the ones they made earlier today, but I notice these ones only have one ingredient per jar. I'm wondering if these are the supplies they were talking about.

My three favorite witches make their selections and pile a bunch of things onto the counter by the register.

It feels good to be in public. Not worried about being found or someone recognizing me. No possibilities of JT coming around a corner and spotting me.

I feel free. And I couldn't be happier.

"Hey there, ladies," the woman behind the counter says.

She's petite with a long black braid that falls over her right shoulder. She's wearing a flowing brown dress and she's decorated with what appears to be one of each bracelet she sells. Her ears are flooded with silver and jewels, along with a cuff that sits halfway down the cartilage on her left ear. Each of her fingers is decked out in layers of various rings, some bigger than the others, and her nails are painted a deep red.

Her eyes are wrapped with lines of happiness and she appears to have lived at least a good fifty or sixty years.

She has to be the owner of this place.

"Hey, Wren," Kiara says, accepting the hand Wren offers her.

"It's so good to see you," Jade says as she comes around the counter to hug her.

"Giselle, my dear," Wren says. "It was so nice of you to bring your significant other to my store."

Giselle looks over her shoulder at me and I look behind me toward the door. "He's a bit new to all of this," Giselle tells her.

"How did you know I was-,"

"The way you look at her," Wren says, interrupting me. "The way you act when you're around her. Your aura. The energy shifted when the two of you stepped into my store. I can continue if you need further clarification."

I shake my head. Her voice is so soft and smooth that I feel she could put anyone into a trance simply by saying their name. Maybe use her as the voice actress for those meditation apps or something.

Wren returns behind the counter and begins ringing up the items. "Seems as though you ladies shouldn't spend so much time away from my shop. Not that I'm complaining about the sale I'll make today, but still." She gives them a wink as she bags up some of the small crystals into a purple mesh bag.

"I'm sorry," Giselle says. "We've kind of had a bit of a snag at the homefront."

"Everything okay?" Wren asks. "I'm assuming it has to do with your putrid ex-husband."

Giselle's eyes glaze over. I can't help wondering how Wren knows all of this. I've pretty much been glued to Giselle's hip and she hasn't talked to anyone on the phone aside from her mother and the asshat attorney.

"You keep dabbling in my mind, Ms. Wren," Giselle says with a teasing voice.

"It's not hard to see what's right in front of me," Wren replies. She scans the last item and bags it into a brown paper bag with her logo on it. A moon, sun, and stars with GET WICKED stamped across it. Simple and to the point. I love it. "Alright, ladies. That will be six-hundred dollars and seventeen cents. Cash or card?"

I almost fall over at the amount they're spending in this store. Six hundred dollars on supplies to fill tiny jars? Maybe the kids can cushion my fall.

"Cash," Kiara says, digging in her wallet. "We never use a card here, Wren. You know we don't want you getting all those silly fees."

Wren reaches out and touches Kiara's cheek. "You girls are too good to me."

"We know," Jade teases as she toys with a necklace hanging next to the register.

I'm completely absorbed by the way Wren moves and talks. She's like one of those women you only see in movies. Almost on the side of living that free hippie lifestyle, but more eclectic and modern. She's one of those people you'd want to have on your side. Someone you'd be happy to know.

"You girls enjoy the rest of your day," Wren says. "And when you come back next time, I'll have a few more inserts for your book of shadows."

This pings something inside me and makes me think back on the witch movies I've watched. They add things to their books to help them with something. Whether it be something they learned or something that happened, and the insert will ease a negative energy.

It's almost an unsettling feeling with Wren's timing to say that, like what she has for their books has something to do with me. Especially since she looks at me when she says it.

"Be safe, girls," Wren says. "Blessed be."

"Blessed be," they say in unison.

I've had an unsettling feeling in my stomach ever since we left Wren's shop. I'm glad the mall isn't busy when we get here because the unsettling feeling leads me to believe something bad really is coming.

Maybe I shouldn't be out in public. Maybe my feeling of enjoying the freedom has set sail and it's time to get back to reality.

I am a drug dealer on the run. Someone wants me dead. I've committed homicide and I'm in hiding.

Apparently hiding in a shopping mall.

"Can we get a pretzel?" Owen asks, tugging at Giselle's shirt.

"No," Abby argues. "I want ice cream!"

I'm glad she seems to be feeling better.

"Looks like we're having a smorgasbord for lunch today," I laugh. I look around as the smell of the food court hits me, but all I can see are clothes stores, jewelry stores, and a store that I remember shopping at when I was a kid to get the newest, coolest, skater shoes. "Where is the food?" I ask.

This mall is a lot different than the one back home. It has two floors instead of one. Escalators that you can ride like Buddy the Elf. And by the smell of it, a food court the size of our local grocery store.

The weariness of being in public is fading as I realize the size of this place. I can totally blend in here.

Then, I look at what I'm wearing.

Oh yeah, I'll *definitely* blend in here.

"We're almost there," Kiara says.

We take a few turns and walk past a few more stores before it comes into view. The place is absolutely packed with a variety of choices. Chinese food, Mexican food, Thai food. In addition to all of the usual greasy American choices. Plus, ice cream, frozen yogurt, smoothies, and even an entire space dedicated to soft pretzels.

It looks like Abby and Owen will both get their wish.

The center of the food court is filled with tables, though not many people are occupying the seats. Probably because lunch was almost three hours ago for most people.

"What do you girls want to eat?" Giselle asks Kiara and Jade.

Jade shrugs. "Something super greasy. I have a date with editing software tonight."

Kiara and Giselle groan as if someone suggested live cockroaches for lunch.

"What's wrong with editing software?" I ask. "Doesn't that mean it does the work for you?"

"Editing itself is the devil," Jade snaps. "Edits make your head throb. They make your eyes burn. And eventually, all of the words look the same. But to the editing software? It tries to turn correct words into incorrect words."

"And you can't do just one round of edits," Kiara adds. "Nooooo. You have to do three or four rounds before you send it to an editor."

Giselle rolls her eyes as she adds, "And then your editor will send back your manuscript with a bunch of comments and corrections that you have to make before you send it back to them for another round of their suggestions."

"That's when you cross your fingers and pray your ARC readers and betas readers don't say anything is wrong with the story itself." Kiara's fists are now clenched at her sides.

"I don't understand anything you just said, but either way, I'm sorry I asked." I put my hands in my pockets like I did at Wren's shop and just wait for them to tell me what to do next.

The three of them shudder and I'm almost sorry they chose this profession.

"Now I need anger food," Jade grumbles.

"Me too," Kiara agrees.

"The greasier the better," Giselle adds.

After we make stops for Chinese food, soft pretzels, sushi, pizza, and two different burger joints, we finally find a table and sit down.

The kids are ecstatic with all of the options and the women are laughing hysterically at the amount of food they chose. I dig into the loaded potato wedges while Giselle gets out her medium-well burger and fries. Jade is happy with her malt milkshake, and Kiara is diving head-first into a full tray of sushi.

The smell of it is making me want to gag.

"Try it," Kiara says with a mouthful of raw fish.

I shake my head. "Not a snowball's chance in hell that is going in my mouth."

"Giselle will do that thing you like," Kiara says with a raised brow.

Giselle stops chewing long enough to glare at Kiara over her burger. The look on her face says 'I'd say some nasty things right now if I didn't have my mouth full of half-cooked cow'.

"Oh, come on," Jade says. "Stuff your trap with the dead ocean critters."

"You make it sound so appealing," Kiara grunts.

"Listen, ladies," I say, wiping my hands on a napkin. "As much as I'd love to listen to you two fail at getting me to eat sushi, I'd rather hear about things like your commune, your writing, or even Wren."

Their ears all perk up at the mention of Wren's name.

"What about Wren?" Jade asks, making that obnoxious sound with her straw when the milkshake gets low.

I take another bite of potato wedge and wash it down with Coke. "How did she do what she did in the store today? It was like she read Giselle's mind. There's no way she knew who I was or what Giselle was going through."

"She's a witch," Kiara says with another mouthful. I try not to look at it as it rolls around her teeth.

"Plain and simple," Jade adds.

"But there has to be more to it than that. You three can't read minds."

"How do you know?" Giselle teases.

"Because you'd have made a comment about what I'm thinking right now," I say with a wink, praying she's lying.

Owen snatches a milkshake from Abby who begins to cry. Owen takes a long drink of it and hands it back before he says, "I was just making sure it wasn't poisonous. Do you want this food to poison you?"

"No," Abby's little voice replies.

"That's what big brothers are for," Owen says. Abby gives him a hug and I have to laugh when Piper and Lexie both fist-bump Owen. Jade chuckles too.

"There's all different kinds of witches," Kiara begins. "Some have more power than others."

"How do they get that power?" I ask.

"Walmart," Jade says.

I glare at her, knowing she's full of shit.

"They come into it," Giselle says, kicking Jade under the table. "Either by genes or by blessing. There's a laundry list of ways you can inherit those powers. It's just a matter of finding them.

"So, you three have the ability to do things like that?"

They all shake their heads, mouths now puffed with their next choice of grub.

Jade picks at the fries on Giselle's plate. "We're just normal moms who like to practice the craft and dance naked under full moons."

"Fully clothed," Kiara says through gritted teeth when Wyatt looks over.

"Sorry," Jade mouths.

I mull over everything they've told me about inheriting magic and the things about Wren. It's fascinating that people can just pick this stuff up and claim it as a lifestyle. Especially when it's things that I've only ever heard about in movies and TV shows.

I'm completely captivated by all of it.

"What did you want to know about the commune?" Kiara asks, cramming one of my potato wedges into her mouth. I cringe knowing her fingers were just touching ocean animals wrapped in seaweed.

I adjust in my chair, leaning back and crossing one leg over the other. "What made you decide it was something you wanted? What sparked your interest in moving to the center of nowhere?"

"Well," Giselle starts. "We trust each other. We all get along. And we're all single moms who have kids around the same age."

"And we hate people." Kiara adds.

"Amen to that," Jade adds. She grabs one of the sodas from the center of the table and pokes a straw into the top. "It just made sense for us, I guess. We all wanted the same things."

"Like being left the hell alone," Giselle murmurs.

This makes me laugh and I look between the three of them. It adds up why they do what they do. They wanted to get away from the chaos of the public. And now that they're together, they co-parent and have the luxury of living a carefree life with flexible work schedules.

"Does that answer your question?" Kiara asks. "Or were you waiting for us to say that we created a commune so we could pleasure each other any time we wanted."

I choke on the mouthful of Coke I'm trying to swallow and spray some of it on Giselle. Giselle then punches Kiara in the arm and they all start laughing as I wipe Giselle off with a handful of napkins.

"Well played," I grunt.

"What was the other thing on the list of topics you mentioned?" Kiara asks.

"Our writing," Giselle says, snapping her fingers as she remembers.

They dive into the details of all the different kinds of readers and what they do. Then, they talk about how they started writing and how much they wish they'd have known before they published their first books. These women are astounding. They've written books in less than a month which is less time than it takes me to read one.

"Did you get all that?" Giselle asks.

I nod slowly though my eyes feel like their whirring behind my lids. "I think so."

"Good," Kiara says. "Because there's a quiz at the end."

"I'm a piss poor test taker," I admit.

"Same," Jade says.

We sit and chat while we finish off most of the things we got on the trays. Owen only tests for poison two more times before lunch is done and over with. And Jade is now sitting back in her chair mentioning something about changing into stretchy pants.

"We probably should get back home soon," Giselle says, looking at her watch. "We can hit a few stores and head out."

"Sounds like a plan to me," Kiara agrees. "By the looks of it, you two are about to fall asleep on the table."

Giselle looks at Abby and Owen and smiles. "They sure do wear out quickly."

"Fully clothed," Kiara says through gritted teeth when Wyatt looks over.

"Sorry," Jade mouths.

I mull over everything they've told me about inheriting magic and the things about Wren. It's fascinating that people can just pick this stuff up and claim it as a lifestyle. Especially when it's things that I've only ever heard about in movies and TV shows.

I'm completely captivated by all of it.

"What did you want to know about the commune?" Kiara asks, cramming one of my potato wedges into her mouth. I cringe knowing her fingers were just touching ocean animals wrapped in seaweed.

I adjust in my chair, leaning back and crossing one leg over the other. "What made you decide it was something you wanted? What sparked your interest in moving to the center of nowhere?"

"Well," Giselle starts. "We trust each other. We all get along. And we're all single moms who have kids around the same age."

"And we hate people." Kiara adds.

"Amen to that," Jade adds. She grabs one of the sodas from the center of the table and pokes a straw into the top. "It just made sense for us, I guess. We all wanted the same things."

"Like being left the hell alone," Giselle murmurs.

This makes me laugh and I look between the three of them. It adds up why they do what they do. They wanted to get away from the chaos of the public. And now that they're together, they co-parent and have the luxury of living a carefree life with flexible work schedules.

"Does that answer your question?" Kiara asks. "Or were you waiting for us to say that we created a commune so we could pleasure each other any time we wanted."

I choke on the mouthful of Coke I'm trying to swallow and spray some of it on Giselle. Giselle then punches Kiara in the arm and they all start laughing as I wipe Giselle off with a handful of napkins.

"Well played," I grunt.

"What was the other thing on the list of topics you mentioned?" Kiara asks.

"Our writing," Giselle says, snapping her fingers as she remembers.

They dive into the details of all the different kinds of readers and what they do. Then, they talk about how they started writing and how much they wish they'd have known before they published their first books. These women are astounding. They've written books in less than a month which is less time than it takes me to read one.

"Did you get all that?" Giselle asks.

I nod slowly though my eyes feel like their whirring behind my lids. "I think so."

"Good," Kiara says. "Because there's a quiz at the end."

"I'm a piss poor test taker," I admit.

"Same," Jade says.

We sit and chat while we finish off most of the things we got on the trays. Owen only tests for poison two more times before lunch is done and over with. And Jade is now sitting back in her chair mentioning something about changing into stretchy pants.

"We probably should get back home soon," Giselle says, looking at her watch. "We can hit a few stores and head out."

"Sounds like a plan to me," Kiara agrees. "By the looks of it, you two are about to fall asleep on the table."

Giselle looks at Abby and Owen and smiles. "They sure do wear out quickly."

"I can wake them up," I say. Giselle, Kiara, and Jade give me a look that says they don't believe me. So, I reach my arms high in the air and let out an exaggerated yawn. "Man... I wish I wasn't so tired right now." I slowly look out the corner of my eye to make sure I have the kids' attention. "Otherwise, I'd totally be up for a game of lava monster back home."

"I'm not tired," Owen says, picking his head up."

"Me either," Lexie adds, though her jaw is tense from fighting the urge to yawn.

"I'm wide awake," Abby says in her tiny little voice.

Piper laughs because she knows the game I'm playing, but thankfully doesn't rat me out. I look over at Giselle, Kiara, and Jade who are all grinning at me, impressed that I proved them wrong.

I take a nonchalant look around the food court before I finish my Coke and say, "Now, let's go finish our shopping."

Chapter Twenty-Three

Giselle

Today was the perfect day. I'm not at all shocked by the amount of decorations we brought home, but I know the kids are excited to get started with the Halloween decor. It's still summer, yes, but we always plan ahead.

And who are we kidding? For us, Halloween is all year.

Once we got back from the mall, Cal kept his word and took the kids over to the playground to play lava monster while I dug my hands into the soul of our garden at the back of the property. It's the first thing people on the trail see and I keep telling everyone that we should move our garden so we don't have stragglers stealing our veggies.

"Hey!" I yell as Abby and Lexie go racing through the flower beds. "Get your butts back over on the playground and stay out of the flowers! What's the matter with you?!"

Cal races over and ushers them back to the equipment. "Sorry, Giselle!" he yells.

The kids all follow suit with apologies and Cal gives me a sly smile. He's such a pain in the ass, but I have completely fallen head over heels for him. The way he treats me, kisses me, touches me, talks to me. Every part of him just melts me into a useless puddle.

I look over my shoulder toward Cal and the kids, watching them play. I swear he loves those kids as much as I do.

Cal races in between the houses and I watch the kids scatter as they start a game of hide and seek.

"Excuse me," a voice says from beside me.

I jump and clutch my chest. "Jesus Christ!"

The man takes a step back and his eyes go wide. "Sorry," he says. "I didn't mean to startle you. I was actually just on the trail and saw your little space. Thought I'd check it out."

"It's private property," I say to him, pointing to the sign that Cal hung with way too many nails.

He follows my finger and shrugs. "I'm sorry, miss. I didn't mean to trespass." He looks around a bit. "Is all of this yours?"

I'm skeptical, but he seems harmless. I try to give him the benefit of the doubt, though his outcome with me won't end the same way Cal's did. I look him up and down. Thin, dark hair, green eyes.

Not bad to look at.

"It's mine," I say, finally replying to him.

"How long have you lived here?"

I don't give him exact dates. He doesn't need that kind of personal information. And quite honestly, he's getting on my nerves the more he pries.

"We've lived here for quite some time now," I say flatly.

"We?" he echoes. "There's more than just you?"

Was he expecting me to be alone? Did he plan on mugging me before he knew I had company?"

"Three families. And we recently accumulated our newest member."

"A baby?" His features soften as he asks, like babies are one of his favorite things. Maybe to kill. Maybe to hold. At this point, I'm not quite sure which.

I don't intend to find out. "No, not a baby," I say. Then, cross my arms over my chest and lean my weight onto one leg so I can use my other one to kick if I need to. "Is there something I can help you with?"

He lets out a heavy breath through his nose and his mouth forms a tight line. "Actually yes," he says. Then, he reaches into his pocket which has me taking a step back. "Just a photo," he says.

Shit. A missing person maybe? Now I kind of feel sorry for the guy.

He pulls out the small photo and I see that the edges are tattered and torn. But I can almost make out the face in the photo.

"I was just seeing if you knew who this was. Or if you've seen them around this area."

I study the photo in his hands and look over my shoulder toward Cal and the kids. The man follows my gaze and I see the look on his face when I turn back toward him.

The look of recognition.

"You're here for Cal?" I ask the stranger.

The man nods, but his eyes never meet mine. They're fixed on the Cal and the kids. The bad feeling in my stomach intensifies and I know now that this man was the root of all that.

Whoever he is was the reason we had to do rituals and spent so much money at Wren's to replenish our supplies.

"Who are you?" I ask. I ask this loud enough that I know Cal will hear me. When I look back, I see Cal running toward me. He stops right beside me and stares at the man, putting an arm in front of me and pushing me behind him, like someone would do to put someone out of harm's way.

"Cal, what's going on?" I ask, hearing my voice shake a little.

Cal stares at the man and he squints a little as if the man is putting off a light so bright that it burns his eyes. "Ash?"

The man gives a half smile and says, "Hey there, Caleb."

"Ash?" I ask. "As in your brother?"

Cal nods. "That's the one."

I stare at both of them, unsure of what's happening. Why didn't Ash just drive here? Why didn't he call first to let us know he was coming? Did Cal invite him without telling us?

"Is it your mom?" I ask before I can filter my thoughts.

Ash shakes his head and I can see the tension in Cal's jaw. His expression changes to one I haven't witnessed before. Something almost animalistic.

"Nothing like that," Ash says. "I have a feeling Cal knows why I'm here."

Cal shakes his head slowly. "How did you find me?"

Ash looks at his feet like his shoe laces will answer for him. I feel my heart leaping in my chest. Something isn't right.

"Evan told me you were here," Ash says, his eyes shifting to me afterward.

I wrack my brain, trying to remember if Cal told me anything about this Evan guy. I can't recall anything and it's making me wonder why his name has Cal taking a deep breath. Why Cal's face went pale and why Ash looks like he's about to cry.

Cal finally peels his eyes away from his brother to look at me.

"Giselle, I need you to take the kids and get inside."

"But I-,"

"Just do it," Cal snaps.

I've never heard him talk like that. He's never talked to me like that before, that's for sure. It almost hurts to hear it, but I listen. This is family business and I don't need to be involved.

They've made that perfectly clear.

Cal's eyes shift back to Ash and I don't know what to think. I race toward the kids and wrap Abby and Owen in my arms. I knew something big was coming. I just wish I knew the details of what hadn't quite been revealed yet.

Why is Ash being here such a bad thing?

I really wish I would have noticed red flags when Cal wouldn't talk about his family or his past. What was I thinking? Why am I so stupid sometimes? Why am I so quick to fall for people that aren't right for me?

I look at the kids and Kiara comes rushing outside. She takes a look at Ash and grins at me. "Who's the hottie?" That's when she sees the look on my face. "Oh no," she groans.

"Grab the kids," I say through clenched teeth. "Get them inside. Lock the doors."

Kiara helps me get the kids inside and I look toward Cal and Ash before I hurry into the kitchen. Jade is looking out the window and can't seem to take her eyes off Ash.

"Who's the hott-,"

"Don't finish that statement," Kiara interrupts. "We don't know what the details are yet."

"All I know is that the man standing on our property right now is Ash," I say. "And Cal isn't exactly thrilled to see him. And something about Evan knowing where he is."

"Evan? Ash?" Jade echoes. "Wait, Ash as in Cal's brother?"

I nod slowly.

When did he get here?" Kiara asks.

"He came in from the trail while I was in the garden," I say, refusing to take my eyes off the two of them.

"So, he didn't drive here," Jade concludes as she cranes her neck to check the driveway.

"Nope," I say.

"Is he in some kind of trouble?" Jade asks.

I shrug. "I know as much as you girls do. At this point, I think we just wait and see what happens."

"Should we go back out there?" Jade asks.

"Ask the guy what the hell he wants?" Kiara adds. "Maybe he's just here to see Cal."

The feeling in my stomach tells me there's much more to it than that.

I hear something break and I turn to see Tarot on the counter. I look down and see a glass of milk shattered on the floor. When I look a little further right, I notice a pile of something, but can't quite tell what is.

"Is that garbage?" I ask as I take a few steps toward it. I kneel down and reach toward the contents on the floor. As I get closer, I notice the salt, rosemary, and black obsidian scattered over broken glass. I look over my shoulder at Jade and Kiara.

"Is that what I think it is?" Jade asks.

I nod. They look back out the window and I follow their gaze. My heart is thumping in my chest and my palms are wet with nerves. I'm completely ignoring the fact that my spell jar is shattered on my kitchen floor.

"Is this the bad feeling we've been having?" Kiara asks.

I nod slowly, feeling their eyes on me now. "Or at least it's the beginning of it."

Chapter Twenty-Four

CALEB

I can't believe my eyes as I stand here with my brother only a few feet away from me. He's not so stable on his feet though. He looks like a wilted flower that's about to lose its last pedal.

He looks awful. And I'm now understanding the feeling that Giselle and the others were talking about. The bad feeling in the pit of their stomachs.

It's not so much the short distance between us that bothers me, or that he found me. What bothers me is that he made it seem as though Evan was the one to tell him where I was.

"Evan is dead," I tell Ash in a low tone even though Giselle can't hear me.

Ash shakes his head. "No, he's not."

I can't even begin to calculate how Ash would know Evan's status. "Yes, he is," I say. "I left him for dead in that hideout that we built way back when. We got into a fight and I left him there."

"He wasn't dead, Cal," Ash says. His face is coated in fear and the glimmer I once remember in his eyes is completely extinguished.

I want to stumble over myself. I want to collapse into a ball on the ground. Not a very manly thing to feel, but it's shocking news to find out that Evan's body won't be discovered because it's out roaming the earth.

"He... Evan is alive?" I repeat. "Are you sure?"

"I'm positive," Ash says. His voice is harsh and I can tell he hasn't had water in a while. He should have stopped at the gas station a few miles back. The clerk there was a real treat.

I shake off the news from Ash and push forward to the next important bit of information. "How does Evan know where I am?"

"JT has people," Ash says, shaking his head like I should know this. "You need to get out of here. You need to leave and never look back."

I face Giselle's house, wondering if they're watching us. My heart breaks at the thought of leaving them. This is my family now. This is where I belong.

Unless Giselle decides she doesn't want me here after she finds out the truth.

"Are they coming here?" I ask.

Ash nods. Right before Ash opens his mouth, everyone comes pouring out of the house. Abby is racing toward the playground and Owen is chasing after her.

"The children," Ash says, watching them scurry like ants. "How many of them do you have here?"

"None of my own, but five total," I tell him. I look toward Giselle, Kiara, and Jade who are all staring at me with urgency in their eyes. They aren't sure what to do. Jade begins to yell for the kids to get back inside, meaning they snuck out and put the three witches in a complete panic.

I nod toward Giselle and say, "You three need to take the kids to the bunker you told me about. I will come get you when it's safe to come back."

"Cal, I'm gonna ki-,"

"No time for threats," I say, interrupting Kiara. "Right now, I need to keep you safe. Go. Now. I'll explain later and you can threaten me with anything and everything you've got. Threaten me with my own gun if you must."

Giselle's eyes are damp with tears of pain and betrayal. I won't recover from this. The way she's looking at me tells me that she's seen and heard too much. At this point, I have to accept that we're over, and focus on my main goal of keeping them alive.

I watch as the three women take the kids and disappear into the woods. I know they'll be safe in the bunker and I know they will wait until I go get them. I watch for a few minutes before I turn back to Ash.

Now, my focus can be on my brother and myself.

"How do we keep them from coming here?" I ask. "I can't have them hurting these people. They've done nothing to deserve this."

"There's no stopping them," Ash says. "You know that. You're acting like this little oasis has completely wiped your memory of who you really are. You don't belong here. This isn't your family."

It's like he could hear my thoughts only moments ago.

I look at Ash and feel my eyes narrow with distrust. What is the possibility that he brought them here?

Before I can make any accusations, I hear footsteps behind us and whirl around, prepared to come face to face with Evan, but instead, feel even worse when I realize it's Giselle.

"You were supposed to be in the bunker with everyone else," I tell her, racing to her side. Giselle shakes her head frantically. I look all around, making sure she didn't come here with an emergency. "Are you okay?" I ask.

She nods slowly, but keeps her eyes squeeze closed. "What's going on?" she demands. "You need to tell me right now."

"Listen, Giselle," I say. "I can't explain right now. At this very moment, I need to keep you and the rest of the family safe."

"You don't get to tell us we're family if you're lying to us," she says with tears streaming down her cheeks. They're obviously tears of anger because she quickly wipes them away and stands her ground.

"I'm not lying to you," I say. "Everything that I've told you thus far is true."

"You're withholding information," she hisses. "It's the same damn thing!"

I put my hands on her shoulders but she shrugs away. "Giselle-,"

"Well, well, well," a male voice says. I stop mid-sentence when I realize it's not Ash who's talking.

My skin crawls at the sound of Evan's voice. "This is not good," I mumble to myself.

"Who is that?" Giselle asks. "And how many more of you are going to walk onto our fucking property from that goddamn trail?!"

"Just me," Evan says. "For now." He grimaces and I almost freeze in place. How is it possible that he made it out of that hideout alive?

"What do you want?" I ask.

"I want you dead," Evan says simply.

The sneer on his face is enough to make anyone hide under a rock. He's such a creep. Like one of those guys at the comic book store that you want to tell yourself is just a nerd, but deep down you wouldn't be surprised if he had someone tied up in his basement.

I feel Giselle gripping the back of my shirt and I don't know how to get her out of here safely. Looking at Evan, I don't see any weapons, but that doesn't mean he isn't concealing one.

"I really don't see that happening," I tell him, trying to sound more like my cocky self. I feel my voice hitch, but nobody reacts, so I assume they don't notice.

"Someone needs to tell me what the hell is going on!" Giselle yells, her fearless side making an appearance at the most inconvenient of times.

Everyone winces at the sound of her high-pitched tone. I reach back and grab her hand, trying to comfort her the best I can. But I know it's not going to help. She knows I've lied and has no reason to trust me.

Now, she's standing face to face with my past and I don't know how to shield her from it.

Perhaps making sure Evan was actually dead would have been a good place to start.

I feel Giselle's small fists pounding against my back. "You stupid sonofabitch! You got us all into trouble and now we're all going to die! I hate you! I hate all of you! I hope you all rot in hell!"

I allow her to get it out, even if it results in tiny bruises on my back. I suppose this is the least I deserve after what I've done to her and her family.

"You're not going to die," I assure her while she keeps punching. "I won't let that happen."

"Don't be so sure," Evan scoffs.

I raise a finger at him and grit my teeth. "Don't you dare fucking talk to her. You don't even get to look at her. I'll dig your goddamn eyes out with a rusty knife."

Giselle shudders against me and I feel so sorry that she has to see this side of me.

Evan laughs and looks at Ash. "I can't make any promises," Evan says, licking his lips at her. "She's a tight little thing. Couldn't imagine what it would feel like to give her a ride."

My insides go hot and I swear I'm seeing red.

I take a step toward Evan and notice him take a step backward. Ash remains still with his hands clasped in front of him.

"Still a coward, I see," I say, looking Evan up and down.

"Don't get smug with me," Evan growls.

He's not that far away from me and I continue to close the gap between us, one step at a time, but keeping myself between Evan and Giselle.

Pretty soon, I'll have to come up with a plan. I still don't know which side my brother is playing on, but I hope to God he's here to help me.

I look at Ash and Evan throws his head back with a boastful laugh. "Don't look at Ash for help," Evan says with a hand on his stomach as though his laugh was painful. I hope it was. I hope it hurt so much that he now has an internal bleed.

"Ash is the one who helped me find you," Evan says with a sly smile. "He's pretty pissed about how you left things with your family back home."

It's like getting stabbed in the gut with a knife. I fight to hold the tears back. "You're a liar," I snarl at Evan. But when I look at Ash, I don't see him denying it. The tears in Ash's eyes are either of guilt or helplessness… or both.

The minute I reach up to run a hand down over my face and regain composure, I feel a blow to my torso. My back hits the ground and the wind is pulled from my lungs. It hurts to breathe. My hands are pinned above my head and I can hear Giselle screaming.

I open my eyes and see a huge smile above me.

Evan's smile.

Chapter Twenty-Five

Giselle

A scream escapes my lips before I'm able to contain it as I watch Evan tackle Cal to the ground. I'm feeling a mix of emotions as I stand and stare at the man that I fell in love with. The man that didn't have crazy people after him and who had a brother that wouldn't throw him to the wolves. The man that played with the kids and made my friends laugh at his stupid jokes. The man who touched me in all the right places and made my heart feel things I never knew were possible.

But as I stand here with him lying on his back, I'm unsure of what to think. I don't know how I'm supposed to feel. He lied to us. He put us in danger. And now, he may be killed by the man who has him pinned to the grass.

I'm hoping Kiara and Jade were able to call the police when we snuck back into the house. It didn't seem like Cal or anyone else noticed us come back, so I'm hopeful this Evan guy is clueless too.

I just hate how far away we are from the station.

I can't peel my eyes away from Cal. My first instinct is to help him, despite what he put us through.

And that's exactly what I try to do.

I rush toward him, but my first step is halted as Evan yields a knife from his sock and holds it to Cal's throat. Cal is still gasping for air and can hardly move with the blow he took to the abdomen.

"Hold it right there, you little bitch," Evan sneers at me. "Or I swear to God I'll slit his damn throat."

Evan looks toward Ash. "Make sure she doesn't interfere," he demands.

Ash comes straight for me and I'm afraid to move for fear of Cal getting hurt even more. I can't let him die. I can't let him get hurt.

I feel Ash's muscular arms wrap around me and my heart sinks. How did it come to this? How did our fun day at the mall turn into such a shit show?

I'm glad we enjoyed our morning and afternoon because it seems like our evening will be our demise.

"Feels a little familiar, doesn't it?" Evan asks Cal as he grips the knife even tighter.

Cal looks at me from the corner of his eye and I watch his chest rise and fall at a normal pace now. Hopefully he's okay. Hopefully nothing is broken. Even though Evan looks a bit scrawny, I'm sure getting hit in the gut by anyone would hurt.

"Take me!" I yell to Evan, unsure of what I'm feeling. Protective? Threatening? Or maybe it's possible that I still love the lying heap of shit in my yard.

I can feel myself wiggling in Ash's grip. "Take me instead. Leave Cal alone."

"After what this fucker did to me?" Evan asks. "I think I'd rather kill the both of you." Evan looks down at Cal and I see Evan run his tongue over his teeth. "You know what? Killing you both sounds like a great idea, actually. I'll torture your little girlfriend over there and make you watch. Leave you both for dead like you left me."

My stomach is twisting while I listen to Evan talk. I don't want to believe Cal left this man for dead, even though the way he's acting tells me he probably deserved it.

"Just leave," Cal says, his voice straining against the weight of Evan and the knife.

"You think it's that easy?" Evan laughs. Then he pauses, and lets out a low laugh again. "Just like you thought it would be easy to get out of the drug business." Evan adjusts on top of Cal. "Let me repeat myself, like I did the day you left me with two broken legs. You. Don't. Get. Out. Of. The. Drug. Business. Alive." His voice gets louder with each word and I feel myself wincing against Ash. "You knew JT would come for you," Evan says. "You had to at least know that I would after what you did to me."

Evan spits on Cal's face and I can't help but look away. Ash still has a strong grip on me and I know that if I try anything, something will happen to Cal. I want to look up at Ash and see the look on his face. See how he's handling the fact that his brother is pinned to the ground with a knife to his neck.

Maybe Evan wasn't lying. Maybe Ash did help Evan find him. That would explain why Ash is holding me back. It would be three against one if Ash would let me go help Cal, but I don't see it happening. I think this is it. This is the end of everything.

I hear a few more footsteps coming up behind Ash and we both turn toward the noise. I know exactly who it is and I wish they would have just stayed inside and waited for the police.

Evan looks up and I swear I can see his eyes grow even darker. Tears begin to pour from my cheeks as Kiara and Jade see what's happening and break into a sprint. They see the knife to Cal's throat and they see me restrained by the 'hottie' they couldn't stop talking about earlier.

They now know the severity of the situation.

"Just stop right there!" Jade shouts. "You don't want to do this."

"There are other ways to handle this situation," Kiara says.

"Girls," I say helpless, tears still streaming down my face.

"What is it with you bitches?" Evan hisses. "And how the fuck many of you are there?"

"A lot," Jade lies. "So you may as well back down."

"You think Cal is going to walk away from this?" Evan asks. He laughs, but it's more menacing than amusement. "You think everything is going to be all hunky dorey?" Evan waves his knife in the air. "I have a knife to this asshole's throat. That should tell you I mean business. Get your asses back inside and I'll deal with you later."

"You can't-,"

At this point, I see the rage in Evan's eyes and watch as he pulls something from under his shirt.

The steel shines in the sunlight and the barrel is long and black. The look on Evan's face says he's done.

Cal looks into my eyes from where he's lying and I can't help but cry helpless tears as I go limp in Ash's arms. A tear trickles from Cal's eye and in this moment, I forgive him. I forgive him because he's just as helpless as the rest of us. All because of that single tear. It shows he loves us and he's hurt that it came to this. It shows that he didn't mean for any of this to happen and he truly wanted to keep us safe.

It shows that we should have stayed where we were so he could have handled it.

Ash isn't moving and I fear what's going to happen once Evan kills Cal. Will they both turn on us? What about the kids?

Panic settles in as Evan points the gun to Cal's face.

"Any last words?" Evan says as he glares downward, head tilted in a cocky manner. "Better to get everything off your chest before it's too late."

Cal says nothing. He closes his eyes and accepts his fate. This is it.

And the air stands still as a bullet leaves the barrel.

Chapter Twenty-Six

CALEB

Death has crossed my mind a few times, sure. In the career path I chose, it crosses everyone's mind. Will I get shot by someone who doesn't want to pay for the product? Will I get stabbed because the product wasn't good enough? Will I get beaten by police because I run away in hopes of escaping a bust?

After a while, I just worked so hard and so fast that I didn't have time to think about the consequences.

Dying at the hands of my partner had never crossed my mind once.

When they say your life flashes before your eyes when you're about to die; they're serious.

It's like watching a movie of your life. Everything I've ever done scrolls through my mind in flashes. The fun I had with my dad before he died. The times I spent with my mom before she got sick. All the things we did together as a family before my dad made the leap into the world of drugs.

Yet another thing I lied about when I told Giselle about my family. He didn't die in a car accident. He died in a shooting.

I feel numb as I look at my past. My entire pathetic life in a flash of light.

I feel the pain in my side and can't tell what's happening. There's another surge of pain, but this time I think it's in my arm. How many times did the asshole shoot me? Why am I still coherent?

Evan is still sitting on me, but the pressure on my wrist begins to decrease. I see the look on Evan's face and I can't tell if he's stunned that he shot me or he's stunned I'm still alive.

Then, Evan begins to lean and the gun falls from his hands, thumping me at the base of my throat. I'm coughing at the impact, but my hands are free and I reach up to rub the spot that the butt of the gun hit me.

Evan falls to the ground beside me and his eyes meet mine as he chokes and gags.

What the actual fuck just happened?

When I look toward Giselle, I see Ash release his grip on her. Giselle runs toward me and Kiara points her gun at Ash.

"Shoot him!" Jade is screaming over and over. "Shoot him! Shoot him!"

Ash walks over to me and extends a hand. I accept it and he helps me to my feet. I'm a little lightheaded, but otherwise I feel alright.

"Don't shoot him," I tell Kiara. "Put the gun down." I look a little closer and see the gun she's using. "You shot him with my gun?"

Kiara shrugs, inspecting the weapon in her hand. "It's the only gun we had that was loaded and easily accessible."

The three women look at Ash. I do the same.

"How did he get to you?" I ask.

"I went to the hideout to see where you were," he explains. "They said there was an explosion at the docks and I didn't know if it was set up to kill you for wanting out of the gig. I had to know if you were alive."

"It was a set up," I tell him.

"I figured," he says. "So I get there and look down to find Evan screaming at the bottom of the ladder. He told me that you broke his legs and left him for dead." At this point, I notice Giselle is covering her mouth as she listens to the details of what I'd done. I try to focus on Ash, knowing I'll try to make things right with her once I have all the answers.

"Evan gave me a sob story, but I knew he was completely full of shit," Ash finishes.

"But how did he get here?" I ask. "What about his legs?"

"Caleb, you were gone for over a month," Ash sighs. "I didn't even know if you were alive until Evan told me that he found you."

"I thought JT found me," I say.

Ash shakes his head. "JT thinks you're dead. Evan just wanted revenge."

I nod. "Got it."

I look back at Evan's lifeless body beside my feet and shake my head. Thinking how much time I spent with him, trusting him to have my back.

What a waste.

"But why didn't you help Cal when Evan attacked him?" Giselle asks, blinking back unshed tears. I can hear the fury in her voice as she interrogates my brother.

"Because Evan took my weapons," Ash admits. "I had to go along with his plan. I had to pretend like I was on his side. Otherwise, I knew he'd call JT and I'd never have found him."

"Who is JT?" Jade asks.

"He's the drug lord for our division," I say. "He's basically our ring leader. He tells us what to do and when to do it. He holds up a hoop; we jump."

Jade is nodding slowly with her tongue tucked in her cheek. It's not a contemplative face. It's more that she's pissed off and has to bite her tongue so she doesn't say what she's thinking.

"Anyway," Ash continues. "I figured if I got him to you, the two of us could take him."

"But you did nothing," Giselle snaps. "You stood there and held me back while Evan had him pinned to the ground with a fucking knife to his throat!"

My eyebrows shoot straight up. I wasn't expecting her to be so mad that Ash wasn't helping me. I have done nothing but lie to her since I got here and yet she still cares about me?

Ash is holding his hands up in surrender while she yells. "Evan is a bit slow," Ash says, trying to calm her down. "I knew what I was doing. And once I saw these two come out," he says, gesturing toward Jade and Kiara, "I figured they had a plan."

"What if we wouldn't have been prepared?" Kiara asks skeptically.

"I'm not stupid," Ash laughs. "Caleb wouldn't have gotten himself mixed up with a bunch of yuppy girls."

This makes me chuckle. Even Giselle smirks and looks down at her shoes. "What about his legs?" I ask. "How did he get this far?"

"How did he get to you?" I ask.

"I went to the hideout to see where you were," he explains. "They said there was an explosion at the docks and I didn't know if it was set up to kill you for wanting out of the gig. I had to know if you were alive."

"It was a set up," I tell him.

"I figured," he says. "So I get there and look down to find Evan screaming at the bottom of the ladder. He told me that you broke his legs and left him for dead." At this point, I notice Giselle is covering her mouth as she listens to the details of what I'd done. I try to focus on Ash, knowing I'll try to make things right with her once I have all the answers.

"Evan gave me a sob story, but I knew he was completely full of shit," Ash finishes.

"But how did he get here?" I ask. "What about his legs?"

"Caleb, you were gone for over a month," Ash sighs. "I didn't even know if you were alive until Evan told me that he found you."

"I thought JT found me," I say.

Ash shakes his head. "JT thinks you're dead. Evan just wanted revenge."

I nod. "Got it."

I look back at Evan's lifeless body beside my feet and shake my head. Thinking how much time I spent with him, trusting him to have my back.

What a waste.

"But why didn't you help Cal when Evan attacked him?" Giselle asks, blinking back unshed tears. I can hear the fury in her voice as she interrogates my brother.

"Because Evan took my weapons," Ash admits. "I had to go along with his plan. I had to pretend like I was on his side. Otherwise, I knew he'd call JT and I'd never have found him."

"Who is JT?" Jade asks.

"He's the drug lord for our division," I say. "He's basically our ring leader. He tells us what to do and when to do it. He holds up a hoop; we jump."

Jade is nodding slowly with her tongue tucked in her cheek. It's not a contemplative face. It's more that she's pissed off and has to bite her tongue so she doesn't say what she's thinking.

"Anyway," Ash continues. "I figured if I got him to you, the two of us could take him."

"But you did nothing," Giselle snaps. "You stood there and held me back while Evan had him pinned to the ground with a fucking knife to his throat!"

My eyebrows shoot straight up. I wasn't expecting her to be so mad that Ash wasn't helping me. I have done nothing but lie to her since I got here and yet she still cares about me?

Ash is holding his hands up in surrender while she yells. "Evan is a bit slow," Ash says, trying to calm her down. "I knew what I was doing. And once I saw these two come out," he says, gesturing toward Jade and Kiara, "I figured they had a plan."

"What if we wouldn't have been prepared?" Kiara asks skeptically.

"I'm not stupid," Ash laughs. "Caleb wouldn't have gotten himself mixed up with a bunch of yuppy girls."

This makes me chuckle. Even Giselle smirks and looks down at her shoes. "What about his legs?" I ask. "How did he get this far?"

Ash points toward the trail. "His crutches are over in the bushes. He ditched them so you wouldn't know he was weak."

"Typical Evan," I groan.

I look toward Giselle who is still staring at her shoes. When she looks up, she starts shaking her head when we make eye contact. "You're a lying sack of shit and I wish I'd never met you."

Kiara and Jade are initially surprised at her reaction, but walk up beside her and put a hand on each of her shoulders.

Maybe she doesn't care about me like I thought.

"I can explain all of this," I say. "If you give me five minutes. I can explain everything."

"It's true," Ash says.

"Well, thanks for finally being on my side," I tell him.

"I was always on your side," Ash says. "You should have known that."

I shrug. "Maybe a small part of me knew it, but you put on a damn good show." I look back toward Giselle and see the tears forming in her eyes again. She's hurt and I'm the one that hurt her. "Giselle..."

"Mark was the lying sack of shit in my life and I got rid of him," Giselle snaps. Her response is far from what I expected. And it hurts me more than I was prepared for. "Now I guess it's time to get rid of the next one."

She storms off and heads for the lake. Kiara and Jade watch her walk away and when I take a step in her direction, they stand in front of me like her personal bodyguards.

"If I can just-,"

"Stay put," Jade says. "Or you'll deal with me."

I swallow hard. Even after everything I've been through today, I'm still a wee bit afraid of Jade.

"Just give her a minute," Kiara says. "You hurt her pretty bad. That was a lot of lying you did to get yourself a place to sleep. Not to mention getting her to fall for you."

Ash's eyes are darting around as he listens to the conversation.

"But I just-,"

"I know this," Kiara says. "You had a shit past. I know what that's like. But you need to give her a minute."

"You're gonna let him go talk to her?" Jade growls defensively.

Kiara nods. "I think he needs a chance to explain himself. Giselle is an advocate for second chances and now she needs to live up to that." She turns back to me. "I heard what your brother said. You were trying to get out of it and they tried to kill you in return so you ran. Does that sum it up?"

"More or less," I say.

"Which is it?" Jade asks.

"More," I say quickly, and a bit afraid.

"Everyone has a past," Kiara says to Jade.

Jade rolls her eyes. Then, she looks at me. "You and I have to start all over again. Remember how long that process took the first time?"

I nod. "It was a hell of a task. But I'm willing to go a second round."

She rolls her eyes again and storms off, much like the first time we met. "I'm going to get the kids," she yells over her shoulder. "We'll deal with the body when I get back."

I look at Evan and back at Ash. "Boy am I glad you're the one that brought him here and not JT. I've never been so happy to have someone think I was dead."

Ash laughs. "You've won the battle," he says. Then, he gestures toward the lake. "Now you have to go win the war."

A long sigh escapes me as I look toward the lake.

"It breaks my heart to know that I made her feel that way," I admit, taking a few deep breaths.

"Don't go crying on us now," Kiara says, punching my arm. "Go tell her the truth. She deserves that much from you, regardless of whether or not she lets you back in."

"She deserves the world from me at this point," I say.

"Start with the truth," Kiara says with a smile. "Then go from there."

I look at Ash. "Don't give these girls too much trouble while I'm down there. I'll only be a few minutes. Then, we need to deal with that," I say, pointing at Evan.

"I'll behave," Ash says.

"Good." I pause for a minute, looking at the path that leads down to the pavilion. I have no idea where to begin. I don't even know if she'll let me near her.

"Are you gonna go?" Ash asks. "Or just stand up here and stare at her like some freak."

I blow out a hard breath. "I will," I say. "I just need a second to gather myself. That was a pretty hectic few minutes."

"Valid," Ash says. "Carry on."

Another deep breath and I jam my hands in my pockets as I walk to the pavilion to tell my life story to the woman I love.

Hoping she still loves me back.

Chapter Twenty-Seven

Giselle

My heart is beyond shattered, but the rest of me just feels numb. I knew I shouldn't have gotten attached to a stranger. This is the exact reason I've stayed out of the dating pool. I don't have the time or the strength to try and trust someone else with my heart.

I fall too hard and too fast. I had red flags with Mark and I ignored them so I wasn't alone. I even thought I saw texts come through his phone once, but I let it go and never asked questions.

And now I've put myself in a position again where the guy can't be trusted. This time, I put everyone I love in danger.

I look up when I hear footsteps, but my gaze drops back to the lake when I see Cal coming toward me. I don't want to move from the pavilion bench. The sound of the lake is all I want to hear right now.

Cal doesn't say anything, he just walks over and sits down on the bench beside me. He leans forward and rests his elbows on his knees while he stares ahead at the rippling water. I want to look at him and say something, but at this point, I don't know what I would say. I fear if I open my mouth, hurtful things will spew out and I'll regret them immediately. It'll be one more thing that keeps me away as I lie there, rethinking all of my life decisions.

I exhale, but remain quiet. He continues to keep his eyes on the lake ahead of him, but he opens his mouth and says, "I'm sorry."

I don't say anything in return, so he exhales again.

"I never should have withheld information from you. Especially something of that magnitude. I guess I wasn't sure how long I would be here. I never expected to fall for you like I did."

He swallows and runs a hand down his face.

"I was just trying to get away from it. I wanted it all in the past and I didn't know how to tell you. Part of me was hoping that the ugly truth of my past died when I left Evan in the hideout with two broken legs."

I wince as he repeats what he's done, and he must notice because he says, "I'm sorry. I guess there's really no easy way to put that."

He sighs and buries his face in his hands.

"I'm sorry too," I say.

He looks up at me with curious eyes. "You have no reason to apologize to me," he says."

"Yes, I do," I tell him. "I'm sorry that I can't sit here and listen to an apology from you." I feel the tears welling up in my eyes. "I don't like being lied to. I don't like being put in harm's way. And I sure as shit don't like when my kids are at risk."

I'm still refusing to look at him, but I wipe the stream from my cheek.

"Well," he says, clearing his throat. "I will always be here for you. And when you're ready to hear my side of the story, I'll be ready to tell it."

Out of the corner of my eye, I see him stand. He takes a few seconds before he walks away from me and heads up the path to the houses.

I want to fall to pieces. I want to wrap him up and hug him tight and tell him it's okay. But it's not okay. It's not okay that he lied to us and it's not okay that his life choices followed him here.

It's not okay.

What kind of mom would I be if I allowed his kind of environment around my kids?

My thoughts pause.

What kind of mom would I be if I took Cal away from the kids without an explanation? To have to lie to them and tell them that Cal just needed to go because he had other places to be. After I got rid of Cal for lying in the first place.

Now it's my turn to bury my face in my hands. I begin to sob, but I feel myself fight it and I suck the tears back in.

"That's it," I say. "I'll feel better about pushing him out of our lives once I've heard what he has to say. Then, I can honestly say it's best that he leaves." I get to my feet and brush the imaginary dirt from my pants. "Here goes nothing."

The small stones crunch under my shoes as I walk up the small path toward the houses. I see everyone gathered by the patio, Cal has his back to me. He's talking, but his words are muffled until I get closer.

"I'm just going to give her space," I hear him say. Kiara is nodding and looks at me, but I shake my head to let her know I don't want my presence known yet. "I guess if she doesn't want me here, then I'll leave. But I really wish she'd give me a chance to explain."

Ash gives me a quick glance, but then turns back toward Cal. I clear my throat and gain everyone's attention.

"You two can stay with us until you find another place to go," I say firmly. It hits me in the stomach when I hear myself dismiss them. My heart is broken by the lying, but it's shattering at the thought of Cal not being here anymore.

Ash nods and Cal looks at his feet.

"We should probably get Evan hidden before the cops show up. We don't have much longer now." I say this so nonchalantly that you'd think we hid dead bodies on a regular basis. "Cal, you will need to hide once they get here. If we want people to think you're dead, we can't have the cops questioning you."

Cal nods slowly and Ash does the same. "Probably a good idea," Jade says.

"Where are we putting him?" Cal asks, jamming his hands in his pockets.

I point to the hills out back of the houses. "Near the flower beds. We already dug up a few spots, so we'll need to use the fresh soil that's been turned over." I look toward the guys. "Cal and Ash, us women will meet you over at the soil. Escort the body, please."

"Once we get him buried, we'll need to get the kids from the bunker," Kiara sighs.

"They'll be fine for a little while longer," Jade says. "When I went to get them the last time, Abby had turned on the gaming console and they were throwing banana peels at each other in the game."

"At least they're having a good day," I groan.

It takes less than twenty minutes to dig the hole between the five of us. I'm grateful for all hands on deck. Otherwise, this would have taken a lifetime for one person.

"I never in my life imagined I'd have to bury a body in my backyard," I say.

"Same," Jade whispers.

"It's kind of exciting," Kiara admits with a shrug.

We all stare at her as though she's lost her damn mind. I give her my 'what the hell did you just say' face.

"We don't get much excitement here," she explains. "I guess I can honestly say that I'm glad Cal showed up."

Jaws all drop at this and Kiara continues.

"I'm not saying I want to shoot people every Thursday night. I guess what I'm saying is that I'm glad Cal chose our commune as his hideout. Regardless of the reason he was on the run, I'm glad we could be the ones to hide him. We learned a lot."

Kiara gives me a look that tells me to say something. I roll my eyes and let my gaze drop to the ground.

"I guess we can take a walk now that the hard part is over," I say. With a quick twitch of my head, I fling my hair over my shoulder. "You deserve a chance to explain yourself."

My tone says that I'm not changing my mind on my decision for them to leave, but that I'm willing to hear him out.

"I wasn't expecting that to be so easy," I hear Kiara tell Jade out of the corner of her mouth.

"I don't have to-,"

"Go!" Kiara and Jade yell in unison.

I jolt at their bark. "Alright," I say. "Calm down. I'm going." I look at the pile of dirt that is now hiding the body of Cal's old drug partner. "Just make sure that's not noticeable. They'll be rolling in any minute."

"Really?" Kiara asks. "Because I was thinking of having little flags made up like they do for vegetables in the garden." She raises her hands as though she's displaying them. "Evan's left arm. Evan's forehead. Evan's Big toe. May he rot in pieces."

"Shut up," I growl. I begin to walk away and look over my shoulder at Cal who is standing beside Ash. "Are you coming or not?"

As though he was given a taser to the side, he leaps forward and follows me while I walk onto the trail that started it all.

Chapter Twenty-Eight

Caleb

I DON'T EVER REMEMBER being this nervous. Maybe the night of prom way back when, but even then it was a toss up because I didn't even have a date. I went with my friends in hopes to score once the dance was over.

Right now, at this very moment, I'm shaken to my core. What I say right now will determine whether or not I get to keep Giselle in my life.

"So," she says as she takes a few more steps down the trail. "I'm giving you a chance to explain your side of the story. However, I don't want you to feel that what you say will have any impact on my wanting you to leave. I've rebuilt the wall around me and it's going to take a long time for me to ever consider bringing it back down."

"I understand," I say softly.

She looks at me and nods as a way of telling me to go ahead.

I sigh nervously and hope I don't choke when I start. "It's going to be a bit of a long story, so I hope this trail is longer on this end than it was for me to get to you."

I see a slight smirk on her face, but I know she doesn't want to be smiling right now, so I pretend I don't see it.

"When I was a kid," I begin, "my dad was involved in this business."

I see her eyes shoot up directly toward me. "You said he was killed…" She shakes her head. "Another lie. Continue."

A chill shoots directly up my spine.

I clear my throat. "He was always disappearing and coming home late at night. I remember he always had multiple cell phones and was constantly throwing phones in the garbage. We were told as kids to never touch those phones. When my dad was killed as a result of JT's commands, Ash and I were taken away from our mom and put into hiding by JT's crew. We were just kids, we didn't know what we were doing."

"How old were you?" Giselle asks, her voice almost trembling.

"I was twelve." When I say this, her eyes clamp shut, so I continue my story to get it over with. "As we got older, we had been acclimated to the world of drugs. JT allowed us to go to school so that we didn't end up in the system as juvenile delinquents, but once the school day was over, we were picked up by his right hand man, Hammer, and trucked back off to the secret location. Our mom was terrified. We got to talk to her once a week, but our conversations were monitored and could only be about school."

"What about holidays?"

"JT allowed us to see mom on the holidays, but only for a few hours. Mom didn't have much money, so JT allowed us to start doing the hands-on work to be able to help mom pay her bills. He let us go back to mom a couple years later since he figured the fuss would be over."

She swallows hard and I want to touch her to soothe her, but I know that's not an option.

"When we were seventeen and twenty, we got the notice that mom was diagnosed with stage three pancreatic cancer. After a long discussion with JT, we convinced him to foot the bills for her medical coverage as long as one of us went to work for him. We had an understanding that if either party were to do him dirty, we would be placed six feet under."

"Including your mom?" she asks. When I nod, a tear falls from her eye and lands on the collar of her tank top.

"Ash went to stay with mom and I went and had a meeting with JT, telling him I could handle the work. I needed the money. I was told that I wasn't to visit with my mom and brother; they didn't need to be involved with what I had going on in his business. Though Ash covered for me a few times when things went south."

I clear my throat as we come around a curve in the trail. A nice breeze is all that's keeping me from sweating my ass off right now. Not so much because of the summer heat, but because of how fucking nervous I am right now.

"Evan joined and partnered up with me a few years after and he became my right hand man. Since JT knew me better than he knew Evan, I was always the lead on the cases and Evan was to follow my orders. Evan didn't like that."

"Shocker," Giselle says, wiping her nose with her finger.

"Evan was after the lead title and wanted me out of the picture. He figured with me gone, he would be able to cozy up to JT and be a part of the higher pay cut. I didn't want to be in anymore, I just wanted to live a normal life. Mom was doing alright financially, but was going downhill quickly when it came to her health. My last call from Ash told me that mom wasn't okay, and the message was relayed through JT. That she was on her last leg and I needed to find a way to go say goodbye."

Giselle's on the verge of sobbing, but I refrain once again from consoling her. It's breaking my heart and I want to hold her, but the last thing I want to do right now is give her a reason to push me further away.

She stops walking and looks over her shoulder at me. "The police should be coming soon. We should probably head back." I nod in agreement, unsure of whether or not to say anything, but then she asks, "What did you do after you got the message from Ash?"

We turn back in the direction of the commune as I tell her about the incident with Evan in the hideout and how I left him for dead. I tell her about the time I spent on the trail and how long I went without any real food or clean water. I even tell her about the gas station I stole from and how I'll never eat another granola bar as long as I live.

"I was feeling a mixture of gratitude and terror when I stepped onto your property that day. I knew I was far enough out that I wouldn't be found, especially with Evan dead, but I was also terrified to put the kids in harms' way. My goal was to only stay for a day or two, just to get myself back on my feet and then continue on the trail for a new place to crash. But one day turned into two and two turned into a week, and before I knew it, a month had passed and I had fallen in love with you."

I hear her breath catch when I mention my love for her, but I keep talking.

"I was torn between keeping you safe, and breaking a heart or two. I wasn't sure how deeply you cared for me and I couldn't run off after the connections I'd made."

Giselle stops and looks at me. She wipes the tears from her face as she stares into my eyes. Her face is red and puffy from crying and I can't tell if she's upset from my story or that we can't continue this any longer.

Maybe she's only upset that she has to tell the kids I won't be around to play on the playground anymore.

She takes a step toward me and reaches out, taking my hands in hers and squeezing. Sobbing, she lets her head fall.

"I'm so sorry that you went through all of that," she whimpers. "It must have been awful."

I don't say anything. I let her stand there and have a moment, hoping that if I allow her to get it all out she will change her mind.

When she looks up at me, I realize that's not going to happen. My brain is telling me to keep quiet, but my heart needs answers. I hear myself say, "Are we okay?"

The tears that Giselle had just wiped away come streaming back and she shakes her head. "You having a terrible past is tragic and I feel awful for you." The tears are spilling over her lips and into her mouth as she talks. She sniffles. "I really do feel awful. But that doesn't change how much you lied to me."

I watch her walk through the break in the bushes toward the commune and have to fight the urge to not hit my knees. I can't believe I just let her walk away.

I hide on the trail until the cops leave the premises and then make my way back toward the group. I give the police about a ten minute head start just to make sure they're really gone.

"How'd it go?" I ask the group.

"Smoother than a baby's bottom," Kiara says. "I know the officer, so it wasn't too bad. How did things go with you two?"

"We're good," Giselle says. Giselle gives me a look that tells me not to say otherwise. Then, she looks at Ash. "He told me about how your dad was in the business, and about the murder, and how you were both taken away as kids. He also told me about the visitation you had with mom, and when you found out about her cancer. Then, I heard about what happened with Evan."

Giselle is staring at Ash. "It wasn't a long story," I say. Ash still doesn't look up.

Looking between Ash and I, Giselle says, "Are you avoiding eye contact with me because Cal bullshitted everything he just told me?" Then, she looks at me. "Did you fucking lie to me again?!"

"No," Ash says. "Caleb is one-hundred percent telling the truth." He clears his throat. "You're just a little scary." I watch Giselle's expression change from pissed off to amused, yet she glares at him simultaneously.

"On that note," Giselle says. "I'm going inside."

She takes off before I have a chance to say anything more.

"She's not nearly as scary as I am," Jade laughs.

"That's also one-hundred percent true," I add. Then, I gesture toward the house. "What's she doing?"

"She'll be a little bit tipsy when she gets back," Jade says.

"Tipsy?" I ask.

"She went to throw back a few shots of tequila," Kiara adds.

"Oh," is all that comes out of my mouth. She's a wine girl, so for her to hit the tequila bottle is saying something.

As I take it all in, Jade and Kiara start asking me about what we discussed on the trail. I give them the full play-by-play and I see the disappointment in their eyes when they realize Giselle hasn't forgiven me.

The door to Giselle's house slides open and she comes walking back toward us. Her cheeks are pinker than they were before she walked away and she's wearing a smile on her face now.

"Feeling better?" Jade asks as Giselle stops beside her and grins at all of us.

"I will be in a few minutes," Giselle says. "But I believe those four shots will hit me pretty hard and I'll be feeling pretty damn great." She looks around at everyone and her eyes land on me. "You're still here?" she asks.

I nod. "We were just getting ready to head to the guest house," Ash says. "We can pack his things."

"Give her time," Kiara whispers. "She'll be drunk any second now. That's when you can win her over."

Ash grins. "Sounds interesting." When Giselle's eyes meet Ash's, I see Ash's imaginary tail tucked between his legs. He's so intimidated by these three.

"Be careful, Ash," Jade says. "You'll bring out the scary in all of us."

"What the hell kind of people have you been staying with?" Ash asks me in a voice that tells me he's only half kidding.

I look directly at Giselle and hear myself say, "I've been staying with the woman I fell in love with."

"You can't say that," she tells me. "You don't lie to people you love."

"I didn't lie," I say with a sigh. "I just didn't bring up my past."

"We all have pasts," Kiara adds. I see Giselle shoot her a trying look and Kiara clams up. She mouths the word 'sorry' and laces her fingers in front of her like a Catholic school girl who just got scolded by a nun.

"I just can't believe you kept it all from me," Gisele says. She shifts on her feet a little and I can tell the alcohol is setting in. She looks around at her surroundings and I'm guessing she just needs a second to gather her thoughts.

"I really liked you, Cal. A lot. But when Evan showed up and everything unraveled, it was like I didn't even know you. That the guy who'd been staying with us didn't exist anymore. I felt like you were one of the characters I'd made up in a story. You were too good to be true."

"But I'm still me," I say, offering her a light smile. "And I'm still madly in love with you. Everything about you." I walk over to Giselle and crush her mouth with mine. It's a ballsy move, but I didn't want my last kiss with her to be my last kiss with her.

I can taste the tequila on her breath and I start to wonder how many shots she actually had in the few minutes she was inside.

She goes to say something, but I cut her off. "No matter how many times you tell me to leave or how many times you tell me you hate me. I will always feel the same way I felt about you the moment I saw you."

She pulls away to say something, but I cut her off again by kissing her. Hard and deep. I can almost feel her melt into me. When I slowly pull away, I say. "We're not fighting anymore. And I'm not leaving."

Giselle shakes her head. "I wasn't going to fight with you," she says. "I was going to say that someone should probably go get the kids."

"They're in the bunker," Jade says. "They'll be alright."

"Yeah," Kiara adds. "It's not like we left them at the cavern."

"You have a bunker? And a cave too?" Ash asks.

I smile and laugh while I shake my head and look back toward Giselle. "Glad we're done fighting."

She pulls my mouth down to hers and I'm thankful for the tequila. "I'm glad we're done fighting too. It's too exhausting and I don't have the energy."

Jade and Kiara chuckle.

"Any sane person would have reacted the way you did," I tell her, hugging her tight. "I would have been scared had you not acted that way." I feel her jiggle against me and I know she's laughing. "Actually, we may have to have a discussion on how well you handle the idea of burying a dead body. But maybe we'll save that for another time."

"Probably for the best," she says, holding up a finger and swaying a bit. "I think I've handled all I can take for one day."

"You and me both," I say, and squeeze her even tighter.

She looks at me and says, "Now, let's go get those tiny humans from the bunker and bring them home." With that, we all head for the break in the bushes and start walking down the trail.

The trail that started it all.

EPILOGUE (GISELLE)

THE SUN IS SHINING down on us as we all stand outside, taking pictures of the kids in the last summer outfits that we'll buy this year. A combination of blues and bright greens surround us while Kiara, Jade, and myself are done up in our usual black attire. Evan Cal was convinced to dress up in a nice outfit, which led to Ash looking nice as well.

A shopping trip was required for their wardrobe which was worse than pathetic.

"Alright," I say. "Everyone in. I'm setting the time for fifteen seconds so I have time to run over and hop in."

Once I push the button on top of the camera, I scurry off toward the group, but I see the flash go off before I get there.

"Damnit!" I yell.

"Mommy said a swear," Owen says with a tsk tsk.

"Sorry," I say, not feeling sorry at all. I walk back over to the camera and laugh when I see the photo. "It's just a picture of my ass."

"Can we get that one printed?" Cal asks with a dash of sass.

Ash punches him in the arm. "She's a lady."

"Don't get them started on that topic," I hear Cal say. "I've been down that road before."

We all laugh and finish up our family pictures, most of which don't include my ass.

"The flower beds sure do look nice," I say, resting a hand on my hips.

"Evan's finally good for something," Cal sniggers.

"Who?" Piper asks.

"It's the brand of fertilizer we used," Kiara says quickly.

I cover my mouth to avoid laughing. I still can't believe we have a body buried in our commune. What a crazy life this is.

"I'm going to head inside and grab the rest of the things we need for lunch at the restaurant," Jade says.

"I'll come too," I tell her, giving Cal a peck on the cheek before I walk inside.

"I guess I'll go too," Kiara says, ruffling Owen's hair and causing him to whine.

We get inside and I say, "What did we need for our trip to the restaurant?"

Jade pops the top on a bottle of bubbly and says, "Celebratory coven drinks."

"Here, here!" Kiara chants.

"That's definitely something I can get on board with," I say, reaching for the champagne flutes.

Jade fills our glasses and grins. "This has been one hell of a month. Crazy ex-husbands and psycho drug murders."

"How did we end up with such crazy lives?" Kiara breaths.

"I don't know," I sigh. "But it gets a little better."

Kiara and Jade both pause and look at me like I better spill it fast.

"Turns out, Cal was loaded before he took off running."

"Loaded as in?"

"Rich," I say, trying not to giggle like a school girl. "With all the money he made from selling drugs, he banked it all to make sure JT wouldn't skimp on his mom. He kept it in a bank account that he left Ash in charge of. Since Ash isn't dead according to the rest of the world, Ash cleared it and we dumped it into my account. I just had a second bank card made so Cal can do the shopping every once in a while."

"No shit," Jade says, lifting her glass. "Cheers to that!"

"Seriously," I say, clinking my glass to theirs.

We take a few sips from our drinks and I put my flute down on the counter. They both look at me as the celebratory mood fades away.

"What is it?" Jade asks.

I shake my head, not wanting to ruin their good time. I force a smile. "Nothing."

"Bullshit," Kiara snaps. "Now just tell us."

A sigh falls from my lips and I slowly look up at them. "Something just doesn't feel right," I admit. "And I still can't shake it. This doesn't feel like it's over."

Kiara and Jade swap a look and sip at their champagne.

"What?" I ask them. "What aren't you telling me?"

Jade swallows her mouthful and wipes a drop from her lip. "I said the same thing to Kiara when she came over to give Piper her outfit for family pictures."

"And I agreed," Kiara adds.

"What the hell is happening now?" I ask, looking toward the window. "Is it Ash that's making us feel like this?"

"Don't blame him," Jade says. "He's really the only family Cal has left and you should be happy that he has someone now."

I smile at her. "I am happy that Cal has his brother. And I'm even happier that you're standing up for him."

"Quite the turn from the first time he stepped onto the property," Kiara says, chuckling.

The sliding glass door opens and Ash steps in with Cal behind him.

"Are we almost ready to go?" Cal asks. "The kids are getting antsy."

The three of us swap a look that says we will finish our conversation later.

Jade nods at Cal and then stares at Ash who gives her a nervous smile.

"Hi," Ash says.

"Hi," Jade replies.

"Hey," Ash says again.

Jade grins and says, "Hey," but with an awkward wave this time.

"Okay," I say. "Everyone's been reconnected since they saw each other in the yard two minutes ago. Can we add a new word to the vocabulary?"

Kiara smirks and sips her champagne. Jade puts her flute on the counter and wipes her hands on her shirt before she looks at Ash and says, "Want to go for a quick walk down by the lake before we go eat?"

Ash's cheeks flush. "Sure," he says, looking as though he may faint.

Jade and Ash go to walk out the front door and Cal hollers after them, "Don't try to kiss her, Ash. Your ass will end up in the lake!"

I punch him, knowing it's a jab at me for threatening to throw him in the first time we were down there alone. I look over my shoulder at Kiara and we all start laughing.

Kiara holds her glass up in the air as her eyes follow Jade. She smiles and shakes her head, allowing the unsettling feeling to dissolve for just a moment as she says, "And so it begins."

I smile at her and follow her gaze toward my friend who's walking down to the lake with a complete stranger. It seems like just yesterday I was talking to Cal for the time as he stood in front of me looking ragged and beaten.

My eyes trail toward him and I feel my insides grow warm. I can't believe how far we've come. I can't believe how fast I fell for him.

And now I can't believe he's actually mine.

But as my gaze trails back toward Jade, even though I can't see her, I feel something pounding in my chest. Something telling me that this isn't right. That maybe Ash is hiding something from us and it will all come out at the worst possible time.

Like brother, like brother.

Hopefully this time, we won't need a gun.

The Series

About the Author

Alyssa Lynn hunkers down in her writing cave in a small town in Central Pennsylvania. Alyssa started writing when she was in her early teens, but only began taking it seriously in the early months of 2019. Known for never following through on projects (i.e. paintings, drawings, household projects) she decided it was time to cross a finish line on something big. Writing a book. Now that she has a "few" stories under her belt, she's conquering the writing world one work-in-progress at a time.

Join Alyssa's VIP Reader group on Facebook: A. Lynn's Readers
Follow Alyssa on social media:

Made in the USA
Coppell, TX
10 April 2023